Praise for
the Novels of Deborah Cooke

Winging It

"[Cooke's] clever ability to convey what it means to be going on sixteen while being faced with dark, world-altering dilemmas has created a unique and compelling young-adult series bursting with magic, mayhem, and danger." —Fresh Fiction

"Zoë is as kick-butt as ever . . . another fast-paced, well-thought-out novel in [Cooke's] Dragonfire universe. Teen readers will love that Zoë and her friends get to be the stars." —*Romantic Times*

Flying Blind

"Whether you're young or just young at heart, you will equally enjoy this brand-new series by Ms. Cooke. . . . It's entertaining, it's exciting, and it's adventurous . . . a wonderful new series." —The Reading Frenzy

"The first of a new dragon series sure to become a classic. . . . Cooke has written a fantastic offshoot of her *Pyr* universe. . . . After turning the final page, I sat for a moment with a sense of excitement I haven't felt since I finished my first of Anne McCaffrey's Pern books." —Fresh Fiction

"This story crosses the boundaries. It will appeal to both teens and adults across the board. The story is engaging and fun. It's bringing to life a world of dragons and magic that appeals to all." —Night Owl Reviews (5 stars, top pick)

"The writing is swift and fun, just like I'd imagine flying on the back of a dragon. . . . If you're looking for a break from vampires and werewolves or you're a fan of Cooke's adult Dragonfire series, you won't be disappointed." —All Things Urban Fantasy

continued . . .

The Dragonfire Novels

Flashfire

"Deborah Cooke is a dragon master of a storyteller. . . . Lorenzo fills the pages with enigmatic glory only rivaled by his mate, Cassie, and I did not stop turning pages until the firestorm had ended."

—The Reading Frenzy

"Thrilling and unpredictable . . . *Flashfire* is another great addition to one of my favorite paranormal romance series."

—Paranormal Haven

Darkfire Kiss

"Over the course of her terrific Dragonfire series, Cooke has introduced numerous intriguing characters. In this book some plot threads are completed while new channels are opened. Cooke's consistent excellence ensures a great read!" —*Romantic Times* (4½ stars)

"Drew me in from the very first page. The premise makes for an interesting read and the sensual intensity between the lead characters could very easily singe the pages." —Fresh Fiction

Whisper Kiss

"Terrific. . . . The author has 'Cooked' another winner with the tattoo artist and the dragon shape-shifter." —The Best Reviews

"Cooke introduces her most unconventional and inspiring heroine to date. . . . The sparks are instantaneous. . . . Cooke aces another one!"

—*Romantic Times* (4½ stars)

Winter Kiss

"A beautiful and emotionally gripping fourth novel, *Winter Kiss* is compelling and will keep readers riveted in their seats . . . a must read!"

—Romance Junkies

"Another stellar addition to this dynamic paranormal saga with the promise of more to come." —Fresh Fiction

Kiss of Fate

"An intense ride. Ms. Cooke has a great talent. . . . If you love paranormal romance in any way, this is a series you should be following." —Night Owl Romance (reviewer top pick)

"Second chances are a key theme in this latest Dragonfire adventure. Cooke keeps the pace intense and the emotions raging in this powerful new read. She's top-notch, as always." —*Romantic Times*

Kiss of Fury

"Entertaining and imaginative . . . a *must read* for paranormal fans." —BookLoons

"Combustible . . . extremely fascinating. . . . Deborah Cooke has only touched the surface about these wonderful men called the *Pyr* and their battle with the evil dragons. . . . I am dying for more." —Romance Junkies

Kiss of Fire

"Wow, what an innovative and dazzling world Ms. Cooke has built with this new Dragonfire series. Her smooth and precise writing quickly draws the reader in and has you believing it could almost be real." —Fresh Fiction

"Brimming with sexy heroes; evil villains threatening mayhem, death, and world domination; ancient prophesies; and an engaging love story . . . an intriguing mythology and various unanswered plot threads set the stage for plenty more adventure to come in future Dragonfire stories." —BookLoons

THE DRAGON DIARIES NOVELS

Flying Blind

Winging It

THE DRAGONFIRE NOVELS

Kiss of Fire

Kiss of Fury

Kiss of Fate

Winter Kiss

Whisper Kiss

Darkfire Kiss

Flashfire

Blazing the Trail

THE
DRAGON
DIARIES

DEBORAH COOKE

NEW AMERICAN LIBRARY

New American Library
Published by New American Library, a division of
Penguin Group (USA) Inc., 375 Hudson Street,
New York, New York 10014, USA
Penguin Group (Canada), 90 Eglinton Avenue East, Suite 700, Toronto,
Ontario M4P 2Y3, Canada (a division of Pearson Penguin Canada Inc.)
Penguin Books Ltd., 80 Strand, London WC2R 0RL, England
Penguin Ireland, 25 St. Stephen's Green, Dublin 2,
Ireland (a division of Penguin Books Ltd.)
Penguin Group (Australia), 250 Camberwell Road, Camberwell, Victoria 3124,
Australia (a division of Pearson Australia Group Pty. Ltd.)
Penguin Books India Pvt. Ltd., 11 Community Centre, Panchsheel Park,
New Delhi - 110 017, India
Penguin Group (NZ), 67 Apollo Drive, Rosedale, Auckland 0632,
New Zealand (a division of Pearson New Zealand Ltd.)
Penguin Books (South Africa) (Pty.) Ltd., 24 Sturdee Avenue,
Rosebank, Johannesburg 2196, South Africa

Penguin Books Ltd., Registered Offices:
80 Strand, London WC2R 0RL, England

First published by New American Library,
a division of Penguin Group (USA) Inc.

First Printing, June 2012
10 9 8 7 6 5 4 3 2 1

 REGISTERED TRADEMARK—MARCA REGISTRADA

LIBRARY OF CONGRESS CATALOGING-IN-PUBLICATION DATA:

Cooke, Deborah.
   Blazing the trail/Deborah Cooke.
      p. cm.—(The dragon diaries; 3)
   ISBN 978-0-451-23682-1 (pbk.)
   1. Supernatural—Fiction.   2. Dragons—Fiction.   3. Shapeshifting—Fiction.
4. Secrets—Fiction.   5. Fantasy.   I. Title.
   PZ7.C774347Bl 2012
   [Fic]—dc23   2011052662

Set in Janson Text STD

Printed in the United States of America

PUBLISHER'S NOTE
This is a work of fiction. Names, characters, places, and incidents either are the product of the author's imagination or are used fictitiously, and any resemblance to actual persons, living or dead, business establishments, events, or locales is entirely coincidental.
   The publisher does not have any control over and does not assume any responsibility for author or third-party Web sites or their content.

Blazing the Trail

Chapter 1

*I*t was Tuesday, the day that stretches so long that you start to think the weekend will never, ever come—and I was actually hoping the weekend would never arrive. I'd avoided my locker all day, but when the last bell rang, I ran out of excuses.

For one thing, it was snowing like crazy outside. The second thing was that I needed my coat. Therefore, I had to go to my locker before I could go home.

And Derek would pounce on me, and Meagan would be there with Jessica, listening to the whole thing, and the day would end even more badly than a normal Tuesday.

I dragged my feet down the corridor, trying to delay the inevitable. Suzanne sailed past me with her cronies and snarled her favorite greeting—that would be "Freak!"—and they all laughed their mean girls' laugh. My dread was enough that I didn't even care about Ms. Popularity.

You would think that my outlook would be more positive. A bunch of great things had happened in the fall—some due to the efforts of yours truly—and it had been quiet in the realm of dragon shape shifters ever since. We'd kicked the proverbial butts of the Mages—that fun group of humans who were bent on wiping all shifters from the face of the earth—by destroying their hive memory; we'd formed alliances with the wolf shifters and the cat shifters against the Mages; and I'd been given the blessing of the previous Wyverns as the new Wyvern. Kohana, a Thunderbird shifter, had stolen the powerful NightBlade from the Mages, thereby rendering them pretty much impotent, and we had a plan to help him destroy it on the next solar eclipse, coming to a sky near you in April. All we had to do was wait for the time to be right to completely consolidate our victory—forever.

My best friend, Meagan, had discovered that she had spellsinger powers and was learning to use them. I'd also had the most awesome sixteenth-birthday party ever at the end of all that drama. Plus I'd gotten my driver's license—a quest that my father insisted had cut at least a century off his life span—and had done so without fulfilling my dad's expectation that the city of Chicago would become a scene of carnage.

Bonus: I got to use my mom's car while they were on vacation together this week. I was staying at Meagan's and we had wheels.

You'd think that after all that a dragon girl would be able to spy the glimmer of gold in her hoard of possibilities.

But no. All I could think about—and dread—was the Valentine's Day dance this coming Friday night.

Derek had asked me to go with him. This wasn't a huge surprise. We'd gone to a few movies and hung out together over the past couple of months. He wasn't much of a talker, but it felt comfortable being with him. We'd kissed twice more and it had been sweet. I knew he wanted more than that, but I wasn't sure if that was what I wanted.

Inviting me to the Valentine's Day dance was big.

And I'd been avoiding him. It was serious finkdom on my part, but I just didn't know what to do.

The thing is, I like Derek. I even like him a lot. He's sweet and thoughtful and occasionally very funny. He's protective of me and pretty quiet, a bit intense. Plus he's a wolf shifter, so he understands the challenge of having two lives and keeping one part of your life secret from the other. We have the shifter thing in common and that makes it easy to be with him. I think it's wicked that he has the gift of foresight, that he can smell the future a couple of minutes before it happens. He calls it his early-warning system. I want some of that, but so far my Wyvern ability to see the future is nonexistent.

The problem is that I don't think I like Derek as much as he likes me.

And that worries me.

Does it matter? I think it does.

Derek is probably the guy I should go for. He's the one chance that could work.

Of course, I have this habit of falling hard for guys who don't fall for me. I did it first with Nick, another dragon shifter, and I'm pretty sure I've done it again.

For Jared. Who is older, elusive, hot, a rebel, and a member of a rock band. He rides a motorcycle, is never around when I want to talk to him, and possibly knows more about dragons than I do. He challenges me and dares me and makes me tingle right down to my toes—and that happened even before I scored my very first kiss from him. He jumbles me up and confuses me—and just the mention of his name makes my dad breathe fire and lock the doors.

I think I could have forgotten Jared—or at least let go of

the possibility of seeing him again—until he sent me the only copy in existence of a book about dragon shifters. At first he said he wouldn't give it to me so I'd need to contact him regularly to see it. He'd called me "dragon girl" then, and his eyes were seventy million shades of green, his grip warm and tight on my hand. My heart did somersaults all over my chest.

Then he sent me the book last fall. What was I supposed to think? I thought he was done and gone and that was that.

I was still trying to reconcile myself to the idea of his being out of my life forever when he called out of the blue. Then he got the tattoo I wanted, the one my mom had forbidden me to get on my back, on *his* back for *my* birthday.

I didn't sleep for three nights.

I've spent way too much time checking out the pictures he sent me of the finished tattoo on his gorgeous muscles.

Plus I still owe him a ride on my own personal Dragon Air.

So, should I hold on to the dream, as crazy and unlikely as it sounds? Or should I accept that Derek is the more practical choice and agree to go to the dance with him? I don't want to be mean to Derek, and maybe love takes time to grow. Or maybe my instincts are right. Or maybe I'm just always going to yearn for guys that don't want me. Maybe that's part of what I like about them.

How twisted would that be? I like to think I'm more emotionally balanced than that.

Maybe Jared just likes the idea of having fan girls, of having me hanging on the line, waiting on him.

That really isn't my style.

At least, it shouldn't be.

I rounded the last corner and saw exactly what I'd wanted to avoid. Derek was leaning beside my locker, waiting for me and my answer. Meagan was at her locker, sorting her books, waiting for me and a ride home.

At least Jessica wasn't there. She and Meagan are still tight, tighter than Jessica and me. (Apparently their both being math whizzes is a stronger force than Jessica and me both being shape shifters and the wildcards of our respective kinds. Go figure.)

Derek's dark hair is straight and still a bit too long. It hangs over his eyes, but doesn't disguise their pale blue hue. They are wolflike in color and intensity. I swear he has X-ray vision. He was wearing his usual dark clothes, a combo that the eye slides over easily and lets him blend into the shadows. He's so quiet that he could be made of shadow.

Of course, he wasn't surprised to see me and had even anticipated my direction. His gaze locked on me as soon as I turned the corner, his attention making my mouth go dry.

I'd have to give him an answer before I left today. But what would it be? Heart or mind? I had a feeling that there would be big consequences from my choice, but, of course, I couldn't even guess what they might be. My Wyvern powers of seeing the future could have helped me out here, but no such luck.

I was on my own.

"Hey," Derek said, a guy of few words, as always. His voice is low and rumbly, kind of like a growl. Sometimes it makes me shiver. "How was art class?"

"Best class of the day," I said with a smile. "Makes the rest tolerable."

As I got to my locker, Meagan laughed, tapping her messenger to pull up a new message. She was laughing a lot more than she used to and no wonder; she'd finally gotten her braces off. Her teeth looked awesome and she was attracting a lot more attention. People saw how cute she was instead of her mouthful of metal. I was happy for her.

In fact, I had an idea that I knew would make her happy if I could make it happen.

"It's Jared again," she said with excitement, scrolling through the new message.

"Again?" I asked as I opened my locker. I gave Derek a smile and tried to keep my tone neutral while referring to Mr. Incredibly Hot.

Derek didn't smile back.

He watched me closely. I knew that the big moment had arrived.

I dodged it just a little bit longer.

I nudged Meagan. "You two have something going on?" I teased, acting as if I didn't care.

Meagan laughed again. "He's sending me all these tips about spellsinging. It's amazing. I'm learning so much."

"Oh, so you hear from him often."

"Yeah! Like every second day. He's in Des Moines this week."

My heart stopped. Des Moines was comparatively close.

But he hadn't called me.

In months.

Meagan held up her messenger to show the image of some club on its screen. "That's where the band is playing tonight. They're sold out!"

"Great," I said, barely glancing at it. I felt a simmer begin deep in my heart.

She heard from him *every other day*?

And I hadn't had one *hello* since November?

I was so out of his life that he hadn't even told me that he'd gotten back with his band.

Even I know enough about guys to understand the implications of that. Jared had been messing with me. He hadn't called me because he didn't want to get in touch. Because he didn't care.

Just thinking that made me wince, but there was no point in ducking the truth.

I shrugged into my coat and met Derek's gaze. He was cautious, uncertain what I would do. "You still want to go to the dance Friday?" I asked him, my tone a little more challenging than necessary.

He straightened. "Only with you." He smiled crookedly and I was struck by just how cute he was. "I thought you weren't sure."

"I'm sure. Let's go."

His smile broadened then and I saw how much I'd pleased him. It is kind of amazing to have that effect on someone. Would it work the other way by Friday? Or after that? "I'll pick you up at seven, talk to your dad and stuff." He was big on the protocol of talking to my dad. Maybe it's a pack thing. A wolf thing. A question of respecting the hierarchy. Either way, my dad likes Derek a bunch.

Probably as much as he dislikes even the idea of Jared.

"They went to the Caribbean today. I'm staying at Meagan's this weekend."

Derek nodded. "Okay. I'll pick you up there." He glanced at Meagan. "You coming to the dance, Meagan?"

She pouted. "I don't have a date and I don't want to go stag. I've done it enough, and this year I really want to go with a guy."

"She's coming," I said to Derek, and Meagan didn't look that surprised. There's a casualty of her being a genius—it's tough to surprise her.

"But . . ." she started to protest.

"She's coming," I insisted, and slammed my locker. Derek looked between us, amused.

Meagan gave me a stern look. "You're not going to fix me up. I won't be a pity date."

"No, you won't be. But, yes, I am going to fix you up." I bumped shoulders with her, the way we always do, and smiled at her. "Trust me. I have a plan and you're going to like it."

I did and she would.

I just had to make it work.

ABOUT THREE MONTHS BEFORE, MEAGAN had gotten her first glimpse of the *Pyr*. That's the name for dragon shape shifters, or, at least, our name for ourselves. That's what I am, although I'm the only female dragon shape shifter in existence. There's only one female *Pyr* at a time, and she's the Wyvern. I'm the Wyvern. And being the Wyvern means having a bonus pack of extra powers, some of which I'm still trying to locate.

But my point is that all the other dragon shifters I know, all of my buddies and the dragons I grew up with, are all guys. And they're pretty hot guys. I think the dragon business works in a big way for the males of the species: it seems to make them fill out and get buff more quickly than plain old human guys. So any female with a speck of interest in the opposite sex would notice them, even when they're in their human form.

In dragon form, they're breathtaking.

In November, Meagan had been targeted by the Mages because of her spellsinging talents. Spellsinging is innate: you're born with it or not. And if you are born with it, the Mages try to enlist you. They thought they could turn Meagan to the dark side, then maybe use her against me and my dragon pals. They weren't counting on Meagan the wunderkind figuring out their plan and deciding to go undercover to learn the real deal. It all culminated at a Halloween party at the house of an apprentice Mage named Trevor who goes to our school. Meagan had been crazy for Trevor forever, until she learned his nasty secret.

Even worse, Trevor offered up Meagan as the sacrifice for his initiation rite.

But then Garrett, one of my dragon friends, came to the rescue. Garrett is garnet and gold in dragon form, his scales like jewels, and just about as magnificent as a dragon can be. He scooped up this damsel in distress, and Meagan has been talking endlessly about Garrett ever since.

Forget Trevor.

So, I can tease Meagan about Jared because I know she's totally nuts for Garrett.

The problem is that we're in Chicago and Garrett lives in Traverse City. Meagan and Garrett haven't seen each other since November. Rotten luck contributed to that—the *Pyr* got together at our place at Christmas, but Meagan and her family were on vacation in California at the exact same time. She was devastated.

And I think Garrett was a bit bummed, too.

He's got the same strong-but-silent-type intensity as Derek. I know Meagan and Garrett talked a bunch, because between the two of them they've managed to translate that treatise on the Mages that he'd found in his mom's used bookstore in the fall.

They didn't really need to do it, given the current state of the Mage population—the Mages who hadn't died had become incoherent messes, with no memories left—but it just seemed mean to take that away. They'd finished a month before and officially had no more excuses to talk to each other or see each other, at least not until the big NightBlade destruction we'd planned for April.

Which I'm sure seemed a very, very long time away for them.

So, that night, when I was supposed to be doing my home-work at the dining room table at Meagan's house, I used my messenger under the table and invited Garrett to the Valentine's Day dance. Meagan watched me from the other side of the table, flicking glances toward the kitchen, where her mom was making dinner. Her mom is serious about homework, and if she caught me, she'd confiscate my messenger pronto.

I closed my hands over it in an attempt to muffle the sound as it chimed to signal an incoming message. I peeked between my fingers and grinned.

Ha! Garrett was coming.

"That had better not be a messenger I hear," Mrs. Jameson said from the kitchen. "We're going to eat in twenty minutes and I want to see that English homework done."

Who? Meagan mouthed.

I smiled as mysteriously as I could.

She wrinkled her nose at me, then glanced at her own messenger. It remained silent.

Geek, I mouthed back at her, and she wadded up a sheet of paper to throw it at me. We have an old joke that we're not geeky enough to message each other when we're sitting in the same room. (Even though we sometimes do.)

"I am talking to you, Zoë Sorensson," Mrs. Jameson added.

"Just finishing the last two questions, Mrs. Jameson," I answered, apparently the most dutiful student alive. Just so you know, I have nobody fooled on that one.

"Meagan?"

"Done, Mom." Meagan frowned and leaned closer to me, flicking another look at the kitchen. "Who?" she whispered.

"Wait for Friday," I replied in kind, and winked. "You'll love it."

Meagan sat back. Of course she knew. Her mouth fell

open and she raised a hand to her lips. *No!* she mouthed, clearly wanting me to say yes.

It is so tedious to try to surprise a brilliant individual, you know. Impossible, maybe.

I tried to act like I didn't understand her, but we've known each other way too long for that. I'd been hoping to make her wait for it, at least until we went to bed, but no luck. Meagan was too excited.

She scribbled a note and shoved it across the table at me, interrupting my consideration of English lit question number 29.

Her expression was expectant as I read it.

Actually, she was bouncing in her chair, vibrating with such excitement that I knew I'd done exactly the right thing.

For once.

GARRETT!?!

I nodded.

Meagan snatched the paper back and scribbled some more. I smiled when I saw what she'd written.

OMG! What am I going to wear?

THAT NIGHT I HAD A familiar dream. I am never really surprised anymore when I dream of snow. It's Wyvern stuff. Snow means that I'll have a dream visit from those two old ladies. I'll see them sitting under that huge tree near a well, their world superimposed on mine, as if I'm standing on the cusp of another realm.

One is soft, like a sweet grandmother who knits and makes cookies and gives perfect presents—you know, exactly what you wanted before you even realized you did. I never knew my grandmothers, so maybe I'm mixing up my wishes with the dream, but I call this one Granny. She is always knitting, silently knitting a big white mound of something. I've thought that she was knitting clouds before. Or snowdrifts. She was the first to show up in my dreams, but she never says anything.

Last fall, when I started to dream about Granny again, she turned up with a friend. This one talks. She says her name is Urd and that Granny is really named Verdandi and that they're sisters. You'd never know it to look at them. Urd has a face like a skull, while Verdandi looks like Mrs. Claus. There's a bit of edge to Urd. She pushed me down the well, for example, the dark, awful well that is right at their feet. I know it was for my own good, but still. I keep my distance from Urd.

So, when I felt cold in the middle of the night in the twin bed in Meagan's room and I opened my eyes to find snow drifting across my comforter, I was pretty sure what was going on. I rolled over, fully expecting to find Granny knitting and Urd spinning. I thought they'd probably turned up to tell me something important.

I doubted that it involved choosing between Jared and Derek, but I could hope.

I rolled over and my eyes just about fell out of my head in shock. Oh, Urd and Verdandi were there, and so was the big tree and even the well. Meagan's room had disappeared, and I was out on the tundra, just like usual.

The big difference was the blood.

It was everywhere. It was crimson and shone wetly against the snow. There was so much of it that my mind boggled. How could there be an ocean of blood? Where was it coming from?

Granny was knitting, but her needles were flying with superhuman speed, as if she were trying to outrun something. Urd was spinning like a crazed woman, her drop spindle a manic blur against the snow and blood. Neither was looking around. Both seemed to be completely oblivious to the change in their surroundings, all that blood. Except, of course, for their speed and determination to ignore it.

I even could smell it, and it made my bile rise.

I knew instinctively that what they were really pretending not to notice was the third woman. She stood between them with a huge pair of silver shears, slashing at the snowdrift that Granny had knit. She turned, laughing, and cut the thread that Urd had just spun with one vicious snip of those scissors. The drop spindle fell and rolled. Urd—who wasn't shy—didn't say boo. She just ducked her head and went after it, rummaging under the cloud of white knitting. Granny continued to knit at warp speed.

And the third one turned her smile on me.

Uh-oh.

She was young, this one, her hair hanging in a long gold braid over her shoulder. She had those scissors in one hand, while a knife gleamed in the other. She was tall and fit, a warrior princess dressed in a laced leather jerkin, jodhpurs, and black leather boots that rose over her knees. They had big, mean silver spurs on them. Her arms were bare and I could see her muscles, as well as the blue tattoos on her skin. Her gaze was steely and her expression was grim. I knew she could whup me without even trying.

I sat up and eased away from her.

Worst of all, there was blood spattered all over her. It dripped from the scissors and pooled on the toe of one boot, gleaming crimson against the black. She even had a few splashes on her cheek.

"I am Skuld," she said, her voice deep and rough. She sounded like she'd been chain-smoking for centuries. She took a step toward me, assessing me, brandishing that knife.

I'd done my research and thought this an ideal moment to show myself an apt student. "The third Wyrd sister," I said, trying to sound as if I wasn't worried. I'm pretty sure I failed. "Your name means 'what will be'."

"No. It means 'what *may* be.'" Her eyes glinted and she laughed at me. I saw the gold crown on her one eyetooth and a hint of what looked like madness in her eyes. Then she flung out her hands, and our surroundings were instantly consumed in fog.

There was just Skuld and me and a whole lot of mist. I couldn't even hear Granny's knitting needles anymore. It was like she and Urd had vanished.

Or been banished.

The blood, however, was still there.

The mist wasn't normal mist, just so you know. It smelled wrong. Dirty. Like smoke. Blood. Trouble. There was also a glimmer to it, as if a red light was being reflected by the fog. Skuld didn't seem concerned by it. She shoved her knife into the holster on her belt on one side and the scissors into a second holster on the other. A bird screamed and there was the shadow of wings flying through the mist. She smiled.

You have to know that I was not thrilled when Skuld extended her hardened hand to me. "Come along, Wyvern. I've got something to show you."

There was a determination about her that had me on my feet in record time. I was pretty sure she'd just toss me over her shoulder if I didn't go with her. Nothing really bad had happened to me yet in these dreams. I was thinking I couldn't actually get hurt—even though the attitude of the other two sisters worried me. They clearly didn't want to mess with Skuld.

And I was a bit curious as to what she would show me. Urd had given me the key to the past. Verdandi had helped me claim my Wyvern powers in the present. Would Skuld give me a taste of the future?

Was she going to teach me how to claim the foresight that should be part of my Wyvern bonus pack? What about the Wyvern's supposed ability to send dreams? I would have loved to have had both powers, so I went with her.

But when I put my hand in hers, her skin was as cold as ice. Her touch sent a shudder through me, one that nearly stopped my heart. She glanced at me and shook her head, as if I weren't good enough for her trouble, then leapt into the air, tugging me behind her. She became a pitch-black raven, her talons digging into my hand as she hauled me into the sky.

I was reminded of Kohana, the Thunderbird shifter who was sometimes my enemy, sometimes my ally, but her bird form was smaller than his. Her feathers had a blue-black gleam and her eyes were as dark as obsidian. His eyes, in contrast, were filled with the yellow fire of lightning. She didn't have any thunderbolts in her claws, either.

Just yours truly.

Skuld ripped through the fog with a speed and a confidence that seemed crazy under the circumstances.

It wasn't as if she had radar. I couldn't see more than six feet in any direction. Where were we? What else was out here?

I panicked then. I tried to shift to my dragon form, thinking I'd do better under my own steam, but apparently that ability didn't follow me to dreamland. Or maybe Skuld had shut it down. Either way, I couldn't shift. I couldn't free myself from her iron grip. I didn't know where she was going, but I was getting the feeling I wasn't going to like it.

The glimmer of red light was getting brighter.

And it had started pulsing.

Maybe, just maybe, I shouldn't have been so quick to comply.

Skuld descended like a rocket, heading straight for the vivid pulse of red light. As we got closer to the ground, I could see more details. It looked like we had arrived at a garbage dump—broken bottles and twisted metal in every direction I looked. The red light flashed over it all, like there was a cop car in the vicinity.

Except there wasn't.

Maybe it was a beacon, guiding us to Skuld's destination.

Skuld landed with a triumphant cry, shifting shape at the last minute and punctuating her arrival by kicking aside a pile of garbage. It toppled with a crash.

"What's that?" someone demanded. I peered through the mist and saw the silhouettes of three guys. They were standing together maybe thirty feet ahead of us. They seemed vaguely familiar to me, even though I couldn't see them clearly. My Wyvern—or maybe my dragon—sense started to tingle.

"They can't see or hear us," Skuld said. She blew at the fog and it dissipated, just like that. "You've nothing to fear."

Then she laughed in a way that implied exactly the opposite.

"They heard that." I pointed to the toppled trash cans.

She grinned at me. "But can't hear *us*."

It was clear she wasn't interested in arguing the technicalities. And, really, she would know the rules—such as they were—for this dream realm better than I. Paying attention was the best I could do.

I looked around the vacant lot. Now that we were on the ground, standing in the rubble, the red light was gone. It looked like we were in the real world. "What are we doing here?"

Her smile was chilly. "I like battlefields. I like my dead

fresh." With that, she marched toward the guys, pulling her dagger on the way.

Like maybe she was going to get her own fresh kill.

I wasn't sure I wanted to see this.

On the other hand, I was in a dream. Theoretically, I couldn't get hurt. Practically, the Wyrd sisters showed me stuff for a reason. I should pay attention. I might learn something useful.

The guys started to chant, as if they didn't see Skuld coming, but I have to believe that anybody with a pulse would have noticed her. She must be telling the truth, I decided. Or at least some of it. Either way, I followed her.

The chant was creepy. It made the hair stand up on the back of my neck, which gave me a theory about it. I looked closer and, sure enough, I saw the dangerous orange light of a Mage spell. It erupted from their throats, then spun together into a kind of cord. It spiraled up into the air, getting thicker and brighter as it went, then widened into a sphere of molten gold.

So they had to be Mages.

No, they had to be apprentice Mages, who still had their own individual memory.

This was not good.

I looked back at the guys and realized I knew two of them. One was Trevor, the apprentice Mage from school who'd tried to trick and trap us shifters last fall. The other was Adrian, the senior apprentice Mage who had invaded our dragon boot camp the previous spring. I didn't know the third guy, but it looked like he was more junior than Trevor.

At least he looked more nervous than Trevor.

What were they doing? Trying to jump-start the old Mage plan for world domination?

The full Mages had been killed or gone crazy in that big battle in the fall. I'd pretty much assumed that cleaning up the dregs of their nasty group would be easy, since just the amateurs and the damaged were left. Trevor had been sickeningly nice to me at school, as if he were scared of me, which just reinforced my conclusion.

What was this spell for?

Was there something I didn't know?

I moved closer, even without any urging from Skuld. The sphere they were creating with their spell became bigger and brighter. It was a golden globe, expanding in the air over their heads. Like a balloon. It looked more solid by the minute, like it was made of orange glass. And as their chant became a song, I saw shapes form within the sphere.

Human shapes.

Silvery human shapes.

ShadowEaters! I took a step backward, feeling like I was going to puke. The Mages had invoked these beings at that last ceremony, to feed them the shadows of their sacrificial victims. They'd creeped me out then, and didn't give a better impression this time around. There was something ominous and awesome about their presence, like they were visiting from another realm.

The thing was, the Mages had invoked the ShadowEaters last fall using the NightBlade. How could apprentice Mages do this summoning? Kohana had the NightBlade, wherever he was.

There was, though, a full moon shining down on the scene, which had been part of the deal during our big battle in the fall. And there was no mistaking those shapes.

Or my dread at the sight of them.

The shapes in the globe became more substantial.

And more numerous.

So numerous that they strained at the constraints of the spell bubble, elbowing each other for space. Jostling and shoving. There was something aggressive about them this time, and I wasn't glad to see that change.

All the same, I didn't want to blink and risk missing anything.

As the guys chanted their spell, the ShadowEaters started to brighten. The orange light of the spell seemed to fill them, making their shapes luminescent, radiant with pulsing orange spell light.

This could not be good.

The guys were staring upward, rapt at the results of their spell, even as they were fortifying it. The sphere became so crowded with shapes that it bulged. I saw fists and feet and elbows as the ShadowEaters tried to fight their way loose of the orb's constraint. The sphere looked to be stretched thin and I worried that it would burst. They struggled with more force. The guys sang louder. My heart pounded. . . .

Then Adrian threw his hands up and shouted, "Be with us, O exalted ones!"

With a flash, the globe shattered into a thousand shards of gold. Hundreds of ShadowEaters leapt to the earth with purpose. Now they looked like menacing shadows, dark silhouettes with no features.

Except for their gleaming golden eyes. Their eyes were filled with spell light. They were silent but terrifying.

Adrian had time to laugh at his victory. "I told you we could do it!" he crowed to Trevor. "We made the Invocation of Destruction!" He turned to high-five Trevor, jubilant in his success.

But the ShadowEaters fell on the third guy like a pack of vultures. He screamed as they pulled him away from Trevor and Adrian, but there were so many of them that he couldn't fight them off. They snatched him and surrounded him and held him down. I saw their teeth flash as they bit and snapped.

When they retreated just seconds later, smacking their lips, he had collapsed on the ground. And he had no shadow.

I would have seen it in the light of that moon. They'd devoured it.

When ShadowEaters ate a shifter's shadow, the shifter died. It was like the shifter ceased to exist, because he or she couldn't cast a shadow—or because in eating the shadow, the ShadowEaters stole the shifter's abilities.

Did it work the same way for apprentice Mages?

I took a deep breath, using my keen *Pyr* sense of hearing to check his vitals.

He wasn't breathing. And he had no pulse.

They'd killed him.

Without the NightBlade cutting his shadow free, without him being a shifter.

This was new—and horrible.

The ShadowEaters swirled around the two apprentice Mages like leaves dancing in a gusty fall wind, looking hungry and predatory.

"Holy shit," Trevor whispered. "What the fuck is happening?" Adrian was flipping through the book in a panic. Obviously, they hadn't invoked the particular destruction they'd anticipated.

The ShadowEaters pressed closer around the pair, and I heard Trevor squeal like a girl; then the ShadowEaters swept into the sky. They soared like a golden tide, as if they'd been freed from some kind of captivity, a thought that didn't fill me with delight.

High above us, they disappeared into the night.

I saw the glow of their eyes shine longer, like nasty stars, until they winked out, as well. Where had they gone?

"You have to stop them!" Trevor shouted at Adrian, and I heard his fear.

"I don't know how." Adrian turned the pages of that book so fast that I thought they'd tear. He kept looking up, but the ShadowEaters were long gone from view. "It'll take me ages to figure it out!"

"We don't have ages! They're hungry and they're here," Trevor said, his horror echoing mine.

The two looked at the fallen kid, then at each other. I could taste their terror.

"I can't fix it," Adrian said quietly. He looked around, his eyes a bit wild. "Not yet. Maybe not ever."

Trevor swore. They stared at each other as a triumphant bellow echoed through the night. It came from above and sent shivers down my spine.

They pivoted and fled from the garbage dump, racing into the street. I heard two car engines start and tires squeal.

Did this mean that the apprentice Mages and the Shadow-Eaters weren't allies anymore? Had Adrian messed up, or had the ShadowEaters wrested control of the ceremony to serve their own purposes?

That was not an optimistic thought.

Who or what would they eat next?

I could only hope the ShadowEaters would feast on all the remaining Mages and apprentice Mages. They didn't look like discerning eaters, but it still seemed like a long shot that they'd do our dirty work.

Speaking of discerning eaters, Skuld was strolling toward the dead guy. He looked to be my age or maybe a year younger. She squatted down beside him, poked him, and then sniffed his corpse with satisfaction.

I supposed that this was as fresh as dead got.

"Wasted soul," she said with a shake of her head. "Oh, well." She sniffed again. "But a very nice liver." She cast me a look. "Hungry?"

I shook my head, unable to look away.

I watched in horror as Skuld shifted shape right before my eyes. She hopped onto his chest in her raven form and ripped his flesh open with her beak. When she tore into his body cavity, presumably looking for that liver, I couldn't stand it anymore.

I spun around and ran. I didn't know where I was or whether I could get back to the real world, but wherever I ended up had to be better than this place.

Chapter 2

I woke up with a start, my heart leaping around my chest and my breath coming in anxious spurts. Even when I closed my eyes, I could see the ShadowEaters falling on that kid, surrounding him and killing him. It was just as horrible remembering it as witnessing it. He'd been swarmed and overcome.

I had to think that he had been convenient. I had to think that they'd be more interested in continuing the Mage plan of eliminating all shifters than in snacking on their own kind.

Come to think of it, every ceremony of the Mages seemed to involve a sacrifice. So, Adrian had called down the ShadowEaters and someone had to die to finish the ritual. The kid had been in the wrong place at the wrong time. Maybe the ShadowEaters had done all the feasting they needed to do.

I had my doubts. I thought about the ShadowEaters

leaping into the sky and disappearing. Like they'd run out of energy. Would they come after the shifters next?

But wait. Skuld said she was about the future. Had this happened already or not?

Was it going to happen—or was it just possible?

That calmed me down a little bit. I pulled out my messenger and began tapping madly. When we had interrupted the Mages' ceremony in the fall, it had been held on the night of a full moon. I found a lunar calendar and checked the dates. The next full moon would be Wednesday, February 12.

This week. My eyes fell on the clock in Meagan's room and I saw that it was two forty-five in the morning. Technically it *was* Wednesday. Had my dream come true yet? I went to the window and looked out, unable to see any golden spell light in the winter sky beyond Meagan's window.

"Scared?" a guy asked from behind me, and I nearly jumped out of my skin.

My older brother, Sigmund, was sitting on the end of the bed, looking as scruffy and disreputable as he usually did. That would be my *dead* older brother, Sigmund. He appeared to me from time to time.

He hadn't been there when I woke up. I would have noticed that.

I looked around the room, which looked perfectly normal as Meagan slept on her bed with the cat, King, curled up near her feet.

Had my brother come to help or to complicate things? With Sigmund, you never knew. "What are you doing here?"

"I'm not really here, am I?" he asked, looking amused. "Being dead and all." He held up one hand, and I could see right through it to the wallpaper on the wall behind him. He grinned.

"I can see you."

He leaned back, completely at ease. "So, do you usually talk to dead people?"

"Apparently, it happens sometimes." I watched him with some suspicion. Sigmund usually turns up to tell me something, but he never just drops the news. It's kind of irritating how I have to work it out of him. "What did you come to tell me?"

He smiled and got up, stretching elaborately. "Just checking on you, sis."

"Why?"

"Bad dream?" His eyes were glinting, as if he knew something I didn't—which wasn't exactly a long shot.

Two could play this game. "What makes you ask?"

"It's a Wyvern thing, you know." He bent and scratched King's ears.

Kincaid, that is. This cat shifter had adopted me in the fall, just as his pal—named Mozart by Meagan—had adopted Meagan. They were both vigilant sentinels in cat form, and good-looking—if enigmatic—guys in human form. They both seemed to prefer being cats. I'd only seen either of them as guys once, in that last fight with the Mages.

Maybe they hated school.

Maybe they'd run away from home.

I couldn't figure out why they didn't seem to have human lives, like we *Pyr* do, but they weren't telling.

Even though I'm not much for cats, there was no shaking King. I'd thought he'd move on after that fight, but he'd stuck to me like glue.

Never mind that he was a huge Maine coon in his cat form and had to weigh thirty pounds. He's no more enamored of dragons than I am of cats, so we have a relationship based on mutual respect and mild animosity.

Yes, I have been known to call him Fish Breath.

Usually when I have a bad dream, I wake up to find him watching me.

But he was out cold on the end of Meagan's bed.

King didn't even move when Sigmund rubbed his ears. What was going on? Was this another, strangely realistic dream? The emergence of a new Wyvern power? Or was everything in some kind of flux?

Come to think of it, where *was* Mozart? Usually he and King crashed together on Meagan's bed.

I spoke with caution. "Casting dreams is a Wyvern thing, from what I understand."

"So is having them. It's the whole seeing-past-present-and-future-simultaneously trick." Sigmund shot a glance at me. "You can't do it yet, can you?"

I shook my head.

"Mastering it drives some Wyverns crazy, you know, so I thought I'd check on you."

Great. That was not news I needed to hear.

Sigmund arched a brow. "Feeling sane?"

"Pretty much."

He grinned. "Other than talking to dead people in the middle of the night."

I smiled back. "Other than that." Plus seeing ShadowEaters come to life, and talking to mythical beings who ate livers from corpses that were still warm. My platter of the strange and unusual was pretty full, and getting more so.

I glanced at King again, amazed that he was comatose.

In the blink of an eye, Sigmund disappeared, so quickly and surely that he might never have been there. King slept on, as did Meagan. The air hadn't changed temperature, the way it sometimes does when ghosts make an appearance. I looked in and under the bed for a frog—that's a typical joke of Sigmund's—but there was nothing. Just me.

But I had talked to my dead brother. I knew it.
Even though it seemed like he could have been an illusion.
Or a delusion.
Evidence that this Wyvern could go crazy.
You know I wasn't going back to sleep anytime soon.

I HAD TO FIGURE OUT the significance of what Skuld had shown me. It was like a riddle. Or a test. What were Adrian and Trevor going to do? (I'd decided to go with the assumption that the ritual I'd witnessed hadn't happened yet.) I trolled through that ancient document that Meagan and Garrett had translated—safely stored on my messenger in English—and composed a list.

I like lists.

You'll get used to it.

SIX THINGS ABOUT MAGES

1. Mages recruit humans with an innate musical
   ability. This power—called spellsinging—allows
   those gifted humans to enchant other humans
   with their music or their songs. (They naturally
   hold their audiences spellbound. Ha ha.) Not all
   born spellsingers choose to sign up for the Mage
   program. Meagan is a spellsinger and so is Jared.
   Both have passed on the invitation to use their
   powers for evil.
2. Those spellsingers who do join the Mages become
   apprentices and are trained in the art of casting
   spells. Like Trevor. Mages have an appetite for
   shadows, and it seems to be an acquired taste—
   even apprentice Mages can bite shadows, as we
   learned in the fall when Jessica was captured.

3. There are at least two levels of apprenticeship in Mage Land, and the ceremony to move from the lowest level to the next tier involves a sacrifice—presumably as well as some level of competence. Adrian must be more advanced, because he can do more things than Trevor—like voluntarily take on the shapes of all the shifter species eliminated by the Mages so far.

4. Full Mages share a hive memory—or they did until last fall. Kohana and I burned this memory to oblivion, so the full Mages either died or became incoherent. Since then, we've had only apprentice Mages underfoot, and they've been twitchy, as if insecure about their future.

5. The Mages had a plan to destroy all surviving shape shifters in order to assume their powers. They did this by cutting away their shadows in a ceremony that requires the NightBlade, a black knife. They invoked the ShadowEaters and offered the shadow of the victim as a sacrifice, which incidentally killed the victim, too. (Nice.)

6. There is supposed to be some kind of bonus energy surge available to the Mages when all shifters are eliminated, which is why they were actively hunting we last four kinds. Details are sketchy.

I looked over the list, tapping my fingers on the edge of my messenger. Essentially, each kind of surviving shifter has a new coming-of-age member with special powers. Kohana, the Thunderbird, calls us wildcards and says we're important. Of course, he won't say how. Derek, the wolf shifter, says his kind has a prophecy that we have to band together in a new

pack and follow the dragon. As wildcard of his kind, he transferred to my school to make that alliance with me, the wildcard of my kind. Jessica, the jaguar shifter and wildcard, also
transferred to our school and insists that the future is in the
hands of the four of us.

I initiated the alliance of wildcards—and, by extension,
surviving shifter species—and led the fight in November. It
seems to be working, even if Kohana is more of a wildcard
than the other three of us put together.

But what had actually happened in my dream? How had
Adrian invoked the ShadowEaters without the NightBlade,
or even any full Mages? What did it mean that they'd broken
free? It didn't seem as if that had been Adrian's plan. Had he
screwed up? Or had they taken charge?

I realized I knew very little about ShadowEaters, and that
this might not be ideal. I'd been thinking that without full
Mages to invoke ShadowEaters and with the NightBlade
safely in Kohana's custody, they weren't important.

Time to think again.

I STARED AT THE CEILING for hours, fretting, but must have
finally fallen asleep.

Because I woke up again suddenly to find Meagan's room
still dark.

This time there was a large cat sitting on my chest, swat-
ting my face with one paw.

King.

"There's a litter box in this house, too," I complained as
I shoved him off my chest. I was cranky and tired and not
interested in waking up to play catch the mousie. Predictably,
I was covered in the hair he'd shed while harassing me. I'm
convinced that he's always shedding, to a greater or lesser
degree, which I guess is the price of a luxurious coat. It also

means that everything I own, most of which is black, has been garnished with cat hair.

This does not work for me.

King doesn't appear to care.

He didn't care about what I said, either. He went to the door and waited, giving me a steady look. There's something regal about him, and even in cat form he has a commanding presence.

I got it. This was an order.

"Something's up," I guessed. He gave a meow of epic proportions and paced from left to right in front of the closed doorway.

Impatient for me to get a move on.

"Go out in the hall. No peeking," I instructed as I opened the door an increment. If a cat could grin, he did—but he did what I told him to do, as well. He slipped through the gap like a wraith. I knew he'd be waiting right outside. I could hear him pacing. I tugged on my jeans and a hoodie, then debated the merit of waking up Meagan.

I decided to go alone and crept after King, wanting to be sure I didn't wake the Jamesons. Once I left the bedroom, King made a beeline for the front door, moving faster than I'd ever seen him move. I winced as I turned the dead bolt, trying to do it as silently as possible, and he streaked out into the night at the first opportunity.

I was right behind him.

"Should we fly?" I asked, intending to shift shape if it would help. I wasn't sure how far we had to go.

He didn't answer. He just leapt off the porch and into the shadows beside the step. One second he was standing in the snow, glaring at me, and the next he had hunkered down to peer into the shadows of the evergreens planted there. I could see only the swish of his tail.

I wondered whether he'd done some disgusting cat thing and brought me a "present" of a bird with its head bitten off. I had not come out in the night for that kind of token of his so-called esteem.

On the other hand, I was up, so I might as well look. I bent and pushed the greenery aside.

Mozart was lying in the snow. He wasn't moving. He wasn't even rapidly rotating between forms, which is a sign of distress in a shifter. He's a soot-colored cat with a white bib and white socks. He was terrifyingly still.

"Is he dead?" I asked, wondering what had happened to him.

King narrowed his eyes, and then I noticed the faint whisper of Mozart's breath.

The subtle beat of his heart.

He wasn't dead, but he wasn't exactly in the prime of health, either. I crouched down beside King and touched Mozart's fur. His body wasn't as warm as usual, but the feel of his heart beating beneath his ribs made me feel better.

I looked at King. "You brought him here." He bowed his head regally. "But you couldn't bring him into the house without my help." King crouched down beside his friend's body, as if standing guard over it. It must have been terrifying to leave him alone, even for a few minutes.

No wonder he'd been so agitated.

"But what happened to him?" I still was thinking that this was some kind of cat-related injury. Cat shifters are more savvy about navigating the human world than regular cats, but still, their form has its risks.

King gave me an intent look, as if I was missing something really obvious. Then he batted at the snow beside Mozart with one paw, indicating something. At his gesture, I did see it. The porch light shone on Mozart, casting his shadow across the white snow.

But his shadow was wrong.

There was a bite out of it.

This was not the most encouraging sign possible. I looked around for spell light or apprentice Mages or even ShadowEaters but couldn't see anything.

King was watching me closely, so I tried to hide that I was freaking. I didn't know what we could do to help Mozart or fix his shadow, but him lying wounded in the snow on a winter night—when his attacker could still be at large—couldn't be the right answer.

I scooped Mozart up into my arms and headed for the doorway, casting a glance at the night sky. I couldn't see any ShadowEaters, which had to be better than the alternative. King was right against my legs, slipping into the house when I opened the door. His eyes shone as he watched me lock the door; then he followed me to the bedroom on silent feet.

Mozart remained limp.

But alive.

I realized then that we had never learned his real name, that he just responded to the name Meagan had given his cat form, as if he were a cat. I knew so little about either of these cat shifters. They were mysterious to me, and maybe they liked it that way. Maybe they stayed in cat form to avoid discussion. To keep their secrets.

I had a feeling we'd have to find out more to help Mozart recover.

And one look at King told me they weren't going to like that.

MEAGAN WAS AWAKE WHEN WE got back to her room and her eyes widened at the sight of Mozart. I shut the door behind us so her parents wouldn't hear that we were talking.

She nearly tripped over the hem of her nightgown coming to get him from me.

"What happened?" She cuddled him close.

"I don't know. King woke me up and took me to him." I turned on the light beside her bed, trying to sound calm. In charge. Competent even. "There's something wrong with his shadow."

Meagan gasped. "Mages! But how?" She sat down hard and chewed her lip as she cradled Mozart. "Or it could be apprentice Mages. But why now?"

I had to love having the brilliant student on my side. I told Meagan all about my dream as we tucked Mozart into the blankets on her bed. King immediately leapt up to sit vigil. He would have just hunkered down there to watch, but I wasn't having any of his mystery right now.

"No way," I said, shaking a finger at him. "You have to tell us what you know if we're going to help him."

"Absolutely," Meagan agreed. "We have to know how much of this has happened already."

He narrowed his eyes at me and looked hostile.

"Shift and spill it, Fish Breath," I said, sounding tougher than I felt. "What happened? What did you see?"

He gave a mewl of protest and glared at both of us; then there was a familiar shimmer of blue light. I closed my eyes to be diplomatic about it all, and when I opened them, there was a guy sitting on the end of Meagan's bed.

In human form, King has sandy hair and is built like a football player. He carries himself as if he owns the world. People step aside for him, even when he's a cat. He doesn't say much, and when he does, he's surprisingly soft-spoken.

"I woke up and he was gone," he said even more quietly than usual, flicking a glance at the closed door. He gently rubbed Mozart's chin as he spoke, but the other cat didn't respond at all. "I went looking for him, found him halfway down the block, dragging himself back here. He was exhausted. As soon as he saw me, he gave it up."

"He knew you'd bring him home," Meagan said, sitting down on the other side of the injured cat.

"I didn't know how else to bring him into the house," King said. "I had to shift to human form to carry him home, but couldn't enter the house that way. So I hid him and came to get Zoë."

"Thank goodness your parents installed that cat door," I said.

King's lips tightened. "He would have been better off if they hadn't."

"Did he tell you what happened?" Meagan asked.

King shook his head.

"Did you see anything? Was anyone else around?" I asked.

King frowned. "There was something strange in the air. Like electricity. I felt like my hair was standing up the minute I went outside." He shuddered. "It felt bad, like something evil was brewing."

I sat down, thinking, on the twin bed on the other side of the room. "Why Mozart?" I asked. "I wonder what he saw." You know I was thinking about ShadowEaters walking the earth.

"He can't tell us, not when he's like this," Meagan said, gently touching his ears. "How do we help him? How do cat shifters heal?"

"I can't tell you more," King said forcefully. His heated reaction surprised me a bit. "You need to ask Jessica."

I would have asked him more despite that warning, but he shifted shape, effectively ending the conversation. What had he been worried about? He gave me a lethal look in his cat form, then curled himself behind and around Mozart, his lush tail wrapping protectively around his friend.

Like a guardian.

One that wouldn't be bypassed easily.

Meagan was stroking Mozart's head with a care that King was prepared to tolerate. "My mom's going to want to take him to the vet in the morning."

"The vet isn't going to be able to do anything about this," I said. "We need to figure out how to heal his shadow, and I don't think they teach shifter physiology in college. Like King says, we'll have to ask Jessica."

King purred approval.

"Maybe we could hide him here." Meagan looked up. "Will you stay with him while we're at school, King?"

King lowered his head protectively. He seemed to enfold Mozart and I knew that the other cat shifter couldn't have a better defender.

Even if I wasn't sure what he could do against apprentice Mages or ShadowEaters on the hunt.

MEAGAN WAS SURE THAT IF my dream had already happened, then Mozart would have died. She had a point—the apprentice Mages nibbled at shadows, but the ShadowEaters consumed them. So, we knew two apprentice Mages, and we knew where one of them was.

"I have to talk to Trevor at school," I said. "Find out what he knows."

Meagan caught her breath. "It's dangerous."

"Not stopping them would be worse."

Meagan frowned as she reviewed my list with record speed. She and I agreed that the ultimate key had to lie in the alliance of shifters we'd formed. Skuld had been warning me of pending disaster. We had to prevent it from happening.

I could see that Meagan was drooping, so I told her to get some sleep while she could. She curled up in bed with both cats, one hand on Mozart, and soon I was the only one awake in the room. I wasn't going back to sleep anytime soon.

First things first. I composed a message to Liam, Garrett, and Nick, my best guy friends and dragon shifters, too, briefly explaining my dream and asking them to come to Chicago ASAP. This was an emergency. Nick answered right away in the affirmative, I guess because he was awake. That made me feel a bit better. If there was fighting to be done, Nick was the dragon to call.

Next up, the other shifters. I'd see both Jessica and Derek at school in the morning, just hours away. I had no idea where to find Kohana, much less how to warn him, other than sending him a text message. He had a tendency—like another guy I knew—to ignore text messages.

That got me to thinking about the alliance.

And King's reaction.

Wasn't it funny that we didn't know what the cat shifters even called themselves? Actually, we didn't know what Derek's wolf shifters called themselves, either, just that they had a prophecy to follow a dragon when "the stars stood still." That would be now, during the Great Lunar Standstill. There was quite a lot we didn't know about one another, so we'd better get started if we were going to solve this riddle.

By tonight.

No pressure.

I pulled out my messenger and sent another message to Garrett. I didn't think I'd forgotten those names for the other kinds of shifters, but it was possible. Garrett would remember if I had. Or he might be able to find out in his mom's bookstore. I asked him to score any details about shifters he could find.

I hesitated a moment, then sent a message to Derek, asking what the wolf shifters called themselves. It suddenly seemed important to define what was similar about us remaining shifters and what was different.

Were we four kinds the survivors for a reason?

One that Team Mage knew and we didn't?

Because there was exactly zero chance of my falling back asleep and it was only 5:14 in the morning, I made a chart on my messenger of what I knew about the four remaining kinds of shifters. It was pretty thin but looked like this:

Shape	Dragon	Thunderbird	Wolf	Cat
Name for Self	*Pyr*	*Wakiya*	?	?
Wildcard	Zoë	Kohana	Derek	Jessica
Origin	Europe	North America	?	?

I should have sent a message to Jessica then, but I hesitated. Meagan could do it.

Things weren't great between me and Jessica. I still felt that there was a barrier between us. I'd thought it was just the math proficiency that fed her bond with Meagan, but now I realized we hadn't talked about shifter stuff since discovering our respective powers in November.

Not at all.

And it was strange. I mean, having that in common had to be more important than sharing a talent for math. Both of us being wildcards gave us common ground, too. That was certainly more rare than acing math. Meagan had said before that Jessica was an only child, under a lot of pressure from her folks.

If she was the cat shifter equivalent of the Wyvern, why didn't we have more of a bond?

I had tried to open the topic a bunch of times. But she always changed the subject, like she was avoiding my questions. And I was starting to think that she was avoiding me, too.

What didn't she want me to know?

I wished I could have been less suspicious of her, but given her behavior, I couldn't. That was partly because she'd been compelled to help the Mages in the past, but mostly it was because of her evasiveness ever since.

Were the cat shifters still aligned with the Mages?

Or were they just naturally secretive?

It was almost time for the alarm to go off, so I seized the opportunity and claimed the shower first.

WHEN I CAME BACK INTO her room, Meagan was awake, sitting up in bed and typing on her messenger. The light from the handheld device was bluish and made her features look spooky.

Or maybe it was my mood.

"Jessica says something is going on," she whispered by way of greeting. I sat down hard, fighting my doubts. "She has to go someplace. Do you think it has anything to do with Mozart?"

"I don't know. Didn't she say?"

"No." Meagan had her Einstein look as she surveyed me. "There's one part of your dream that doesn't make sense."

"What's that?"

"Trevor and Adrian don't have the NightBlade," she said. "Kohana does."

"Maybe they don't need it for the Invocation of Destruction ceremony."

Meagan shook her head. "No. When Garrett and I translated that old book of the Mages', it was clear that the NightBlade was needed for *any* ceremony." Meagan pursed her lips. "It must be that they'll do this on the *next* full moon. Not tonight's."

Instinctively I felt that it had to be sooner. I thought of Derek and his ability to see two or three minutes into the future. A month's warning seemed like too much, even for a Wyvern. "I think we four wildcards need to work together to solve this, like it's a test of the alliance, too. Can you ask Jessica to meet us before school?"

"You could ask her."

"You're already talking to her." It was an excuse and we both knew it.

Meagan frowned at her messenger. "She's not answering anymore."

I didn't much like the sound of that, but Meagan seemed untroubled. "Don't worry, Zoë. We'll see her at school. Whatever she has to do can't take that long."

But I did worry.

It seems to come with the territory.

My mom's red electric Toyota didn't start right away that morning, which just figured. Meagan's parents were gone already, so we were on our own. If the engine didn't start, we'd have to walk, and I did not want to walk in this snow.

"I hate this piece of junk," I said as I opened the hood. I tried to look like I had a clue what to do, but, of course, I had no idea.

"At least you have a car."

"Not mine, really. Just a loaner." I sighed and frowned at the mystery of the engine. "I wish my dad had let me use the Lamborghini."

"Did you ask?"

I smiled. "Of course!"

"And?"

"He laughed and tossed me the keys to this one."

"Well, he is crazy for that car."

"He never even drives it anymore. It's like a shrine or something."

"What about that flashy new sedan he just bought? What is it, anyway?"

"Another Maserati," I said. "He says he likes Italian cars best."

"Well?"

"He drove it to the airport and parked it there."

"So you couldn't drive it?"

"I'm thinking so." I jiggled a pair of wires, then opened and closed the reservoir for the windshield-wiper fluid. You never knew.

"Is it charged up?" Meagan asked.

I nodded. That was one part I understood. I closed the hood, knowing there was nothing else I could do. "Let's try it again." We got back in and I turned the key. To my astonishment, the car started. Meagan hooted with glee. The engine wasn't running very well, but it settled into a choppy purr that was an approximation of its usual noise.

"What did you do?" Meagan asked. "What was that cap?"

"The windshield-fluid reservoir."

She laughed. "I thought you knew what you were doing."

"No idea." I counted off on my fingers as the car warmed up. "I know how to fill the wiper fluid, to top up the oil, to charge the battery, and to lock the doors. Not that anyone would want to steal this heap."

"Maybe your mom will get a new car and you'll be able to drive that."

"Maybe." It was an optimistic thought, one that got me

through the painful moment of driving into the school parking lot. It seemed as if everybody turned to stare.

And snicker.

I drove the battered and rusted red car through the array of shiny, beautiful luxury vehicles and felt like the poor country cousin. I could not figure out why my mom didn't want a new one, but she said she loved this one—and that it was more environmentally responsible to keep using it.

I just wished it looked better.

"It runs," Meagan insisted when I'd parked. "It's free and we get to use it." She gave me a look. "All good."

"All good," I agreed. "But the Lamborghini would be better. Just once, I'd like to drive it into this lot. Everyone would notice that!"

Meagan grinned and opened her door. "Sounds like your dad isn't the only one who likes Italian cars." She slammed the door as I got out. "My dad just likes Italian concertos, and you can't drive them anywhere."

We laughed together and headed to school.

She bumped my shoulder on the way. "You never know. Take care of this one and he might let you take your dream drive."

I didn't argue with her. It could theoretically happen. It would have had a better chance of happening with any other father and any other car.

Still, a dragon girl could hope.

DESPITE THE FACT THAT WE were later than usual, there was no sign of Jessica. Usually, she was waiting for Meagan outside the doors, but not today.

I deliberately forced my suspicions out of my mind. Maybe Jessica was actually in danger. The Mages had nearly sacrificed her at Halloween.

Skuld had corrected me—not what *will* be but what *might* be. Could Trevor and Adrian save the third kid if they had another victim ready?

"We've got to find Jessica," I said. "Is she answering her messenger yet?"

"No, but she'll be in math class," Meagan said with a confidence I didn't feel.

"I really need to talk to her. Do you know where she was going?"

"Relax, Zoë. Maybe it's a family thing."

I couldn't relax.

"What's going on?" Derek asked. He was suddenly at my side, appearing with that silence that still unnerved me. His eyes twinkled a little when I jumped. I was pretty sure he did it on purpose, just to show off.

Or maybe to remind me that he had special powers, too.

"I smell trouble," he said when I didn't immediately answer. "And you're wearing the necklace I gave you."

On instinct, I had put on the silver necklace with a sterling hand of Fatima he'd given me for my birthday, and I touched the charm now. "It seemed like a good idea. I had this dream."

I told him in an undertone about my nightmare. His eyes became brighter than usual, a striking pale blue, and his gaze danced over my features as I spoke. I wondered how much else he sensed.

"Find Jessica," he said to Meagan, an undercurrent of command in his tone. She nodded and loaded up her books with purpose. She gave me a smile, then headed off to class.

"She'll find her," I said, hoping it was true.

Derek watched her go; then he tugged a book out of his pocket. It was warm from being inside his coat. It was called *The Histories* by Herodotus. I read the title, then looked at Derek with surprise.

He had a secretive little smile. "As good a source as any."
He shrugged. "You asked."

So this Herodotus guy had said something about the wolf
shifters. Huh. I fanned through the book. It was pretty thick,
but there was a bookmark in it.

"Any ideas where we can find Kohana?" Derek asked,
glancing down the hall. His words recalled me to the moment,
and I shoved the book into my pack. When I slung it back
over my shoulder and closed my locker, he took my hand in
his. I wasn't expecting that, which maybe was why his touch
made my heart skip. I liked the warmth of his grip.

Never mind the steadiness of his gaze. I stared at him,
unable to look away.

His fingers entangled with mine, his thumb sliding across
my palm very slowly, slowly enough to give me heart failure.

It certainly was slow enough to distract me.

"Because it would be good to confirm that he still has the
NightBlade," he added, as if I needed the strategy explained
to me.

I wasn't, actually, thinking about Kohana in that precise
moment, or even the Wyvern's supposed ability to see past,
present, and future simultaneously. I was thinking about
Derek, about how steadily he looks into my eyes and how
slowly he moves. I was thinking about the warm caress of his
thumb, and I was thinking about Friday night's dance, and
I was wondering just what he had planned.

A slow dance?

A slow kiss?

I am the worst dancer in the world, and I'm not sure I'm
much of a kisser, either. I have been kissed and I have kissed
back some, but that doesn't exactly make me a pro.

Derek smiled and I wondered whether he could smell what
I was thinking.

I blushed. You knew it had to happen.

"I've got my dad's car for Friday," he murmured, and that small piece of information seemed fraught with expectations.

I was well aware that Derek was watching me closely. It was becoming clear to me that this date wasn't anything casual. I was, in fact, remembering his words from the fall, about his taking the task in his pack to ensure the alliance with the Wyvern was made. Wolves are not the most subtle intellectuals, in my limited experience. They put more value in action than in words.

What particular action would secure the alliance, as far as Derek was concerned? Going steady? Doing more than sharing a kiss? I stood and felt his thumb caress my hand and had a pretty good idea that he wanted a bigger commitment from me.

Which meant that my dad wasn't going to like Derek any more than he liked Jared.

Before I could think of anything brilliant to say, the bell for class rang. Derek squeezed my fingers, bolder now, then, to my astonishment, leaned closer and kissed my temple. "Later," he murmured in a low growl that made my stomach quiver. He gave me an intent look, then turned to lope down the hall.

Leaving me staring after him, my mouth dry.

"SORRY TO INTERRUPT A TENDER moment," Suzanne drawled from my other side, her tone snarky. "But Trevor wants to talk to you, freak."

I spun to find her glaring at me. I was as shocked by her words as her presence. Suzanne had never initiated a conversation with me—and Trevor never wanted to talk to me unless he was making trouble.

I had wanted to talk to Trevor. Suddenly, he wanted to talk to me. This was far too easy. Careful what you wish for.

To say that I was suspicious would have been the understatement of the century.

"Me?"

"At least you're as shocked as I am," Suzanne said. She jabbed her finger at me. "Do *not* get any ideas."

"Ideas?"

She leaned closer to whisper, "You're not his type. Don't imagine for one second that you are."

I laughed. I couldn't help it. The idea of me and Trevor becoming a couple was just that funny. He belonged to a group bent on destroying my kind forever, after all. "Don't worry. He's not my type, either."

She flicked a disparaging glance after Derek. "I guess not."

My temper flared because she was putting Derek down. "If Trevor wants to talk to me, why doesn't he?" I challenged. "Are you his minion now?"

Or was he afraid of me? Trevor did know what I was, after all, and we dragons had kicked major Mage butt in the fall.

Suzanne checked that there were other people at the end of the hall, then leaned closer, her eyes flashing. "Never call me that, freak."

She was always brave when others were around; it was when she and I were alone that her bravado slipped. "Then don't act like his minion."

"I am so going to get you," she muttered. "One of these days, I won't be the only one to see, and I'll make sure to take you down."

I mocked a shudder. "Gosh, I'm afraid."

She didn't like that, not one bit. She opened her mouth to say something bitchy, but the hall was empty. I saw my chance and went with it, too mad to care about repercussions.

I let my eye change to a dragon eye just for a heartbeat.

Suzanne paled and retreated quickly.

"What's the matter?" I asked sweetly, knowing my eye was back to normal.

She looked away, then back at me, then shook a finger. "One of these days, Sorensson."

I pretended to tremble, then grinned at her. There must have been some dragon in that look, because she stepped back.

Suzanne jerked her thumb toward the parking lot. "Trevor's in his car." Then she arched a brow, more confident now that there was distance between us. "Unless you don't have the nerve to cut class."

If it had been art class, I might have hesitated. Science meant it was an easy choice. I pushed past Suzanne and headed out of the school, in search of Trevor.

I didn't have to look far.

Chapter 3

*T*revor's green MG was idling at the closest entry to the parking lot. It's a convertible, but he had the black ragtop up. I was surprised he was even driving it in February. Snowflakes tumbled out of the pewter clouds that filled the sky, and it was more damp than cold.

I bent down, cautious now, and he unrolled the passenger's-side window. "We need to talk," he said grimly.

I have to say that Trevor was looking less than his best. His hair was disheveled and I would have bet that he hadn't slept the night before. Maybe for a few nights. There were dark circles under his eyes and his skin was pale.

He looked a lot worse than he had in my dream. He is usually the squeaky-clean type, his jeans practically ironed and every hair in place. The contrast was startling.

Plus he couldn't stop fidgeting. His fingers drummed on

the steering wheel, his agitation obvious. He kept looking around, scanning the parking lot, as if he expected boogeymen to jump him from every side.

Interesting. Was he really spooked or was it an act? I couldn't tell.

I actually had a moment when I wished I knew him better, just so I could assess his honesty, then realized how nutty a thought that was.

"So talk," I said, shoving my hands into my pockets. I would go with the bold Wyvern routine, I decided.

"Not here," he said. "Get in."

I laughed.

"Seriously, Zoë." His eyes were wide and he looked terrified. Again I wondered: Was that the truth or an illusion? It seemed a smidge over the top, especially if my dream hadn't happened yet. He should still be cocky about their plan, at least the way I figured it. "Look, Adrian's got this crazy idea and I don't know how to talk him out of it. I need your help."

I leaned back against the fence beside the sidewalk, keeping my distance. "That has to be a first."

He shoved a hand through his hair. "He found this old book, and he thinks he can manage this spell, but I know he's not skilled enough. I'm worried that it will all go wrong and no one will be able to stop it. He won't listen to me!"

I straightened at that. "What kind of spell?" When he didn't answer, I guessed. "The Invocation of Destruction?"

He stared at me in shock. "How do you know that?"

I shrugged. "How can you do it, though, without the NightBlade?"

And how could I stop them from even trying?

Trevor averted his gaze and shoved a hand through his hair. "It's a special rite. I've never seen it done before. Adrian's sure he can nail it, but I'm afraid." He did look freaked. I felt a teensy bit sorry for him. "This isn't a joke, Zoë. You don't know what he did last night."

My Wyvern sense was on full alert. "Then why don't you tell me?"

Trevor looked from side to side, as if there would be anyone stupid enough to stand out here in the snow and eavesdrop on us. His voice dropped to a hiss. "He went out to eat shadows. He said it would build his strength."

"Whose shadows?" I thought I already knew the answer, but had to ask.

"Just get in. We have to stop him!"

"What makes you think I can change Adrian's mind?"

"Maybe we should be on the same side, Zoë. Maybe this is important enough."

Maybe Trevor wasn't bad to the bone.

"Look, Zoë, there's no time. The ritual has to be done tonight. If we're going to stop him, we have to do it now. Who knows what he's done while I've been gone? Just get in!"

"Do you have a plan?"

He nodded. "There's only one copy of the book, at this library, in the reserves. I want you to incinerate it so everything in it is lost forever."

"Can't you destroy it yourself?"

His lips tightened. "I've tried. I think it needs dragonfire." He looked at me. "Shifter power."

That was news. "Why?"

"Trust me on this. Get in!"

Trust Trevor. That was a stretch.

On the other hand, it sounded like Adrian had been the one who had attacked Mozart—and he might be stalking more shifters. He knew what enough of us looked like in our human skins to find us. I didn't trust Trevor to have my best interests at heart, but I did trust him to understand Mage lore better than me.

And I wanted to believe that he had some redeeming features.

I pulled out my messenger and sent a message to Meagan that I was going with Trevor and hoping to stop Adrian from attacking more shifters. She'd figure out that I meant Mozart.

"Come on!" Trevor said, revving the engine.

I still hesitated a moment more before I got in.

That was all the time it took for me to check for spell light. There wasn't any, so I figured that it would take Trevor longer to conjure a spell to trap me than it would take me to spontaneously manifest elsewhere. I had confidence in my dragon abilities—and also feared this might be my own chance to turn the tide and stop the ceremony. That was a risk I was prepared to take.

In hindsight, I can see that my decision was chock-full of assumptions.

TREVOR'S CAR WAS PRETTY PLUSH inside, with leather seats and a dashboard that looked as if it had been carved of wood. (Did they ever really do that?) I felt as if I should be wearing mirrored sunglasses, or a swinging '60s Mondrian-inspired dress, go-go boots (white ones), or some other throwback fashion item.

Then he reached the main road beyond our school and I forgot about fashion statements. I was too busy hanging on.

Trevor drove like a maniac. Waaaaaaaaaaay too fast. I appreciated that he was worried about finding Adrian sooner rather than later, but wished I was under my own steam. Speeding was one thing, but he didn't seem to be entirely in control. This did not reassure me. Neither did his white-knuckle grip on the steering wheel.

I took this as a sign that he really was scared.

"You could slow down," I said, when he took a corner on two (squealing) wheels.

"No time to waste," he muttered, and, I swear, he drove even faster.

We left the part of the city I know really well, lunging into an area I'd never visited before. The buildings were neither new enough to be sleek nor old enough to have the grace of bygone days. They were all square and practical, made of brick and concrete, so similar that they could have been poured from the same mold. I saw a paved schoolyard with a chain-link fence around it, little kids running back and forth inside their cage, and was glad I didn't live around here.

Then Trevor took a couple of quick turns and screeched to a halt. He turned off the car engine. He'd parked in front of a building with broad concrete steps and double doors. The sign over the doors said it was a public library.

I still felt that foreboding of doom, but it seemed to me that we couldn't get into too much trouble in a library.

Shouldn't hindsight have served me better? I'd assumed myself to be safe before and been wrong.

Misplaced confidence was the first sign of trouble.

"The book is in the reserved collection," Trevor said in a hushed voice. "They won't let it leave the building." He came around the car with purpose. "Come on!"

"You don't think people will notice if I shift shape and start a fire?"

He was dismissive. "I'll launch some spellsong. Don't worry about the details—just fry that book and leave the rest to me!" He leapt out of the car and came around to my side.

I took a good look at the building. What was wrong? I had a very, very bad feeling.

"I'm not sure about this," I said, just as the passenger's door was opened. "Maybe it's not a good idea."

Trevor smiled as he tugged me out of the car, and I did not trust that smile.

Note sign of trouble number 2.

The street was deserted. Completely empty.

Portent of disaster number 3 present and accounted for.

Or was I just being chicken? Because if there was a book, I wanted to see it. I liked the idea of destroying a Mage tome. Breathe a little fire and terminate the possibility of anyone following those instructions ever again. It also sounded like there was something special about shifter power, something that worried the apprentice Mages, and I definitely wanted to know more about that. I didn't mind taking a small risk in order to get the job done and change the future for the better.

I knew I couldn't truly trust Trevor, but I'd beaten him before; even if Adrian was here, I'd thumped him a couple of times, as well. I rationalized that I could always spontaneously manifest elsewhere to get myself out of trouble. Even if I wasn't entirely accurate in targeting locations when I did that, all I had to do was be anywhere else.

Piece of cake.

"The book's inside," Trevor said. "Only copy in the world."

I was curious. You know what they say about curiosity and cats. I was pretty sure that didn't apply to dragons.

Trevor and I started up the steps; then the building did a very odd thing.

It wavered.

Like a sheet in the wind.

That was when I knew it was a glamour. Whatever it was disguising couldn't be good.

The book wasn't here.

It was all a ruse.

A trap.

I spun to run, but Adrian lunged out of the glamour and snatched my other elbow. He'd been waiting there for me, disguised by the spell. Now there were two of them, one on either side of me. Adrian pulled hard to enough to make me stumble, and when I yelled in protest, he laughed.

When I looked up, I saw the orange spell light dancing in his eyes. He could have been filled with it, brimming with it, the spell light boiling up inside of him to fill his eyes.

Oh, shit.

In the heartbeat it took me to process that new data, Trevor kicked my feet out from beneath me. I fell, skinning my hands. I shouted and tried to shift shape, but an orange bolt of spell light slapped me across the face.

I trembled, too stunned by its impact to even respond. The pair of them hauled me up those steps while I was disoriented. They weren't actually steps at all. They dissolved as we moved forward, disappearing as surely as if they'd never been.

Guess what the glamour was hiding?

You've got it. A vacant lot.

Unless I was very much mistaken, this was the same vacant lot where Skuld had brought me. That other kid from my dream was there, singing his Mage chant, holding a gleaming golden orb of spell light captive like a balloon on a string. It was filled to bursting with ShadowEaters, and they pressed against the side closest to me as Trevor and Adrian carried me into the lot.

"It's not the full moon yet!" I protested.

"Sure it is," Adrian said. "You just can't see it in the day-light."

No! I couldn't screw up this badly. I couldn't be the reason their spell succeeded and my dream came true. I had to get out of there ASAP. I called to the shimmer, intent upon being anywhere else on the planet, but I couldn't find it. Somehow it had been shut down or turned off or blocked. I panicked and felt for it frantically, but no luck. I could only find a hard wall of orange in my thoughts.

A spell barrier that kept me from the power of what I was.

You can believe that I lost it.

I struggled and I twisted. I fought and I kicked and I swore and I screamed. None of it made any difference. Trevor and Adrian sang a nasty spell, one that I'd heard before and liked even less this time. As soon as they started, golden ropes of spells appeared in the air, growing longer and thicker as they wound all around me. I was trussed up in no time and power-less to escape, just like a shifter I'd seen sacrificed when I infiltrated the Mages' hive memory; just like Jessica and the guys had been in the fall.

And my blue shimmer was AWOL.

I didn't stop trying to summon it, even though I knew it wasn't going to answer. Meanwhile, Trevor and Adrian hauled me ever deeper into the vacant lot, the one that wasn't very vacant after all. They joined in the chant with the other kid, making the globe overhead get bigger and brighter, the silhouettes inside moving with greater agitation. The Shadow-Eaters pressed against the barrier of the spell orb, so close that I could see their eyes.

They glowed orange, just like in my dream. They had no pupils, no irises, nothing but orange spell light shining like beacons where their eyes should have been. The

ShadowEaters could have been just skins filled with orange spell light. It was like the light in Adrian's eyes but a hundred times worse, and a thousand times more terrifying.

They were going to eat my shadow and destroy me, and there wasn't one thing I could do about it.

Except panic. I had that covered.

And my terror only increased when I saw Kohana.

The Thunderbird shifter who had tried to betray my kind to the Mages the previous spring, who had attacked me in the fall, and who had worked with me under protest to destroy the Mages' collective memory sauntered toward us, working his way through the broken bottles and discarded car fenders and busted furniture.

He still had dark hair and dark eyes, a secretive smile, and a tight pair of jeans. He was wearing a dark T-shirt this time, one that covered the feather tattoo I knew he had on his shoulder, and it seemed to me that his expression was a little bit mean.

Was he enchanted? I dared to hope, but there was no spell light around Kohana.

My heart stopped cold when I saw that he had the Night-Blade, the weapon he had stolen from the Mages in November. He'd said then that he was going to destroy it, as it was the tool they used to cut the shadows away from the bodies of their victims, the better to offer sacrifices to the Shadow-Eaters. But he was back, he still had it, and it didn't look damaged in the least.

Plus he held it up, as if intending to use it.

This was how they were going to complete the ceremony—they *had* the NightBlade. Kohana had brought it to them.

No! Kohana's expression turned resolute, and my very bad feeling became forty-seven thousand times worse.

Because it didn't take much to figure out whose shadow was the plat du jour.

THE SHADOWEATERS CLEARLY KNEW WHAT was going to happen. Their forms were moving more quickly, shifting and shimmering, vibrating with excitement and anticipation. The orb was being stretched in every direction as they fought to become free. And there was a point in the orb where they strained toward Kohana, their fingers grasping in the direction of the NightBlade.

Even though they were still inside that orb of spell light that had conjured them, I could hear them salivating, licking their lips and clicking their teeth together. I swear their bellies growled—even though they didn't appear to have any.

They were the stuff of nightmares.

I struggled as I heard Trevor and Adrian and the other kid sing the spell of sacrifice. I knew I was next, that I was feeling the same horror and futility the other sacrificed shifters must have felt. I did not want to know how it felt to be eaten alive by ShadowEaters.

If they took me out, as Wyvern of the *Pyr*, I feared the rest of the dragon shifters would lose heart. My dad would be easy to trap then, in his grief, and he's the leader of our kind. I feared that all the dragon shifters would seek revenge, only to follow me and my dad to oblivion.

Because I'd been too cocky.

Big mistake.

I knew there was nothing I could do, but I still fought. I watched the mesh of spell light grow brighter and denser. Kohana's form was like a shadow falling over the spell light. He held the NightBlade high and called the invocation, the same invocation that the Mages had sung in the fall.

It was obscene hearing that song fall from his lips, to see that spell wind out of his mouth to join the others.

I couldn't believe he would do it, but my eyes told me the truth. I saw the curved blade of the knife rise high. I saw its darkness silhouetted against the vivid light of the spell. I saw the ShadowEaters become frenzied. I saw the sphere get thinner in preparation for shattering. I felt Adrian and Trevor tremble in anticipation.

I struggled all the while, but I knew I was doomed.

"Now!" Kohana shouted. He leapt down toward me, and I squeezed my eyes shut.

But he sliced down the length of me with one savage stroke, severing the spells that bound me helpless. I sprang to my feet as he pivoted and sliced at Adrian, hacking off a big chunk of his shadow. Adrian screamed. The Shadow-Eaters sighed with lust and moved in new frenzy, licking and slurping and gobbling as they pushed at the spell that held them captive. The orb shimmered but held.

Just.

Trevor shouted in terror and tried to help Adrian, who had fallen to his knees.

I ran.

I heard footsteps behind me, and looked back to find Kohana closing fast, the NightBlade high in his hand. "You!" I shouted, once again unable to guess his allegiances. He'd lied to me and deceived me and helped me, and I never knew what to expect.

"Me!" he agreed, laughing.

I heard Trevor and the other kid singing and glanced back to see a spell being mustered.

It was shaped like a spear.

"Look out!" I shouted.

Kohana lunged past me and sliced at the air. I saw a golden barrier before us part in a shower of sparks. As if he had cut a hole in the side of a balloon, the glamour that had disguised us from the world fell like sliced cloth.

Then the NightBlade did a strange thing. It wriggled in Kohana's grip, as if it had come alive, as if it were an eel or a snake. As if it were trying to work itself free.

Kohana swore and snatched at it with his other hand, but it sliced at him.

He yelled, and it jumped from his grip, catapulting through the air toward Adrian and Trevor.

"Holy shit," Kohana said. "It's got a will of its own."

Trevor and the third kid stopped singing immediately and the spell they'd been conjuring fell to the ground, lifeless. They snatched at the NightBlade in unison, bumping into each other. The handle of the knife bounced off Trevor's head, rebounded—or leapt of its own accord—

And sliced open the orb that held the ShadowEaters captive.

They surged through the space, gleeful and frenzied.

Free.

"They called to it," Kohana said, his features ashen, and I knew he was right. The ShadowEaters spilled through the opening in the globe, milling on the ground, a great crowd of ravenous demons.

"How can we stop them?" I asked, but I knew the answer.

We couldn't. Not now, not when they were hungry and fervid.

As I watched in horror, Adrian got to his feet. He snatched the NightBlade out of the air, seized the new kid, and muttered an invocation. "Blood and shadow!" he cried, and slit his throat.

The kid gurgled. Blood spurted from his throat. Adrian laughed and shimmered.

Then, before our eyes, Adrian became a ShadowEater himself. His features melted into shadow, and he turned into a silhouette, one filled with spell light. He hooted, and it was only by his position that I could tell which one of the Shadow-Eaters he was.

I was so stunned that I could have been rooted to the ground. This was an initiation rite. And Adrian had passed. Was this where all of these ShadowEaters had come from? Had they once been humans? Mages?

Kohana seized my hand and hauled me through the shattered glamour. I couldn't help looking back at the Shadow-Eaters. I had wanted my dream to be wrong. I wanted them to be benign, or easily defeated, or genies who happily went back into their respective jar.

No luck. They fell on the third kid, just like they had in my dream, surrounding him and overwhelming him. He tried to run, despite the wound on his throat. There was nothing anyone could do to save him, and nothing could have stopped their feasting. I shuddered as he fell, buried beneath them.

There was something deeply wrong with the sight of the ShadowEaters. They were shaped like humans but insubstantial. Their human forms had no real faces. Just those golden eyes and forms that couldn't be distinguished one from another. They were all the same, interchangeable, all exuding menace.

And hunger.

Were they the next step in Mage evolution?

What came after that?

"Hurry up!" Kohana cried, and it was probably the first time I'd heard fear in his voice.

That was when I saw that Trevor had the NightBlade and was looking at us.

We raced forward together, and when Kohana yelled, "Now!" I knew what he meant.

I hoped like hell I could do it.

We both shifted shape as soon as we were through the space. I was so relieved that my shimmer was back that I was trembling. Kohana was holding one of my claws tightly, as if he would have hauled me into the sky with force, regardless of whether I'd been able to shift or not.

I roared at the welcome power of my shift. That barrier was gone. I delighted in the unfurling of my wings and the majestic power of my tail. I pivoted, not twenty feet above the ground, and exhaled fire at the collapsing shell of the Mage glamour.

I had nearly died.

I would have died, without Kohana's help.

Just like that third kid, who was lifeless on the ground now, his blood staining the snow.

As we soared into the sky, the ShadowEaters retreated from his body. They were sated temporarily. They looked upward, all those golden eyes shining as they focused on us hovering overheard. I saw them leap into the air and didn't need any encouragement from Kohana to boot it out of there.

He took off like a shot, flying with terrifying speed in the opposite direction.

I was right on his tail.

I saw the ShadowEaters leap into the sky behind us and knew we wouldn't outrace them. They could fly through the air, too—I'd seen them do it in my dream.

There was only one way to save us. I tightened my grip on Kohana's claw, closed my eyes, and flung us both through space and time.

WE WERE INSTANTLY OVER A park beside the lake, one I recognized as being close to my school. Lake Michigan was choppy and pewter in color, and the snow was still falling lazily. There was about a foot of snow in the park.

And I was a white salamander clutched in Kohana's talons. It was one of two forms I could take as the Wyvern.

"Thanks," he said, exhaling as he ensured that his grip on me was firm but not too tight. (Newts squish.) He circled, choosing a spot in the middle of an open area, then landed with care. He shifted shape in the last instant, touching the earth in his human form, tossing my salamander self into the air.

His expression was expectant and I knew what to do. I shifted shape and landed beside him in human form, then took a deep steadying breath.

"That was close," he said, then flashed me a devilish grin.

His eyes glinted like jet, like he had a million secrets, and I wondered whether he really was about the same age as me or whether that was an illusion of some kind.

I looked at him, uncertain what to expect.

The thing was, I wasn't sure whether Kohana had saved me for good or just for now.

I certainly wasn't sure he'd tell me either way.

"Perfect, untouched snow in every direction," he said, surveying the field with satisfaction. "We walk away from here, and the next person who comes along and sees the tracks will wonder where the walkers came from."

I watched him smile. "You like messing with people's perceptions."

"I like giving others something to think about." He gave me a hard look. "I guess we'll call it square, *Unktehila*." With that, he walked away.

"Square?" I said, astonished. "You just freed the Shadow-Eaters!"

"I did not." He cast the words over his shoulder, not pausing or turning back.

"You brought the NightBlade back to them."

He pivoted and flung out his hands, raising his voice for the first time. "Maybe it brought itself back to them."

"But it's supposed to be on the other side of the continent. In *your* safekeeping."

"Oops." Kohana turned to walk away again.

I raced behind him, catching up in about twenty feet. (It's possible that this was because he let me catch up. I'm tall, but he's taller.) "Why didn't you just destroy the NightBlade when you had it?"

Kohana cast me a look. "Who says I didn't try?"

I remembered that wriggling and had nothing to say.

Kohana's eyes became impossibly darker. "The problem is that it's not easily shattered."

"King said that after you left with it," I remembered.

"I shouldn't have been surprised that it has a will of its own. That explains a lot."

"What do you mean?"

"I didn't know for sure until just now. But at home, it started to turn our elders against each other. I thought maybe I was seeing things that weren't there, but the disputes escalated and—" He frowned and fell silent.

"What?"

His lips tightened. "On the equinox, one elder was found dead."

I was shocked. "The NightBlade killed him?"

"No. It persuaded one of our own to wield it as a weapon."

"How could it do that?"

"I don't know," he admitted. "But I saw it. Things got so ugly so fast. They were arguing about who should be custodian of the NightBlade. You should have heard the things people were saying to each other—no. No one should hear that."

I thought of the effect of the Mage spells on the dragon

guys when we'd been at boot camp and Adrian had been messing with our thoughts. Even though I knew they hadn't meant what they'd said while under the influence of the spell, those words were hard to forget. "I've heard it," I said.

"I'd never seen such dissent among our kind, and when that elder was found dead, my grandfather and I both knew what had caused it. He hadn't liked my bringing it there, not from the start. I promised my grandfather that I would take the NightBlade away and not return until it was destroyed forever."

"You're an exile."

He nodded once. "A willing one. This weapon has to be smashed down to molecules." He spoke with such severity that I shivered.

"What were you even doing with Trevor and Adrian?"

Kohana frowned. "I can't break the NightBlade. I can't even scratch it. It seemed to me that the ones who made it would be the most likely to know how to destroy it."

"Maybe it made you think that."

His eyes glinted. "Maybe."

"Did you lie to them?"

His smile flashed, so irreverent that I couldn't help but smile in return. "Wouldn't you?"

"In a heartbeat."

He studied me, and his smile faded once more. "They didn't believe me any more than you do," he said quietly. "They said I had to prove that I wanted to join them, that I had to participate in the ceremony to prove my intent."

"You had the NightBlade," I pointed out. "You had to know what would be part of the ceremony."

"Eliminate a shifter, preferably a wildcard. Yes, I knew." He nodded, his expression hardening. "I would have done it, too, because it might have given me the secret to destroy that weapon forever." His gaze locked with mine, his intensity making my mouth go dry. "If it had been any shifter but you, Zoë."

Before I could wrap my mind around that—not just what he'd said but that he'd called me by my name—Kohana bent and swiftly touched his lips to mine. His kiss burned against my mouth, even with the contact being as short as it was.

He looked deep into my eyes and spoke softly. "Remember, *Unktehila*, they get their power from eating shadows, and they like shifter shadows best."

Then he walked away, leaving me standing alone in the snow.

Astonished.

And shaken.

Which had nothing on my reaction when I saw the wolf watching us from the shrubbery that surrounded the clearing. The wolf was silvery gray and utterly still, unblinking, its expression that of a predator.

Derek.

Before I could do anything, the wolf disappeared into the undergrowth as surely as a shadow fades from view. Kohana, meanwhile, had also vanished.

I was alone in the middle of a snowy field.

Good. I glanced at the time on my messenger and took a deep breath. Excellent. I had English in ten minutes. A little spontaneous manifestation—arriving in one of the school restrooms—and I just might make it.

Derek was in my English class, but it would take me a bit longer than the trip over to figure out what to say to him about what he'd seen.

I MADE IT TO MY locker, hyperventilating and desperately in need of a sugar hit (with no time to get any), only to find a note taped to it.

It seemed I had an appointment in guidance counseling.
And I was late.

Fantabulous.

The day just kept getting better.

The counselor, Muriel, was on the phone, so I took the
seat outside her office and peeled off my coat. I checked my
messenger and found roughly forty-five thousand anxious
messages from Meagan, including the update that Jessica still
wasn't answering her messenger. She hadn't turned up at
school, either. I quickly let Meagan know where I was, my
concern for Jessica growing by the second. She was the one,
after all, who had nearly been sacrificed to the ShadowEaters
in the fall. That might make her more vulnerable.

I sent a frantic message to Nick and Liam and Garrett,
copying them all, explaining that the ShadowEaters really
were raging through the world. I managed to send one to
Meagan before my messenger started to chime with such
urgency that I had to turn it off or else it would be confis-
cated. I'd have to tell Derek myself.

Where had Kohana gone?

Where was Jessica?

I refused to give any more weight to the idea that she
might be working with the apprentice Mages. That was probably what they wanted me to think, as it would divide us when
we needed to pull together.

If only there was a way I could track her down. The
Wyvern was supposed to be able to dispatch dreams. I hadn't
had much luck with that, but it couldn't hurt to try again.
I closed my eyes and thought about my fear for Jessica,
focused it, then tried to send her an urgent alert, independent
of modern technology.

I had no idea whether it would work.

When I opened my eyes, Muriel was still on the phone.

That was when I remembered the book that Derek had given me. I tugged it out of my backpack and opened it to the bookmark he'd inserted.

It couldn't be all bad to be found reading Herodotus.

Herodotus, it turned out, was a traveler who wrote up his adventures and experiences for other travelers or for the entertainment of those who stayed home. Fodor's for the B.C. era. For a guy who's been dead for a couple of millennia, he reads pretty well. This was the passage Derek had marked—4:105, in case you don't believe me:

> The Neuroi practise the Scythian customs: and one generation before the expedition of Dareios it so befell them that they were forced to quit their land altogether by reason of serpents: for their land produced serpents in vast numbers, and they fell upon them in still larger numbers from the desert country above their borders; until at last being hard pressed they left their own land and settled among the Budinoi. These men it would seem are wizards; for it is said of them by the Scythians and by the Hellenes who are settled in the Scythian land that once in every year each of the Neuroi becomes a wolf for a few days and then returns again to his original form. For my part I do not believe them when they say this, but they say it nevertheless, and swear it moreover.

Wolf shifters driven from their land by serpents.

You know I had a pretty good idea who those serpents might have been—and glimpsed another reason why some of the wolves were not so hot about making alliances with dragon shifters. Kohana's Thunderbirds had made a treaty with some reptiles they called *Unktehila*. It was an agreement that dragons would surrender North America to the Thunderbirds. That's why he'd called me an oathbreaker when we'd first met.

Had my ancestors really needed to piss everybody off?

Or did that just come with the territory of being a dragon shifter?

I wasn't doing a very good job of ensuring peace, love, and understanding myself. Maybe we're meant to be solitary and grumpy. But with apprentice Mages hunting shifters and ShadowEaters set free, we needed to keep this alliance with the cats and the wolves and the Thunderbirds to ensure the survival of all of us.

Regardless of our innate tendencies. I made a mental note to ask Derek if the wolves really did call themselves Neuroi, and closed the book as Muriel came out of her office.

She looked at the book.

She smiled.

I smiled.

But when she gestured me into the hot seat in her office, Muriel's smile disappeared.

IT SEEMED THAT I WAS officially troubled, and my disappearance that morning was proof that I was unreliable in terms of attending classes. This was perceived to be a result of my parents' marital difficulties, a continuation of my bad attendance in the fall, and a natural if unfortunate emotional progression for a sixteen-year-old whose domestic life had become unmoored.

She did actually use the word *unmoored*.

Muriel didn't know the half of it.

Of course, I couldn't say anything in my own defense, even when it came to cutting class. *I had to leave school this morning in an attempt to stop the apprentice Mages from invoking the ShadowEaters, which is part of their plan to eliminate all remaining shape shifters from the world. Sadly, I failed so it's on to plan B.*

Uh-huh.

Even better: *I was late getting back because the apprentice Mages trapped me, deceiving me with a glamour, then binding me with spells so they could cut away my shadow. Fortunately, a Thunderbird shifter saved me and we both flew out of danger to the park just around the corner. Phew.*

Or best of all: *The wildcards have been drawn to this school to make an alliance to ensure the survival of our respective kinds. Derek Black is a wolf shifter and Jessica d'Angelo is a jaguar shifter and I'm a dragon shifter. Suzanne really did see a dragon in the girl's bathroom last fall, and it was me.*

Maybe not.

Trust me. It's much better to just hang your head and let them think you cut class to buy cigarettes.

Given the current absence of my parents and Muriel's unwillingness to compromise their last chance to rebuild their marriage (no, I have no idea where she got that interpretation of their vacation plan—ha) and her reluctance to draw Mrs. Jameson into this "disappointing situation," Muriel had a plan under which I'd check in with her before and after each class. My observation that this could, in fact, make me late for class made no difference. We were partners, Muriel and I, from this point forward, driven to ensure my attendance, which would henceforth be perfect.

The timing on this strategy completely bit.

I might as well be a poodle on a jeweled leash.

It's not my look. Just so you know.

Chapter 4

So, I was in a pretty crap mood when I got to English class late, one that was not improved by Derek glowering at me from the back of the room when I entered. I could feel his gaze boring into the back of my skull throughout the whole class, and he was ticked enough to not know the answer when he was called on.

I think that had to be a first. I hoped he'd be mad enough to ignore me afterward, but no luck; he followed me out of class and back to my Muriel check.

I was really not interested in getting chewed out, but Derek's heightened sense of smell apparently wasn't sharp enough to pick up on that.

Or else he didn't care.

"So, what was that all about?" he demanded in his growly

undertone. "Where did you go? And why were you in Trevor's car?"

"You saw that?"

"I had a feeling. I turned back to find you." He glared at me. "I saw you leave, but I couldn't catch up with you." His tone turned fierce. "You never should have gone anywhere with him. You know he's dangerous."

"He told me that Adrian had been eating shifter shadows. I went with him to try to stop Adrian." It seemed like a good idea not to mention—yet—that I'd completely, totally, and utterly failed in that goal. I marched down the hallway and he walked beside me.

"Alone? Dumb, Zoë. Dumb."

That stung, because it had been dumb. It would have been nice for him to have had some confidence in me, though. "I told Meagan."

"Well, you didn't tell me."

I strode onward. I hadn't exactly had time to update everyone on the planet on my situation.

"We're a team," he said with force. "We have an alliance, in case you've forgotten. We're supposed to work together but you acted alone." I guess the fact that I didn't immediately defend myself made him even more angry, because he took a deep breath and a step back. "If you got yourself in danger, you deserved it."

Deserved it? I was with him until those last two words.

"Excuse me?" I halted in the hallway and spun to face him. I didn't care who saw me and I didn't care what my eyes did. I was feeling the need to breathe some fire.

"I *deserved* to be spellbound?" I demanded in an undertone. "I *deserved* to be cornered and nearly sacrificed to the ShadowEaters? Is that really what you think? Just because I didn't tell you what I was doing, I should *die*?"

Derek, to his credit, looked shocked. His eyes widened as he surveyed me. It was a bit late, to my thinking, to worry about the details.

"No," he whispered.

"Yes," I hissed with force. "The ShadowEaters are free. I tried to stop Trevor and Adrian, but I failed. Not only that, but they're hungry and they've already killed someone by eating his shadow."

Derek paled.

"Plus Adrian has become one."

Derek took a step back.

"Zoë!" Muriel called from the end of the hall. "You don't have time to socialize."

"No way," he muttered, but I could see his doubt.

"Yes! I would have been *lunch* if Kohana hadn't helped me."

His eyes flashed. "I would have helped you. You should have told me where you were going. I found you by scent, even though you disappeared. I would have followed you anywhere. . . ."

"Obviously I made a mistake," I said, interrupting him. "But since I'm the one who was nearly sacrificed as a result, I'm not feeling like I owe you an apology."

Oh, he didn't like that. I saw the flash of anger in his eyes and the way his gaze dropped to my lips. That was when I knew that it was the kiss that really bothered him, not my leaving alone with Trevor or even endangering myself.

That made me see red. Because Kohana had kissed me. It hadn't been my choice, I hadn't invited it, and I sure hadn't drawn it out.

"You don't own me," I whispered, and Derek's features set.

"Coming, Muriel!" I shouted with false cheer, and marched toward the guidance office. She smiled at me, all sweet concern, but I nearly snarled at her. There must have been a little bit of dragon in my expression, because her smile disappeared in record time. She swallowed and marked the time on her sheet so I could sign it, then ushered me off to math class.

Standing in the hallway to make sure I went right there.

I was feeling, if you must know, a little bit pissed.

I BANGED OPEN MY LOCKER at lunch and flung my books into the bottom.

"Bad morning?" Nick asked from right beside me, and I could have jumped for joy.

Then I practically fell on him, giving him a hug so tight that I nearly squished the stuffing out of him.

If dragons had stuffing. They don't, in case you aren't sure. All the usual blood and bones and guts inside. No sage-and-onion stuffing. Not even chestnut.

He hugged me back just as hard. "Okay, Z?" he asked, pulling back to look at me. He'd taken to calling me Z since my birthday. I'm not sure why, but I kind of liked it. The nickname had a buddy feel to it, which perfectly suited our friendship now that I'd abandoned my lifetime crush on him.

"Bad morning." I tried to compose myself, with—it must be said—mixed success. "What are you doing here?"

Nick smiled sheepishly. "You called."

I propped my hands on my hips to survey him. "I called you only an hour ago. Even you couldn't get here from Minneapolis that fast."

"So maybe I was here already."

What?

Nick flicked a glance up and down the hall. "I wanted to talk to you."

He had my undivided attention with that. "About?"

Nick's neck reddened but he didn't avert his gaze. "Isabelle." He said her name in a long whisper. Then he shoved his hand through his hair, leaving it all standing up, and looked unsettled.

Isabelle.

Well, the plot had thickened.

Just to fill you in on the gaps, Isabelle and I are convinced that she's the reincarnation of the previous Wyvern, Sophie. Sophie died with her *Pyr* lover, Nikolas, and once she died, I was conceived. Only one Wyvern at a time. The story is that they chose to sacrifice themselves because they couldn't be together, anyway—their love was forbidden stuff. Nick's dad was convinced that Nick was Nikolas reincarnated, and I thought it was incredibly cool that he'd been so determined to find his Sophie again that he'd started a new life just months after his last one had ended. Isabelle says she's been dreaming about Nick all her life, and that her dreams always come true.

Destined love? Sounds like it, in all its romantic glory—hopefully with a better ending this time around.

The trick is that Nick has been a little uncertain about all of this. Maybe more than a little. I know he likes Isabelle, I know he's not daunted by the fact that she's older than us, and it certainly doesn't hurt that she's gorgeous and kind and pretty much everything anyone would ever want in a girlfriend.

He just didn't want to promise what he couldn't deliver.

I respect that, even if it isn't the happy ending I—or Isabelle—might hope for.

"What about Isabelle?" I asked, pretending that I hadn't guessed.

"Well, you're a girl."

I had to tease him. He looked so earnest. "True."

He grinned and gave me a nudge. "Seriously." He pulled a jewelry box from his pocket. "Do you think this is a sucky birthday gift?"

"Her birthday's not for another couple of weeks," I said,

taking the box. I didn't need to say that. Nick is one person who always remembers other people's birthdays. He's like a birthday calendar. He knows them all and makes sure he remembers everyone on their day.

It's quite sweet, and it's not just because he loves a party or loves to be remembered on his own birthday.

"Two weeks from Saturday." Nick grimaced. "I want to make sure I picked out something good while there's still time to fix it if I didn't."

He *was* worried about it. I opened the box and caught my breath. Inside was a pendant, set in silver, with two stones in the center. One was yellow and faceted, while the other was opalescent and rounded. They weren't huge stones, but they were pretty together. The yellow one had a silver setting that made it look like it was the orb of the sun, while the opalescent one was set into a silver crescent of a moon.

"The sun and the moon," I said.

Nick and Isabelle, I thought. In his dragon form Nick has glorious golden scales and glowing amber eyes. Seeing him as a dragon is like looking into the radiance of the sun. Isabelle, meanwhile, is ethereal and a bit dreamy. When I'd dreamed of the past Wyvern, Sophie, her dragon scales had been so pale that they could have been made of moonbeams. I touched the pendant with a fingertip.

"Well?" Nick was practically bouncing in his anxiety. He swallowed visibly, obviously concerned that I wasn't saying more. "Do you think she'll like it?"

"I know she'll love it." I met his gaze. "It must have cost you."

He shoved a hand through his hair again and grinned, as nervous as I'd ever seen him. This was saying something. Nick does confidence like he invented it. "Yeah. I had the jeweler make it special. I wanted it to be right."

I looked down at the pendant, awed and wary, too.

I had to say it. "It's not a trinket, though, Nick. You shouldn't give it to her unless you're going to see her more than you do now." He looked worried when I said that. "Isabelle—well, anybody—would think this was a pretty serious gift. A declaration, maybe."

"Yeah, I know." He shuffled his feet again. "I guess that's what I really wanted to see you about. You know that night after the big fight with the Mages, before your birthday?"

"Yeah."

"I went back to her room at the dorm and we sat and talked. . . ."

"Uh-huh."

He grinned. "Really. We talked all night. It was awesome." He shoved his hands into his pockets and heaved a sigh. "It was easy, but electric, too." He grimaced, but I knew exactly what he meant. "I don't know, Z. I don't know what to do. Can you see some future for me?"

That was not an easy question to answer.

The hall had emptied out and Nick's stomach growled right on cue. "You hungry?" I asked. "Let's get something to eat while we talk about it."

"Good idea," he said, and slung an arm around my shoulders. We headed to the cafeteria, grabbed some pizza, and sat in the corner together, talking—which gave all sorts of people all sorts of things to speculate about.

Nick is the kind of guy people notice.

No: *girls* notice him.

I felt every female eye in the place on us, even after we sat down. In fact, I felt more than one gaze boring into my back. I bit into my pizza—they actually had my favorite combo today, feta and green pepper, a sign from heaven that I was intended to eat lunch in the cafeteria on this day—and glanced over my shoulder.

Suzanne and her cronies were obviously talking about Nick. I knew this because Fiona and Yvonne were looking our way, Trish was snickering, and Anna was whispering something to Suzanne that made the Queen Bee smile. I also could hear what Anna said, courtesy of my sharp *Pyr* hearing.

Her comment made Nick and me smile, too. We exchanged a glance at the conviction that he must be my cousin to be seen eating with me.

"Right," Nick said with a teasing grin. "I should kiss you just to mess them up."

"Who cares what they think?" I said, dismissing them. "Anyway, a few months ago you were sure it wouldn't be fair to spend more time with Isabelle, in case you have a firestorm with someone else."

"In case destiny isn't on our side," Nick agreed, making a slice of pizza disappear in record time. He met my gaze. "But what if it is?"

"Something changed your mind," I insisted. "Was it really a night of talking?"

"I can't stop thinking about her." Nick flung out his hand. "It pisses me off a bit. I've never had this happen before."

"Could it be love?" I teased, and he flashed his usual confident grin.

"Well, doesn't it make sense to find out?" He leaned closer. "I mean, maybe I'm blowing a chance to find out for sure. She finishes her year here and goes back to England in two months, you know."

"It's not another planet. You could go there sometime."

Nick sat back and drummed his fingers on the table with impatience. "But I've got this feeling, Z, that I'm screwing up an opportunity. It just keeps getting stronger, like—I don't know. This sounds stupid."

"Tell me."

He looked right at me. "Like someone or something is trying to kick my ass before it's too late. I thought maybe it was you, since you're the Wyvern."

"Not me. Not yet." I smiled at him. "Maybe it's the Great Wyvern."

He rolled his eyes at that.

Maybe it was the last Wyvern. Sophie. Hmm.

"So, maybe you *should* find out. Go and talk to her." I nodded at the pocket where he'd shoved that jewelry box. "But I'd keep that in my pocket until I knew for sure."

He was cocky then, maybe because I'd convinced him that his instincts were right. "I've got two weeks to figure it out."

"Wait a minute. Are you cutting school for this?"

"You'd better believe it." He leaned across the table to whisper, mischief in his eyes. "But I told my dad I had to come and defend you while your folks are away."

"I am not your cover story!"

"Sure! It turned out to be true before I even got here. You've got to tell me all about this morning and those Shadow-Eaters." Nick cocked a finger at me. "But first, promise to cover for me." And he smiled at me, his auburn hair tousled, his amber eyes gleaming, and even though I didn't have a crush on him anymore, I still couldn't say no to him.

"All right, I'll cover for you." I shook a finger at him when his grin widened. "But you owe me big-time."

"Tell you what. I'll get you another slice of pizza."

"More than that!"

He looked at me in mock horror. "You want *two* more? Z, you're not going to have a skinny butt for long if you eat like that."

I threw the wadded-up paper plate at him, and he laughed all the way back to the line.

Then I smiled to myself. I knew this was going to work. Maybe not this month or even this year, but this would lay the groundwork for their future together.

Nick and Isabelle, together at last. It would be perfect.

The thing was that now I knew exactly what I'd give to Isabelle for her birthday. I'd wanted to give her the drawing I'd done of her and Nick at the lake the previous spring, but with Nick AWOL, it had seemed inappropriate.

I'd better get the final touches on that drawing before her birthday.

NICK INSISTED ON GOING TO check out the vacant lot after I finished school. Visit the scene of the crime, as it were, and see the evidence. He was adamant that everyone had to gather and hear my story right where it happened, as well as look for clues about the ShadowEaters. I was afraid Trevor and the ShadowEaters might still be there, but Nick was ready to kick their butts immediately if they were.

He was acting like a protective older brother, and I couldn't argue with him very easily, especially after he got Liam and Garrett on his side. They wouldn't be here, but they agreed with Nick. Nick thought Isabelle's instincts would be helpful and I thought her presence would suit him well, so I pinged her and asked if Nick could pick her up. She agreed quickly, which I had to think was a good thing. My job was to tell Meagan and Derek and find Jessica before the end of the school day.

Overall, I was less than thrilled about this plan but could see the logic of it. At least we'd all be together. I was deeply afraid that we'd find a welcome committee there, one that wasn't very welcoming, but they couldn't take us all down at once.

Could they?

We'd beaten them before.

But I was afraid the rules might have changed.

Or was I just being chicken because I'd made one mistake already?

We'd go in with the full alliance, and see if we could save the day.

I took a deep breath when Nick took my car keys and went to get Isabelle, his heart obviously in his throat. We bumped fists before he headed out, and I was well aware of Trish watching from her locker on the other side of Meagan's.

Out of the corner of my eye, I thought I caught a glimmer of golden spell light. When I turned to look, Trish was whispering to Yvonne and sashaying down the hall and there was no spell light at all.

Great. I was so exhausted that I was hallucinating.

Belatedly, I tried to remember what homework I should have done at lunch. Being hunted was messing with my academic performance, that was for sure.

"Hey," Derek said, appearing silently beside me as he always did.

I ignored him.

"I don't want to fight with you."

I was still mad about his crack that I'd deserved to get in trouble.

I straightened and looked him in the eye. "How could I tell?" I asked, then bent to get my books.

But not before I saw him flinch.

"She's already upgraded," Trish shouted, taunting him from down the hall, and Yvonne giggled.

"If you change your mind, freak, you can toss the new boy to me," she said, rolling her eyes as she sighed. "What's his name?"

"Where does he live?" Trish added.

"What's he see in the freak?" they asked together, then collapsed in laughter and left.

"Their work here is done," I muttered, and dug for my books again.

"I'm trying to apologize," Derek said, sounding a bit hesitant.

"Try harder," I suggested, but my own tone had softened. "I made a mistake and I know it. I won't do it again. Don't you think tasting death was enough negative reinforcement?"

He folded his arms across his chest and leaned against the lockers, watching me intently. "What happened?"

I glanced up and down the hall. "It was a lot like my dream. Adrian conjured the ShadowEaters and they were trapped in an orb, like in my dream."

Derek didn't say anything.

"But the difference was that Kohana was there with the NightBlade, and they intended to sacrifice me. Kohana pretended to play along, but cut me free instead."

Derek's eyes brightened but he was still listening.

"We ran, but the NightBlade—this is going to sound weird—struggled free and went to the ShadowEaters. It flew into the air and cut the orb and they swarmed out. They ate the shadow of a Mage recruit, then dispersed over the city." I grimaced, remembering the sight. "Hey, have you seen Jessica yet today?"

He shook his head, and I could tell he wasn't that interested in Jessica.

"So, you were saying thanks to Kohana?"

I met his gaze. "I didn't kiss Kohana. He kissed me."

"Why?"

"I don't know. Why does he do anything?"

Derek exhaled shakily. He looked up and down the hall, and I could almost hear him thinking. "Okay," he said, and

I wondered who he was trying to convince. "Okay. Sorry I came down so hard." He fell silent as Meagan arrived at her locker beside mine.

"Hey, Derek," she said, then turned to me. "Have you seen Jessica? She's still not answering her messenger and I'm getting worried, since you said the ShadowEaters are free."

"How do you know that?" Derek asked Meagan.

"Zoë sent me a message."

"Really?" he said, giving me a hard look. I had a sense of a barrier solidifying between Derek and me. "When?"

"Before lunch." Meagan smiled and opened her locker, while Derek seethed.

I tried to make it better. "I couldn't send you one," I said to Derek. "I was waiting on Muriel, and after I told the guys, my messenger went crazy with incoming messages."

"The guys?" he echoed, clearly incredulous. "So you told Liam, Garrett, Nick, *and* Meagan, but not me?"

It did sound bad when he said it that way. "I told you in person. . . ."

"An hour later and only because I asked." He folded his arms across his chest and glared at me. "Is this about getting even?"

I felt as if I were trying to hold on to something slippery, something that was wiggling out of my grasp despite my efforts.

"No! I just couldn't do it right then. . . ."

Meagan looked between us, watching my total failure to win Derek's understanding. "Don't argue about details. We need to find Jessica and stick together." She turned to me. "I don't understand how they could free them without the NightBlade."

"Kohana was there with the NightBlade." I hesitated, knowing she wouldn't like this bit. "He was supposed to make the sacrifice, but he bailed on them at the last minute."

"At least he lies to everyone," Derek muttered. "Points for consistency."

"But the NightBlade flung itself back at the apprentice Mages. It freed the ShadowEaters, like it had a will of its own."

Meagan's eyes widened in horror at that, and she pushed her glasses up her nose to peer at me. "Really?"

"The NightBlade was doing what the ShadowEaters wanted."

"Or Kohana threw it," Derek muttered. "Whose side is this guy on?"

"No," I said. "They summoned it."

Derek shook his head, apparently believing that I was covering for Kohana.

"We wildcards have to stick together—" I started, but Derek interrupted me.

"Convince Kohana of that first." He glared at me, and the air was charged between us.

Meagan cleared her throat, obviously trying to help me hold things together. "I don't understand why Kohana would even be here."

"He thought it was turning his elders against each other, so he exiled himself until he destroyed it."

"I'd say he failed," Derek commented.

I ignored him because I was having no luck changing his mind. "He said that he needed to know more about how it worked to find a weakness, because he couldn't even scratch it himself. He figured the apprentice Mages were the only ones who would know, so he tricked them."

"You don't actually believe this garbage, do you?" Derek asked.

Meagan was watching me closely and I knew she knew there was something more I wasn't saying. I thought about telling her, but didn't think it would help anything for Derek to know that Kohana would have happily sacrificed him in my stead if it had meant learning more about the NightBlade.

I was thinking, actually, that the NightBlade itself might have been twisting Kohana's thoughts in that arena, too.

"Do you think he's telling the truth?" Meagan asked.

"I do." I shrugged. "Even though he's been known to be less than straight with me."

"There's an understatement," Derek said.

I turned on him. "Look, it's not to Kohana's advantage for the ShadowEaters to be on the prowl, either. I don't think he expected that to happen. And I think he's in as much trouble as we all are. . . ."

I saw that Derek wasn't really listening to me, but I kept talking all the same. I guess I was hoping that I'd say *something* he'd find persuasive.

But I realized suddenly that Derek was very still. It was more than not listening. He was looking at someone behind me, and I swear his nostrils flared.

I turned, wondering who he disliked that much, and found a girl I didn't know standing behind me. No consolation that she, too, had appeared silently, without my hearing her.

Was I losing my dragon mojo completely?

Or just going crazy, as Sigmund had suggested?

MEAGAN STARTED AT THE SIGHT of her. "Hi," she said, scanning the girl, who ignored her.

This girl was beautiful, maybe in her early twenties, with that kind of long silky hair you see in shampoo commercials. It flowed over her shoulders like a dark river, so black that it looked like it had blue highlights in it. Her eyes, if anything, were even darker, like black velvet. She seemed mysterious and powerful all at once, sexy right to her bones, and I could guess why Derek was staring. My heart nearly broke with yearning to be so confident in my own skin.

And that was before she said anything.

"Jessica said you're looking for her," she said, and her voice was exactly as low and sultry as I would have expected.

Wait a minute. Had Jessica heard my plea? Or just finally turned on her messenger?

"Where is she?" I asked.

"Who are you?" Derek demanded. He took a step forward, as if to protect me.

She didn't even look at him. "Are you coming?" she asked me.

"Where is she?" Meagan asked, since the girl hadn't answered me.

The girl just started to turn away, glancing back over her shoulder at me with a question in those dark eyes.

Again, I was supposed to accept an invitation on trust.

It would have been smart to decline, but I really wanted to know that Jessica was safe.

As long as Meagan and I would be safe with this girl.

I took a deep breath and sensed feline. The girl met my gaze and smiled ever so slightly. There was something in that expression that reminded me of the way Jessica smiled—a secretive feminine allure, maybe—and I decided to follow my instinct.

It couldn't steer me wrong twice in one day, right?

"Okay, we'll come," I said. Meagan and I stepped forward, Derek right behind us, but the girl gave Derek a hostile glance.

"Not you," she said, the words low and hot.

Oh, this was not good.

Derek glared at her. "Why not?"

The girl smiled, then took Meagan and me by the hand,

leading us out of the school. I glanced back, but Derek had already disappeared.

Was he following us?

I didn't think that would be a good idea.

On the other hand, after what I'd already faced today, additional backup was probably a good idea.

There wasn't much I could do about his choice, anyway. The girl had a strong grip on my wrist and was practically dragging me behind her. Meagan and I exchanged a glance, and Meagan shrugged. We were going to see Jessica, wherever she was.

Black Velvet was on a mission.

BLACK VELVET TOOK US TO a fancy apartment building downtown. I was kind of surprised. I knew that Jessica lived close to us—after all, she went to our school—but I'd thought her parents were tight for cash. Meagan had told me that they'd come from Argentina to improve Jessica's chances of getting into an Ivy League school, but that her dad wasn't able to use his license as a doctor here. He was driving a cab, which didn't lead me to believe that they were living in such fancy real estate.

Was Jessica sick?

Or in some kind of trouble? You know I was worried about her shadow.

Black Velvet wasn't answering any questions, so we stopped asking after a while.

The lobby of the building was magnificent. All Art Deco brass and dark marble, with a doorman in livery guarding the entry. His expression was stern, as if his face were carved of stone. I was a bit daunted by him, but he clearly knew Black Velvet. He just gave her a nod and summoned the elevator. He even knew where she was going, apparently.

Was she the one who lived here? She certainly looked like she belonged.

Yes, I did feel scruffy.

Just in case you were wondering.

The inside of the elevator was all mirrored, a bit of a dizzying effect, as there were hundreds of us extending to infinity in every direction. No missing the frayed hems of my jeans or the fact that my fave black boots could have used a buff.

Come to think of it, I needed a haircut.

Fortunately, my eyeliner was perfect.

A girl needs some constants.

Given that I'd nearly been a sacrificial victim today, I thought I was holding it together reasonably well.

Meagan flashed her killer smile at the doorman when we were on the elevator, just before the doors shut, and to my astonishment, he smiled back.

But Meagan is really pretty. I couldn't help noticing that she seemed more at ease than I felt, maybe because she'd been to this kind of apartment before. With her dad being a concert pianist, the Jamesons did dip their toes into some different social circles than my family did.

Meanwhile, Black Velvet had hit the very top button.

The doors closed and we zoomed straight for the penthouse.

I know. It shouldn't have surprised me. Black Velvet was luxe all the way. She hadn't said a dozen words to me yet, but I had all these ideas about her. She must be a model. An heiress. A princess in exile.

There certainly was a feeling of security in this place. I felt safe, and more confident that Jessica was okay, which made no sense at all.

The elevator door opened, as smooth as butter and just

about as quiet, and there was only one apartment door facing us. My eyes widened. The whole top floor of the building was a single suite? It would be like living in the clouds, with a full surround view. Meagan and I exchanged a glance, and now she looked a bit more impressed.

The foyer wasn't a whole lot bigger than the elevator, and there was only that one door opposite us. It was a nice door, painted a very shiny black, but a bit odd in that it had no knocker, doorbell, or keyhole. The knob was one of those you just push, but I didn't believe for a minute that the door was unsecured.

To the right, framed in heavy silver, was a square black pad, about five inches on a side. It had to be a scanner of some kind, but one I'd never seen before. On the other hand, this wasn't the kind of area where I usually hung out. The black square was too big for a fingerprint pad and really big for a doorbell, and I couldn't see the kind of light in it that iris scanners tended to have. There was no peephole in the door, either.

Black Velvet stepped forward and reached for the pad by the door as if she did it all the time.

So she wasn't going to knock.

She must live here.

I thought I had used up my daily allotment of surprise, but Black Velvet had one more for me.

Just before her hand touched the keypad, she shifted shape.

Black Velvet did shimmer blue, just before she made the transition, exactly the way all of us shifters do, but she changed really fast. Faster, actually, than any shift I'd ever seen—and we dragons compete on the basis of speed. I know from fast.

When she reached for the keypad, she cast a coy glance over her shoulder—that should have warned me—and then there was the blue shimmer and a panther holding one paw to the keypad.

A very large, sleek black panther.

She laid her paw on the black pad. There was a hum and a click; then she leapt forward and bumped the door with her shoulder. It was an elegant, easy move, once again making me think she did it all the time. She cast us a glance that seemed to be a challenge, especially as her eyes had become a vivid yellow, then she slipped into the apartment, like a shadow in the darkness.

Meagan and I took one look at each other, then followed. It was dark in the apartment, so we moved slowly, waiting for our eyes to adjust to the shadows there. As far as I could tell, the apartment was spacious and luxuriously furnished. The carpet was really thick under our feet.

But dark. Dark like midnight. Dark like the windows that had to surround the penthouse had been draped. Sound was muffled, as well, as if there was a lot of fabric around us, and the darkness seemed to press against our ears.

Never mind that as soon as we stepped over the threshold, the door slammed behind us. There was that same whir and click, echoing loudly in the silence. I reached back immediately, but the door was locked. There was no lock hardware on this side, either.

I didn't need to see the future to know that this was not good. I felt the pulse of several dozen heartbeats and panicked.

"You're all shimmery," Meagan whispered. "What's wrong?"

"We're not alone," I told her, because it was true.

I didn't say any more to Meagan because that was when a woman screamed.

Chapter 5

My blue shimmer—generated because I was on the cusp of change and unable to do anything to stop it, not after that scream—illuminated the foyer of the apartment a little bit. It took me a second to hear the muffled murmuring of many, many women.

The ones whose heartbeats I'd heard first.

Black Velvet nudged open another door then, because we saw her silhouetted in a rectangle of bright light to our left. The woman screamed again and I could hear women trying to reassure her. Black Velvet disappeared into the room and the door didn't quite close behind her.

I took that as an invitation. I nodded at Meagan and we went to the door together. I peeked around the edge as the woman screamed for a third time; then someone hauled the door open wide to reveal us standing there.

There was a big bed in the middle of the room; that was the first thing I saw. And a woman was lying on it, her expression anguished and her knees up. She was surrounded by about a dozen women, and Jessica, too. All of them were focused on her, and the one who had opened the door indicated that we should be silent.

All of the women, even Jessica, were wearing red dresses. They were like tubes of sheer fabric, gathered on a drawstring at their shoulders and tied at the waist with a gold cord. They were all barefoot, and the cloth was sheer enough that I could see their legs silhouetted beneath. Even Jessica had abandoned her usual baggy clothes and baseball cap for the sheer red dress. She was clearly the youngest present, but the others treated her with deference. She looked as gorgeous and feminine as she had at Halloween, but more glam.

Was this some kind of ceremony? The bed was more like a platform than a bed you'd sleep on, or maybe like an altar. It had four large golden pillars, one at each corner, which actually connected to the gilded ceiling. I'd thought at first that the light emanating from the room must be sunlight, but it was candlelight reflecting on gold.

The walls were lined with cat sculptures. Most of them were gold, and most of them had red stones for eyes, like rubies. There were candles placed between them on the shelves, the flickering light making the cats seem alive, as if their red eyes were scanning the room.

The whole room shimmered gold and looked exotic. It felt to me as if there were many more present than just the women we could see.

I heard Meagan catch her breath when she saw Jessica, but I'm not sure Jessica knew we were there. Her attention was fixed on the woman on the bed and she looked a bit nervous. Why was Jessica here? Was she related to this woman? Or did she know her well? Black Velvet climbed onto the bed and lay beside the woman like a pet—or maybe a sentry.

"Push next time," advised one of the attending women. "It's close."

The woman on the bed was delivering a baby.

She had time to nod before the next contraction rippled through her body. She tipped her head back and bared her teeth but didn't scream. I saw her clench a fistful of Black Velvet's fur, and Black Velvet's eyes narrowed, but she didn't move away or protest. One of the attending women reached to coax the baby into the world, and another firmly guided Jessica to the foot of the bed.

Jessica swallowed.

The baby's crown appeared, wet and dark.

"Push," advised the woman who must be the midwife. "Push."

The next contraction came; the mother pushed. The women leaned closer.

The candles flickered simultaneously.

Meagan and I grasped each other's hands.

And the baby surged forth in a rush. The midwife lifted the baby and cleared the mucus from its face. She cut the cord, and the baby cried out for the first time, its yowl nearly bouncing off the walls. The midwife tied the cord expertly, as if she'd done this a thousand times. The mother gasped with relief, smiling as the midwife put the child in her arms.

I'd never seen a baby born before. I wasn't sure whether it was gross or amazing.

The thing was that even though the baby seemed okay, tension remained in the air. The mother rose to her knees, her gaze locked on her baby, and the attending women gathered closer. Jessica looked as if she were facing down a terrible midterm.

What were they worried about?

One woman gave Jessica a nudge, and she stepped forward. She reached for the child, who was still naked. It was a girl. The attending women watched with obvious anticipation; then one woman began to sing.

It was singing but not like choir practice. She made a wordless cry, kind of *lalalala*, one that reminded me a bit of Jessica's ability to sing scat. The woman beside her joined in, adding her voice. At regular intervals, another woman would join the cry. The ululation rose in volume as each woman added her voice to what became a chorus. It vibrated in my ears and made me shiver.

Jessica closed her eyes as if concentrating and held the child high. Every gaze was locked on the baby. What was supposed to happen? The song grew in intensity as the baby flickered blue and gold in her grip. The candle flames danced all around the room. There was a crackle of energy in the room, as if something had been summoned.

I gasped when I saw the cat sculptures on the wall move. At first I thought they'd come to life, but it wasn't that. There were ghostly cats between the sculptures, so many of them that the sculptures seemed to disappear in their midst. The golden ghost cats with red eyes mewled the same note as the women, watching Jessica.

In the same instant, a shape became visible in the haze of color around the child, a shape other than the child's own shape.

Superimposed on the shape of the child—or maybe coexisting with it—was the shape of a great golden cat.

The women gasped with relief and pleasure.

Meagan caught her breath. "She's a puma!" she whispered.

The chorus ended with a triumphant cry. The attendants smiled in relief at each other, then embraced as the mother fell back with obvious satisfaction. The candle flames stilled, flickering normally as they had before, and when I looked at the sculptures on the wall, there were no more cat ghosts.

One woman held up a finger for silence. "She *will* be a puma," she corrected, then she smiled at Jessica. "The new Oracle of Bast has awakened the ancestors to reveal the child's future. It is as all should be."

Jessica kissed the child, once on each cheek and once on her forehead. "Her name will be Safiya," she said with greater confidence, and I recognized that summoning the vision of the child's future had been a test for her. Or maybe the test had been awakening the ghosts. "Hold it sacred for Bast. May Safiya live long and bear many."

"May Safiya live long and bear many!" echoed the women.

Jessica handed the child to the mother, who kissed the little girl just as Jessica had.

Then she handed off the baby to the midwife and clapped her hands. An older woman brought her a golden box, like a little lidded casket. Jessica caught her breath at the sight of it, and the new mother smiled. She opened the box, revealing a golden necklace. It was made of linked squares, the hinges hidden so that the necklace appeared to be a solid gold band. It was more supple than that, though, because of the links. It was about two inches wide and there was a red gem mounted on the front square.

I saw that when she fastened the necklace around Jessica's neck. "Praise be that the power continues. Praise be that the ancestors have acknowledged a new Oracle. Praise be that Bast continues to show her favor to her faithful." She gave Jessica the same trio of kisses that seemed to be their habitual salute, then spun her around. "Hail the new Oracle!" she said, and the assembled women cheered.

Jessica touched the necklace with her fingertips and bowed

her head. I could see that she was both jubilant and over-whelmed.

Kind of the way I'd felt when Urd had first called me Wyvern.

The new mother guided Jessica toward us, her eyes glinting with purpose. I was amazed at her energy, given that she'd just had a child. "And so you have been permitted to enter our sanctuary," she said to Meagan and me.

"This is our Oracle," Jessica said, her awe obvious. From that and the attitude of the other women, I assumed this new mother was the Bastian equivalent of my dad.

She nodded, her gaze never leaving me. I felt interrogated before she even asked a question. "I allowed you to enter our sanctuary because of the depth of Jessica's concern. I needed her to be able to concentrate. But now you must tell me, Wyvern—why are you seeking Jessica?"

I told her and Jessica about Mozart's shadow and about King's instructions.

"He did as should be done. He kept his vow," she said with approval, then turned to Jessica. "You have the power to heal his shadow, and I am too tired to do it well. It must be done today, after sunset. He will be safe until then, but act quickly once the darkness falls."

"Yes, Oracle," Jessica said, and bowed.

I wanted to ask the Oracle a whole bunch of questions, but she spoke crisply, ensuring I had no chance. "And so you have witnessed one of the great mysteries of our kind, Wyvern. I allowed this because of the treaty between us, but you will not leave this sanctuary without making a pledge of secrecy."

Her gaze turned even more steely then, and I was pretty sure I didn't imagine the flicker of red in the depths of her eyes. She reminded me a little bit of Skuld, to tell you the truth.

"What do we need to promise?" Meagan asked.

The woman looked at Jessica, who squared her shoulders and spoke. "The mysteries of the vessels of Bast shall not be shared with any of the male gender. You must swear to say nothing of what you have seen to any man or boy, of any kind."

The Oracle nodded approval of Jessica's words.

So that was why King had refused to talk. Either he didn't know more or it was smarter to keep what he knew to himself.

The problem was that I wasn't so good with this request.

"But there are other male shifters in our alliance," I began to argue, and the Oracle's eyes narrowed.

"We, the vessels of Bast, have endured for five thousand years," she said, her tone inflexible. "And we shall survive for five thousand more, alliance or no."

I thought it tactless to point out that the lion shifters, who were of their kind, had been exterminated by the Mages and that the remaining cat shifters had been enslaved by them afterward.

But I thought it.

And she knew it.

"I have made an exception for you, because you freed us from captivity, but do not press me too far, Wyvern. We survive because of our ability to keep our secrets."

"But we all need to survive. I saw the ShadowEaters summoned. . . ."

She smiled, and her tone turned condescending. "And what should we care? Do you not know what the Shadow-Eaters are, Wyvern?"

I had to shake my head.

"They are Mages who failed." She sneered this last word. "They are Mages who tried to perform the final ceremony, to become pure spirit and merge with the universe, thereby turning all to malice. In that form, they would fill the thoughts of men with poison and hatred, inciting wars and strife and feeding greed. In the dissent, the remaining Mages could build their powers without interference, then ultimately dominate us all."

This was horrifying stuff.

Her eyes shone. "But they *failed* in making that critical transition. They are snared between our sphere and the realm of pure spirit, and this renders them harmless to anyone in either realm. Only the Mages can invoke them, and thanks to your efforts, the Mages are impotent, or close to it."

"But I saw them here. . . ."

"You could not have." She shook her head firmly. "What ShadowEaters can influence is dreams. It is the highest form of spellcasting. They can give nightmares, Wyvern, and undermine your faith in what you know." She regarded me, her eyes glittering. "Do not believe everything you dream to be true."

I felt slapped down. Stupid. Like a kid.

That was her intent.

The Oracle leaned closer to me, her eyes now shining with that red glow. I could see a golden cat shape surrounding her, like an aura or a ghost, and guessed that she was on the cusp of shifting shape. Which meant she either felt threatened or was mad.

Or both.

"Now promise," she hissed.

I couldn't just give in, not after she'd spoken to me like that.

"No guys? Absolutely none?" I asked. All the dragon shifters were guys, and they were my friends. How could secrets not divide us? "Not my dragon friends or the wolf shifters? What about guy cat shifters, like King and Mozart?"

"No males may know of this divine secret," she said with resolve. "Those you call King and Mozart have accepted this truth."

Wow. Did guys even have names in the realm of the Bastians?

The Oracle put out her hand. "Pledge your silence, Wyvern. Pledge it now." She smiled coldly, her gaze flicking to the cat sculptures on all sides of the room. "Or you will remain the guest of the ancestors forever."

I looked again and realized that the sculptures were actually jars. I could see now that the cat head on each one was a lid. What was inside them? She was talking about ancestors, and I was thinking about remains.

Was there a jar in this room with my name on it? I shuddered despite myself at the very idea. I could see them again, those shadowy cat ghosts, shimmering and gathering, slipping around our small group. The Oracle kept her attention fixed on me, her gaze unblinking. I thought about that door with no hardware. Jessica was watching, still fingering her necklace, and I could hear Meagan's heart thumping.

I did not have a lot of options.

"I pledge it," I said, not having any idea how I was going to make this work.

The Oracle's smile flashed. She kissed me then, with that same trio of kisses, and when her face was close to mine, she whispered. "Make no mistake: I shall know if you break your word."

There was a brilliant shimmer of gold and I saw those milling ghost cats on all sides again. They were all looking at me, their red eyes gleaming, and I knew they would be the ones to rat on me—ha—if there was cause to do so.

I had to hope she was right about the ShadowEaters.

But I didn't believe it.

With one last smile, the Oracle turned to her new daughter and the midwife, dismissing us from her attention. Jessica watched the other women for a minute, a kind of yearning in her eyes. She was one of the Bastians, I saw, but not really like them.

A wildcard, just like me.

"Did you ever do that before?" Meagan asked.

Jessica shook her head. "Never." She glanced over her shoulder at the women. "The mother is the current Oracle, so she couldn't do the ceremony this time. I knew theoretically how to awaken the ancestors, because she taught me how to do it, but it's a lot different in real life. My mom was sure I could do it. I just hoped I wouldn't screw it up."

"No pressure," I said, understanding completely. She flashed me a smile. "You look like you could use a chocolate bar."

"Ice cream." Jessica grinned and nodded. "Definitely ice cream. Just let me get changed."

"And we've got big news," Meagan said.

"I figured that when I heard Zoë in my thoughts." Jessica gave me an intent look.

So that, at least, had worked.

"Can you really heal Mozart's shadow?" I asked.

Jessica nodded with confidence. She tapped her necklace. "I can, now that I have this."

That was good news. I had to think that things were finally looking up.

Relatively speaking.

IT DIDN'T TAKE JESSICA LONG to get back into her usual clothes, complete with the baseball hat jammed over her ponytail. I couldn't even see the golden necklace under her T-shirt and hoodie, but I was sure it was there. It wasn't the kind of thing you just forgot and left behind.

The apartment was lit normally now, the women having opened the blinds and drapes. It was a beautiful apartment, decorated in black and gold with Art Deco furniture. There were big vases of flowers, everything so perfect that it looked like a photograph. I caught a glimpse of a fantastic view of the lake out the windows on the far side.

I wondered a bit about our exit, but as soon as we stepped into the foyer, the door opened, seemingly of its own volition. Jessica pushed the elevator button as the door clicked shut behind us. It looked as if she was used to this.

I had so many questions, I wasn't sure where to start.

Meagan didn't have that trouble. "Is this why you didn't answer me?"

"It wasn't up to me to tell you where I was. The Oracle had to decide, and she was a bit busy."

"But the panther girl," I said.

"The Oracle sent her," Jessica confirmed. "She asked me why I was worried, and I told her that you were concerned about me. She said I didn't have time for distractions."

Meagan pushed up her glasses. "Did you really call to the dead?"

Jessica nodded. "The ashes of all past Oracles are here in the sanctuary, and the current Oracle calls on them for guidance." She grinned. "Apparently, even an Oracle in training can get them to show up."

"How do you ask ashes for guidance?" Meagan asked as we got into the elevator.

"Because they're more than ashes," I said, understanding now what I had seen. "The past Oracles came alive, like ghosts, right when the baby was shimmering in your grip. They were there again when I had to promise."

Both of them looked at me in astonishment.

"You *saw* the ancestors?" Jessica asked. There was an edge to her tone, as if she didn't believe me, as if she thought I was making up that part.

As if maybe I was trying to steal some of her thunder.

But I had seen them.

The elevator zoomed toward the lobby, moving so fast that my ears popped a bit. It was a smooth ride, but the bottom of my stomach felt weird.

"I think so," I said, pretending to have more doubt than I did. "There were lots of gold cats, transparent ones with red eyes. They were walking between the sculptures, kind of weaving their way along the shelves, and meowing."

"That's them," Jessica said, looking at me in awe and maybe, just maybe, a teensy bit of resentment. "You shouldn't be able to see them. You're not initiated into our rites or one of our kind or anything."

Oops.

"Don't you see them?" I asked.

She shook her head. "Not yet. But I've been told about them." She smiled. "I know what to look for."

"We both saw the puma," Meagan said.

Jessica nodded. "Everybody does. I never heard of anyone other than an Oracle seeing the ancestors before, though." She looked at me again, consideration in her eyes.

"If you can't see them, how do you know whether they come?" Meagan asked.

"I hear them," Jessica explained. "Today they told me the baby's name. And I felt their power surrounding her in that moment, revealing her future."

"Why does it matter?" I asked. "I mean, is it important what kind of cat the baby will be able to become?"

"Just that she can." Jessica exhaled and looked suddenly tired. "We never know, you know. A child might not have the power to shift and become one of us. It's not a gimme anymore, even for the child of an Oracle. Ever since the Mages—well, since we were their slaves—things have been erratic. This ceremony used to just be routine, but now it's really important. If the child will fully be one of us, the ancestors share that truth."

"And if they don't answer the summons?" I asked, sensing that she wasn't telling me the whole story. The Bastians sure were big on their privacy.

"Then the child will just be human." Jessica grimaced. "Or maybe the Oracle doesn't really have the gift to conjure them." She smiled wearily as the doors opened to the lobby. "I'm so relieved that they came today."

"You were great," Meagan said, giving Jessica a quick hug.

The doorman smiled at the sight of us, and it did not crack his face. He nodded at Jessica as if they were old pals, then swept open the door to the street. We walked through like queens, and I thought I could get used to living in a place like this.

Then Derek, looking ticked off, separated himself from the shadows to stride toward us.

"Remember your vow," Jessica muttered under her breath.

Derek gave me an electric look, like he'd heard what she said, and I wondered what I could tell him that wouldn't break my shiny new promise. I was thinking there was something to be said for my dad's skills with diplomacy and negotiation, and that maybe I should have paid a bit more attention when he'd explained all that to me.

"Did you tell her about the ShadowEaters this morning?" he demanded, flicking a look at Jessica.

"We didn't have time to talk about it yet," I said. I slipped my hand into his and he visibly relaxed. "Let's find Jessica some ice cream and bring her up-to-date before we get back to class." Derek's eyes narrowed and he looked more closely at Jessica, but she held his gaze.

As if daring him to imagine she'd share her secrets.

I watched her and wasn't at all sure that the cat shifters *had* lost their royalty.

WE SCORED SOME ICE CREAM and claimed a pair of benches in a concrete park off Michigan Avenue. It was probably a busy little oasis in the summer, but in February, with the fountain turned off and the snow fluttering down, we had the place to ourselves.

It was hard for me to tell them about my experience with the ShadowEaters. It was gross to remember it, even though the Bastians' Oracle was sure it had been a dream even the second time. I thought she was wrong; the others weren't so sure. Again, I had that sense of things coming apart when they really needed to be together, but couldn't think of a thing to do or say to fix it.

Except maybe prove to them that I was right.

That was when we realized the time and that we'd be late back to school. We started to walk back together, moving pretty quickly.

"What about our alliance of shifters?" Derek asked, and I heard the edge in his tone.

"What about it?" Jessica asked, looking between us.

"Seems like it's not working," he said in a low voice. "Seems that some people would rather keep their own secrets and run their own plans than work together."

Jessica clearly took exception to that. She straightened. "Just because we're allies doesn't mean that I can betray the trust of my kind and share our secrets with everyone."

"We're not talking *everyone*," Derek argued. "We're talking about the four of us." His gaze snapped. "We're talking about trust and teamwork. Isn't that what an alliance is?"

Uh-oh.

"You don't need to know everything about me to fight by my side," Jessica said.

"I think I do. I think that's the way it should be." Derek

had even more than his usual intensity. I remembered his comments in the fall about wolves seeing the world in black and white.

"All or nothing," I murmured.

"Exactly," he said, punctuating the word with another hot look at me.

Jessica folded her arms across her chest. "You can believe whatever you want and you can tell me whatever you want, but we learned the price of trusting in the wrong place when the Mages took out the lion shifters. We keep our secrets, thanks. And let's remember that Mozart, one of my kind, has been injured already."

Derek—predictably—took exception to her tone. "Oh, so now you're assuming that I'm going to betray you!"

"Not you!" Meagan interjected, obviously trying to save the situation.

I wasn't sure it could be done.

"Who else, then?" Derek demanded. "Meagan and Zoë know whatever it was that you were doing, but I don't. Obviously you trust them."

"It's a girl thing," Jessica argued.

"It's a girl-*shifter* thing," Derek retorted, then glared at me. "You don't want wolves in the alliance—that's fine. We can take care of ourselves."

"That's not what's going on," I said, and his pale gaze locked on me.

"That's what you say, but you're not showing me anything that would make me believe you." He gave us each one last glare, then turned and trudged away.

Perfect.

I ran after him, but he pretended not to hear me until I caught his hand and pulled him to a stop. He looked at me with narrowed eyes, obviously wanting to be somewhere else.

Anywhere else.

The alliance was being destroyed and it was my fault.

All I could do was try to save it.

"Look," I said, talking fast and quietly. I knew he'd be able to hear me. "I made a mistake this morning. I'm sorry I did that, and I'm sorry I got mad when you challenged me about it. I really thought I could handle it."

"What happens if they get you?" he demanded through his teeth. "Our prophecy says that the only way forward is to follow the dragon. If there is no dragon to follow, there is no way forward. If you die because you're too confident, you're condemning all of us."

"Gee, no pressure," I said, trying to make him smile.

He didn't. "It's not a joke, Zoë."

"I know." I squeezed his hand. "I was wrong about that, and I won't do it again."

"I can only defend you if you let me go into danger with you."

"I know." I twined my fingers with his. "I promise not to go off on my own again."

"You just did it again!"

"Okay. You were right. I need to trust your instincts, too. I will. I promise."

That seemed to please him a bit. Or at least it calmed him. He took a deep breath and turned his hand so that his fingers tangled with mine.

"But you need to trust me, too," I said. "Secrecy is really important to the Bastians. They will leave the alliance over it, and I have sworn to defend it."

He looked at me. "That's divisive."

I grimaced. "It's the only way to keep them in the union. I can't lose them, or we're all goners. Come on, she's under pressure and worried about Mozart, too." I tugged at his hand, seeing that he was unconvinced.

But thawing. He was definitely thawing.

"Nick and Isabelle are coming after school. They want to go to the vacant lot and hear the whole story, see if they can pick up any clues. I think we should all go together. Will you come?"

He watched me, his eyes glittering with indecision.

I leaned closer to him, touching my lips to his cheek. I felt him melt. It was strange, realizing that I had some ability to affect his thinking with just a little touch, and it gave me an uncomfortable sense of power.

One I wasn't sure I wanted.

"Can you trust me?" I whispered.

Derek heaved a sigh, then turned to consider me. "The only time you ever kissed me back was on your birthday," he said softly, then pulled his hand from mine and walked away.

I watched him go, feeling like I'd blown it completely. I could have kissed him back any number of times. I could have initiated a kiss right this minute—well, two minutes before. I could have used that new power I'd felt to bring him completely to my side.

But it didn't feel right.

When I return someone's kiss, I'm going to mean it.

Which sounds really good and principled—except if it looks like that principle is going to trash the alliance that could save the last four kinds of shifters left in the world.

Did I care more about being honest with Derek? Or with ensuring the survival of our respective kinds? How much would I compromise for the greater good?

I knew Derek wouldn't have compromised anything, but it seemed that dragons saw more shades of gray.

Bonus.

Or not.

I DON'T KNOW HOW I got through the rest of the day. Muriel chewed me out for not telling her where I'd gone at lunch—never mind that I was late getting back—and I knew there was yet another black mark beside my name.

That I refused to confide in her compelled her to write a lengthy note in my file.

Meet Zoë the troubled teen, signed up for detention.

I hoped the others would wait for me.

They did.

Meagan and Jessica were still at my locker when I got free of Muriel and detention, but there was no sign of Derek. I figured he wasn't coming, even though I wished I could have had the chance to change his mind.

When we came out of school Nick was waiting outside, leaning on my car and spinning the keys on his finger. I'd sent him a message and knew he'd give me a hard time about my detention. The three of us ran for it. Isabelle hopped out and gave us each a hug while Nick razzed me about being a troublemaker.

I had a feeling then and looked back, only to find Trevor leaning on his MG. He was surrounded by Suzanne and her crew, all of them flirting shamelessly with him. The spell light danced around them, giving me a sick feeling in my stomach.

I felt sicker when he turned to me and I saw the glimmer of spell light in his eyes. There was something odd about him, something that didn't look quite right, but I hoped my response was residue from earlier in the day.

I felt Nick beside me then, the weight of his hand on my shoulder. He glared at Trevor, who turned away quickly, as if intimidated.

I didn't believe it for a minute.

"He's going to follow us there," I whispered.

"Then we'll kick his ass," Nick said. "Let's go."

Let's face facts. My mom's car is not a big car. It's a teensy vehicle designed for commuters who travel alone, maybe with a briefcase and a bag of groceries. There were five of us. Five. Isabelle pulled the passenger's seat forward as far as possible. Meagan got into the back; then Jessica and I piled in after her. By some miracle, we managed to make room for Isabelle to put the seat back and shut the door, but I was glad we weren't going far.

There was still no sign of Derek as Nick drove away.

"Where's Derek?" Isabelle asked. Everyone looked at me.

"I'm not sure he's coming."

There was a heavy silence after that. I sensed that they blamed me for his absence, and, really, I did, too. The trouble was that I wasn't at all sure how to fix it.

It took me a while to direct Nick to the vacant lot, because the area had been unfamiliar to me. We went around a couple of blocks several times. The fact that there was no sign of the library—even though I knew it had been a glamour—didn't help me to get oriented.

"Are you sure, Z?" Nick asked for the forty-third time.

"Maybe it was another vision," Isabelle said. "Maybe it didn't really happen in this plane of existence."

"That's what our Oracle said," Jessica agreed.

"Don't you believe me?"

Isabelle smiled at me, but it was forced. "You have such vivid dreams, Zoë, and the realm of the Wyvern includes dreams and possibilities."

"The Oracle says the ShadowEaters can't touch us in this realm," Jessica added.

"You could be confusing reality and your vision," Nick said. "It makes sense to me."

"It would make sense to me if you believed me," I muttered.

"What did it look like again?" Meagan asked, trying to be helpful.

Skepticism threw my game a bit and we drove around for another half an hour, the tension mounting in the car. I ignored Nick's deep sigh, as well as the way Isabelle reached out to touch him, ensuring his silence.

Finally, I thought I spotted it, and Nick parked where I indicated.

I got out and looked around, confirming my memories.

"Here?" Meagan asked, and I saw that she wanted me to be right.

I nodded. "I saw that convenience store when we arrived, when I noticed that the street was empty." I pointed. "And I saw that locksmith with the grates over the shop windows when Kohana and I took off."

"So, you see," Meagan said triumphantly. "Zoë did find it."

I didn't wait for a reply, just marched into the vacant lot. Yes, that was the streetlight that shone in my dream, and those were the boarded windows on the other side of the far street. This was the garbage can that Skuld had toppled over, still lying on its side. I headed straight toward the clearing I'd seen several times now, bracing myself for what we'd find there.

That kid might be there still, dead.

Or at least there would be his blood in the snow.

Even though I couldn't smell it.

I halfway expected apprentice Mages to leap out from behind the piled trash, or ShadowEaters to pounce on us from the sky. Would Kohana reveal himself again? My heart was pounding as I walked to the clearing where the orb had been suspended overhead. I braced myself and looked.

But there was nothing there. There was nothing but

discarded and broken bikes, bashed-up trash cans, dented car fenders, some barbed wire, and a lot of litter. The snow fell steadily and silently all around. The sky was a bright gray overhead.

It was just an empty lot.

With no body or blood.

Worse, the snow was pristine, as if we were the first ones to step onto this lot in a week. How could this be?

"Are you sure this is the right place?" Meagan asked. Even she was fighting to believe me now.

"There are no footprints," Isabelle said. "The snow is completely undisturbed."

"Like no one's been here all week," Nick agreed. "I don't think anyone's been here in a long time." He inhaled deeply, then shook his head.

He was right. There was no scent of anyone having been in this space.

No spell light, either.

How could that be? I turned around and around, staring at the lot, seeing the things that verified that I was in the right place.

And not seeing the really important things that would have proven it.

"So it was just a bad dream," Jessica said with satisfaction. She repeated what her Oracle had said about ShadowEaters. I could tell that the others liked this answer a lot.

"They're just messing with Zoë," Nick said with approval.

"Or it could have been a vision," Isabelle suggested, maybe seeing that I was disappointed. "Something that *could* happen." She smiled. "You must be coming into your ability to see the future."

"That must be it," Nick agreed amiably. "It's not necessarily going to happen, but it could."

"And it hasn't yet," Jessica said.

But that wasn't it and I knew it.

I just didn't know how to convince them.

Again, I had that sense of the alliance weakening, and a growing sense that it needed to be more robust.

For . . . *something*.

"Maybe there's a glamour disguising the truth," I suggested, and I sounded a bit desperate even to myself. "The library was a glamour, after all." I turned to Meagan in desperation. "Can you sense any spell light?"

She shook her head. "There must be many vacant lots that look pretty much like this one."

Nick nodded sympathetically. "We can drive around some more, if it makes you feel better, Z."

"I'm sure it was here," I insisted. "I'm *positive*. It happened right here, just a couple of hours ago." I looked around, scanning for evidence of the dead guy. That would prove that I was right.

No luck.

Isabelle dropped her hand on my shoulder. "There's no energy here, Zoë."

"They could have disguised it."

They all smiled at me, their false encouragement doing nothing to hide the fact that they didn't believe me.

"I think it happened," I insisted. "I think I dreamed it once, but then it happened for real. And I think the rules have changed, no matter what the Oracle says. I think that the ShadowEaters are here and . . ."

"Then where are they, Z? Here we are, fresh bait, and they're AWOL." Nick flung his hands skyward, cocky as ever. "Hey, ShadowEaters! Come on down! We're two wildcards, a shifter, and a spellsinger. Shadows all around! Lunch is served!"

"Nick!" Isabelle said in horror.

He grinned.

Because there was no reply. The sky looked normal. The hum of the city surrounded us. The snow fell steadily. Nick looked at me, and turned to go back to the car.

The others stood for a minute, then began to follow Nick.

"What about Mozart getting hurt last night?" I called after them. "That was real."

"That just means there are apprentice Mages around," Jessica said. "And we knew that already." She and Meagan came to me, as if they were going to help an invalid.

"You said that Trevor said Adrian did it," Meagan reminded me.

I looked at each of them in turn. "What about Trevor bringing me here in his car?"

Meagan grimaced. "You should know, Zoë, that he was in class this morning. I checked with a couple of people this afternoon when I was trying to find out what had happened to you. He was there. He didn't miss a thing."

"A glamour," I muttered. "He used a glamour."

We walked back to the car in silence, where Nick and Isabelle waited.

"I think you're seeing past, present, and future simultaneously," Isabelle said kindly. "That's supposed to be one of the Wyvern's abilities, and I'm sure it's confusing."

"I am not confused!" I shouted. "I saw the ShadowEaters invoked by Trevor and Adrian. I saw the NightBlade free them. I saw Adrian become a ShadowEater himself. I saw the ShadowEaters swarm that kid and eat his shadow."

"Twice," Jessica noted. "Who's to say that both times weren't dreams?"

"What we need to do is make a plan to ensure that your vision doesn't come true," Nick said firmly.

"Look at it this way," Meagan said. "Maybe the Night-Blade does have a power of its own. Maybe it wants to be returned to the apprentice Mages for this very purpose. Maybe it's what is messing with your mind, so that you'll go to Kohana and get it." She linked her arm through mine. "Let's go home. Nick's going to keep vigil on the roof tonight."

I looked at him and he nodded. They'd made plans without talking to me?

They really were treating me like a crazy person.

"It's getting dark," Jessica added. "I have to take care of Mozart."

Nick pulled out his messenger. "I'll send a message to Kohana, confirm that we're still on for the spring equinox to destroy the NightBlade. Let's meet in the morning and make a plan."

"It'll all be just fine," Isabelle said.

Meagan smiled. "Don't worry, Zoë. We'll defend you."

But I was trying to defend them.

THE SUN HAD JUST BARELY set when we got to the Jamesons' place. We'd dropped off Nick and Isabelle at the L because there wasn't much time left until dinner and we didn't want to be late. Mrs. Jameson immediately asked Jessica to stay to eat.

Then we headed for Meagan's room. King sat up when he saw Jessica, his tail thrashing at the air and his eyes bright with anticipation.

Just her presence seemed to improve Mozart's state. His eyes opened a little and he mewled, and that was even before she touched him. I had the feeling that she communicated with King on a different level than I could hear, but I sensed his reverence for her. She stroked Mozart and his breathing became more comfortable.

Like he knew she'd take care of him.

"Can you turn that light on?" she asked Meagan, who quickly did what she requested. The lamp was on the nightstand, so its light shone across Mozart, casting his shadow across the bed. Jessica traced its outline with her fingertip, murmuring softly. She looked to be in a kind of a trance. She winced as her fingertips passed over the bite in the shadow, and King shuddered.

Then she pulled out the necklace she'd been given. She kept it on, but left it on the outside of her shirt now, instead of hidden underneath. The red stone seemed to have a spark trapped within it, a glow that hadn't been there before. I could see the light reflecting off the opposite wall. Mozart opened his eyes to stare at her, and the light was mirrored in his gaze, too.

She murmured softly, maybe so that neither we nor the guys could hear her incantation clearly. The stone flashed red, making the cats' eyes look red.

I jumped when a dozen golden ghostly cats appeared in the room. Meagan shivered at the sudden chill in the air. I watched the ghost cats mill around Meagan's bed, their eyes flashing. They twined around Jessica's legs, and the stone's light got even brighter.

Jessica bent quickly and touched the stone to Mozart's forehead. The ghost cats leapt onto the bed and surrounded him tightly, circling with greater speed.

I thought I could hear them purring.

Then Jessica straightened with a flourish. The ghost cats were gone in the blink of an eye, and the stone could have been a piece of red glass. She tucked the necklace back into her shirt and stood up, just another math whiz come to do homework.

But the bite out of Mozart's shadow was starting to fill in.

I could already see that it was smaller and that King curled around his buddy a little less protectively than before. Meagan followed my glance and her face lit.

"You did it!" she said.

Jessica smiled in obvious relief. "I started it. It'll take a couple of days to grow back. Don't let him outside until then."

"I'll secure the cat door," Meagan said.

"You summoned the ancestors again," I said.

Jessica nodded and smiled. "Second time in a row." Then she sobered. "Did you see them again?" I nodded and she studied me. "Careful, Zoë. You don't want to become one of those people who get lost in their visions."

Great. One more thing to worry about.

"What's the stone, though?" I asked. "Is it just for healing?"

Jessica smiled and looked a lot like the Oracle when she did. "I can't tell you its powers, but I can tell you its story." Meagan stopped on her way out of the room, turned back, and shut the door, leaning against it. "When we were enslaved, a plan was made for our escape. The Mages had a treasury then, a collection of talismans they'd taken from different shifters when they eliminated them." She swallowed. "The story is that we stole from the treasury, hoping to bargain for our own freedom. We were caught, and the tiger shifters were eliminated to teach us the price of defiance."

She touched the stone. "But they didn't get everything back that we'd taken. This ruby was one of three hidden from them and passed in secret from Oracle to Oracle over the centuries ever since. The cobra shifters filled these three stones with their powers and wore them on their brows."

She draped the necklace around her head so that the gem was on her forehead. She looked like a queen. "At least until the Mages eliminated them." She sighed and put it around her neck again, touching it with her fingertips. It had no spark in it now. "I can't tell you the secret name of this stone, but it is the one best used for healing."

"And the others?" I asked. "The Oracle must have one of them."

Jessica held my gaze, neither agreeing nor disagreeing. "They are hidden, as the ancestors wish them to be." She really reminded me of the Oracle when she gave me that look and when she left the room walking so regally.

At least one of us wildcards was getting it right.

THE FUNNY THING WAS THAT my doubts multiplied as the evening progressed. I wasn't sure what I'd seen or what to believe anymore. Was I right? Was everyone else right? Was this the road to insanity? I felt like something was eating away at me, devouring my confidence, something that festered in darkness and fed nightmares.

ShadowEaters.

No surprise that I wasn't particularly brilliant with my homework. I was just too twitchy. I couldn't keep my gaze from trailing to the big living room window and the square of night it framed. I couldn't stop thinking about my close call—and the possibility that the ShadowEaters might be hunting me. Kohana had warned me that they liked shifter shadows best. At night, the memory seemed even more creepy.

More real.

And that claustrophobic feeling of them drawing close, hungering for my shadow, isolating me and suffocating me . . . even the memory made me shudder.

What if the Oracle was wrong?

Would Jessica be able to heal damaged dragon shadows?

I really wanted to talk more to Jessica and Meagan about the ShadowEaters and make a plan together, but Mrs. Jameson was hovering. We couldn't use our messengers because she'd take them away while we were doing homework. So I just fretted, which was just about the most ineffective solution possible. It did exactly zero for my confidence.

Mrs. Jameson kept checking on my progress with homework—of which there was little—so I knew that Muriel had found herself an ally. Meagan and Jessica sat on either side of me, periodically touching my hand. I guess they knew I was still freaked.

Mr. Jameson came home late from a rehearsal and was immediately assigned by Mrs. Jameson to drive Jessica home.

"I was going to do that," I said, but everyone shook their heads in unison.

"You're dead on your feet, Zoë," Jessica said, and Meagan nodded agreement. "You should crash."

I tried to not be paranoid. I wanted to think that they were being protective of me, not treating me like a wacko who shouldn't be driving—or a delusional person who couldn't tell the difference between dreams and reality.

"Everything will look better after you get some sleep," Meagan said.

"Maybe you should stay tonight," I said on impulse to Jessica. Mrs. Jameson gave me an odd look, so I made up an excuse. "Help me with this math question in the morning, before we go to school and have that test."

"You'll do fine. You know more than you think you do." Jessica smiled at me, and Meagan went to get her coat to tag along.

Don't go. They're out there, I mouthed to her when she looked back, unable to fully express my fear for her.

She must have seen it all the same. She flicked a glance at

the window, then back at me. *I'll be fine*, she mouthed, as confident of the Oracle's perspective as I was not.

I exhaled, not liking the situation. Again I looked out the window. Was that the glimmer of orange eyes I saw in the shadows? I could hear my friends checking that they had everything and kidding around with Meagan's dad. I couldn't stop staring out the window. I had a feeling of foreboding, one I couldn't shake.

I wondered what Mozart had seen. I thought about doing my Wyvern trick of wandering through another individual's memories. I was pretty worn-out, but I was ready to give it a try.

I closed my eyes and concentrated, but I couldn't find a way into Mozart's mind, much less his memories. With the *Pyr*, I could follow the ley lines that connected all of us. With apprentice Mages, I'd been able to follow spell light. But there was no conduit to Mozart, wherever his thoughts might be.

I checked the ley lines to the *Pyr* and was relieved to find them all pretty much where they should be.

"Milk and a cookie?" Mrs. Jameson asked, startling me so that I jumped.

I thanked her, begged off, and retreated to Meagan's room. I hadn't been physically injured during that encounter in the lot, but I felt psychically roughed up.

I left the curtains open and stared into the night sky, watching for . . . something.

I had a feeling I'd know it when I saw it.

But I had no idea what I was looking for.

That was probably exactly how the ShadowEaters wanted it to be.

Don't you hate when the bad guys are winning?

Chapter 6

*T*he sudden smell of toothpaste jolted me awake and alerted me to Meagan's arrival. She turned out the light that I'd left on and got into bed, making a fuss over both cats before she snuggled in. I kept my eyes closed, not really feeling like talking.

I *was* bagged.

Meagan cleared her throat, as if she were going to say something that was no big deal, but I didn't believe it for a minute. "So, are you still g-g-going to the dance with Derek?" she asked.

It was her stammer that got me.

What was *she* worried about?

I rolled to my side, turning to face her, and opened my eyes. I was just able to see her troubled expression in the darkness. "I don't know, actually. Why?"

"It seems like he's mad at you."

"Well, he is. He thinks I should have taken him with me when I went with Trevor. Or at least told him."

"Well, you did tell me."

"And you discovered that Trevor was still in class, when I said he was with me." I made a face.

Meagan, I could see, was thinking.

This could only be good.

"It is weird, isn't it?" she said, patting Mozart as she frowned. "I've been thinking about it, and I didn't know Trevor could cast a glamour. I thought that was advanced stuff beyond his powers."

"Adrian did it at boot camp."

"Maybe he cast the one you saw today, too." Meagan grimaced. "But who cast the one of Trevor in school? Could Adrian do both at the same time? Or has Trevor learned more?" She turned on the light, pulled out her messenger, and began typing. "I'll ask Jared if there's a way to know for sure." A moment later, she smiled at me, and I ached that I couldn't just send a message to Jared like that, too.

Over. Jared was over.

Meagan turned out the light and put her glasses on the nightstand when she was done. "What else?"

"Derek's mad that I won't tell him what happened with Jessica today."

"You promised not to." She fluffed her pillow. "Isn't there something else? Derek's pretty loyal to you, and you've explained all of this to him."

I fell silent, deciding how much to share.

But Meagan is my best friend, and she is brilliant, and the fact that she was staring at me, waiting for me to go on, made me spill it. "Derek saw Kohana kiss me," I admitted.

"Whoa!" Meagan sat up, grabbed her glasses, and turned

on the light. "When did that happen? And why didn't you tell me?"

"I didn't really want to talk about it in front of everybody."

She was excited. "But that means that Derek could confirm that Kohana was here, which would prove that you weren't dreaming. . . ."

"I don't think he will."

"Just like Kohana won't tell anyone what *he* saw. Guys!"

To tell the truth, it wasn't guys who were frustrating me in this moment.

Meagan sensed as much. She looked at me hard. "What's the matter?"

I was telling her the whole story, wasn't I? "So, you don't believe me, until I say that Derek saw Kohana; then you believe it, even though Derek hasn't said anything to you about it himself?"

"But that explains perfectly why Derek's so mad at you. I couldn't figure that out."

"You could have just believed me!"

"Okay, sorry." Meagan grimaced. "It's not that I didn't believe you. I wanted to believe you. I knew that you believed what you'd seen. I just thought that maybe you didn't have all the information."

"And now?"

"Maybe the Oracle's the one who doesn't have all the information." Meagan fell back against her pillows, thinking. "I mean, let's agree that it did happen and that we couldn't see that kid at the lot today because of a glamour."

"Okay."

"That would mean that the ShadowEaters weren't caught in their own realm anymore. They'd be here. Where?" I shrugged, but Meagan looked at me. "Seriously, why didn't they attack us at the lot today when Nick dared them?"

"I don't know. Maybe they're messing with us."

"No. They would have done it if they could. What's stopping them? And how do we find out?"

"Ask Trevor?" I suggested.

Meagan snorted, then pursed her lips. "Wait a minute." She was drumming her fingers on top of the bed, making enough vibration that King gave her a poisonous glance. She ignored him. "You see it, don't you?"

"See what?"

"Maybe they need more energy. Maybe they don't have enough yet to do whatever they want to do. So they're using what energy they have to target you! If they'd shown themselves today, we would have all believed you. This way, they stay hidden longer." Meagan was excited. "That means you're a threat to their success." She sat up, her expression triumphant. "That means *you* can ruin everything."

She was right. She had to be right.

I felt invigorated again.

"I just have to figure out what their plan is." I smiled at her. "You know, it kicks butt having a genius for a best friend. Thanks." We reached out across the gap between the beds and brushed fingertips.

"You can do it, Zoë. You'll figure it out." She was smiling at me, exuding a confidence that fed mine. I felt again my happiness at her having her braces off, and took a good look at her. She frowned at me. "What's wrong now?"

I smiled. "Nothing. Just that when you get contacts, every guy in the world is going to be at your feet."

She dropped her gaze and pleated the sheet between her fingers. "Well, that's just it, isn't it?"

I sat up, finally understanding. "Wait a minute. You don't think that if I'm not going to the dance with Derek that Garrett won't come?"

She flicked me a look and blushed. "I'd really like to see him again."

"He'll come. He was totally bummed at Christmas that you were away."

"Really?"

"Really. I think you're the only reason he came to Chicago."

She was pleased by that—I could see it.

She settled down to sleep, but I knew I had to fill her in on everything. "Hey, there's one more thing you need to know about Kohana and the NightBlade."

"What?"

"Kohana made a deal with Adrian and Trevor that he'd wield the knife for their ceremony, thinking he'd learn something from it."

"Yes, you said that he'd agreed to do the sacrifice. But he faked them out."

"He said he would have done it if they'd brought Derek or Jessica, just to learn more about the NightBlade, but that he couldn't do it to me. He saved me, then told me all that; then he kissed me."

"So he knew they would sacrifice a wildcard. That must be important." She turned to me. "Do you think Kohana is telling the truth?"

"I have no idea."

"But do you like Derek?" Meagan asked quietly.

"I like him," I admitted, "but I'm not sure I *like* him. I think I should be sure before . . . well, before anything more happens. I know he wants more commitment, but I want it to be honest." Now I was blushing like crazy.

To my astonishment, Meagan smiled. It wasn't like her to enjoy my discomfort. "What about Kohana? Do you like him?"

I shook my head. "I don't trust him. He'll probably turn up again, though."

"He's hot."

I shook my head. "Not really. I think he's just trying to mess with me."

To my astonishment, Meagan seemed delighted by this confession.

"What are you so happy about?" I asked.

"You're the Wyvern," Meagan said with a confidence that warmed my heart. "You're the key to everything, and you're my friend, and I know exactly what I need to do to help you out."

And with that, she went to sleep.

Leaving me in total suspense.

I TOSSED AND TURNED FOR a while, maybe dozed off and on. I was both exhausted and jittery. Running through the sequence of events in the vacant lot over and over again was doing exactly nothing to help me get to sleep. I reviewed it for the umpty-gazillionth time, looking for clues—I wasn't sleeping, so I needed something to think about—when it hit me.

Kohana had been singing the invocation chant.

Kohana had been *casting spells*.

This was huge. It was epic.

And it had slid right past me.

"Kohana's a spellsinger!" I said, sitting straight up in bed. How could I have missed that? Was that his special power as the wildcard of his kind? Was that why he thought he could destroy the NightBlade?

"Yes. I don't know. Yes and yes," said a man with a low, slow voice.

I jumped, then spun in the bed, knotting the sheets around my knees in the process. (Very elegant look, let me tell you.)

There was a guy sitting cross-legged on the floor, smoking a cigarette. He looked pretty old to be sitting like that, and his long dark hair was threaded with silver. His face was both tanned and lined, and so were his hands. He was wearing jeans and a red cowboy shirt.

And he was watching me.

Meagan was still sleeping, and King was out cold, too. (Even though I had pretty much shouted. I took it as a clue that I was in dreamland again.) The room looked completely normal, other than the guy on the rug.

This was like my conversation with Sigmund, chatting with a guy in what looked just like Meagan's room. It was reassuringly Wyvern-like, so probably not some ShadowEater nightmare.

So, who was this guy? I had a feeling he wasn't among the living anymore.

He took another drag, his dark eyes glinting, the end of the cigarette glowing, and watched me as he exhaled. The smoke made a silvery plume, like a snake winding toward the ceiling.

Mrs. Jameson would have a fit that someone was smoking in her house.

That was my first thought.

I said my second one out loud.

"Are you dead?"

"She will. And yes again," he said, and this time he smiled a little. He twisted in place, showing me the bleeding gash in his back. It was a vicious wound.

"No blood on the rug, okay?"

He smiled and smoked. I realized now that I could see a second smaller tendril of smoke winding out of the wound. So his lung had been punctured. Nice.

I sat up, shifting around so I was sitting cross-legged on

the bed facing him, the sheets wound around my lower body. He said nothing more. It seemed that I was going to have to start the conversation. "So, the thing is that when I see other dead people, they come to tell me something. Or give me a clue. Something like that."

I was ready for help—you can believe that.

He glanced at his back, then at me again, and took another drag.

Wait a minute. This guy knew about Kohana's powers. I guessed. "Are you the *Wakiya* elder who was killed by the NightBlade?"

He almost smiled; then he nodded slowly.

I was excited. Dead men might tell no tales, but their ghosts might be able to help me out. "Can you tell me more about the NightBlade? What about the ShadowEaters? What do they want?"

He exhaled, launching three smoke rings in succession. They floated toward the ceiling, then slipped inside each other, changing order as he watched with a smile. I was amazed. "I suspected that there was a connection between the NightBlade and the ShadowEaters."

"I've seen it. It's true. They called it to them." I had a thought. "Is that why you died? Because you were figuring things out?"

He pondered that. "Possibly. It acted seemingly of its own volition, but now I wonder if the ShadowEaters dispatched it—and me. They feed on shadows, but shadows exist in our realm, not theirs."

"So without Mages to offer them shadows, they're hungry?"

"Impotent," he corrected. "Shadows give them power and energy. To be hungry is to be weak."

"And without Mages to offer them sacrifices, they were

starving," I guessed. He nodded. "So, somehow they managed to use the NightBlade to free themselves." He nodded again. "So I *did* see the truth!"

He frowned then. "Kohana plays a dangerous game on behalf of our kind. You must help him. You must save him."

"But I don't know where Kohana is."

He looked at me steadily and I saw the vacant lot in my mind's eye, the snow falling over it.

I frowned. "Why couldn't I see him when I was there?"

"Why couldn't you see the lot when you went to the library?"

Okay. It made sense that if ShadowEaters were Mages who had done a ritual wrong, as the Oracle declared, they would still have some Mage-like abilities. "They can cast glamours in this realm, too, then?"

He nodded. "The more they feed, the more powerful they will become."

"What do they want?"

He smiled. "What they have always wanted."

I remembered what the Bastian Oracle had said. They wanted to become pure spirit but had failed at the ritual. They were trapped between here and there, but still wanted to go *there*. "They came here for more fuel. For shadows."

He smoked calmly, and I thought he was considering this. Eventually, he nodded, then frowned. "You, too, are targeted, *Unktehila*."

I shivered at that.

I realized then that it must have been hard for this elder to come to me, given the broken treaties between our respective kinds. So there must not have been many other options available.

It was up to me to do something.

"What can I do to ruin their plans?"

He smiled and smoked.

I tried again. "Is there a way that I can undermine their glamours and spells, so we can see what they're doing?"

He pursed his lips and hesitated so long that I didn't think he'd answer me. "I can tear the veil of illusion and shred the glamours, *Unktehila*, but only at your command," he said finally. "You are the center of the web."

Well, that had to be a step in the right direction.

In fact, I was thinking that Meagan might be right, that this might be the one thing I could do to trash the ShadowEaters. Tearing the veil would mean that we would have more information to finish them off—instead of arguing about what had really happened.

Worked for me.

"Tear it, then. Tear it, please!"

He watched me for such a long time, just smoking without breaking eye contact, that I feared I'd asked for something terrible. More than I expected. More than he could do. Something was wrong with this choice.

"Zoë?" Mrs. Jameson called. "Who are you talking to? And is that a cigarette I smell?"

Was this a dream or not?

I glanced at the door in uncertainty, then back at the elder.

"Be warned that you must act swiftly, *Unktehila*," he said in an undertone. "You will see all possibilities and realities merged together, but still you must choose with speed."

What did that mean? I was on the verge of asking him for more information when his eyes flashed golden and he leapt straight up with incredible power.

I saw the cigarette drop and glow when it fell on the rug.

I saw the shadow of his Thunderbird shape.

I heard the rumble of thunder.

And I saw his claws shred my view of the room. It was as

if Meagan's room had become a glamour. He tore away the wall with the window like it was a dark curtain, and all I could see was that vacant lot.

The vacant lot was right there, right *here*, two feet away from me.

With blood on the snow and the air filled with spell light and the dead kid on the ground. I crawled back on the bed in horror. It was as if the elder had torn the scales from my eyes. Was I here? Was I there? Everything was merged together.

How could I choose swiftly if I didn't know what was real?

Then Mrs. Jameson rapped on the door and pushed it open, crying out when she saw the burning butt on the carpet. The room reverted to normal in a flash, Meagan woke up, the cigarette was crushed and flushed, and much confusion ensued as I confessed to having snuck a smoke.

It wasn't like I could tell Mrs. Jameson the truth.

If dreams and reality were going to keep mingling like this, maybe I *would* end up going crazy.

HOURS LATER, EVERYONE HAD SETTLED down again, but I was wide-awake. Had anything changed? I was trying to figure out what I was supposed to do—I knew I had to do it swiftly—when I heard the faint sound of music.

The sound was distant, elusive, forcing me to strain my ears to catch the tune. I was tempted to open the window, but I was leery of that wall since the elder had ripped it. Everything looked normal, but I wasn't taking anything at face value.

It could be real. It could be a dream. It could be both.

I was already starting to see the downside of tearing the veil.

I got out of bed without really intending to, opened the bedroom door, and eased down the stairs to the front door.

I had a powerful urge to go outside, to follow the sound of the music.

No, I *yearned* to follow the music.

Like one of those rats following the piper to his death.

I opened the door, even knowing it was stupid. It was like I couldn't stop myself. The melody *was* haunting and beguiling, although I couldn't have named the tune.

It was in a minor key.

Wait a minute. Mages used minor keys.

It was a lure! I could see spell light dancing down the street toward the town house, swirling in the middle of the road, churning up the porch steps. To my surprise, Mozart and King were right next to me. I hadn't even noticed them leave the bedroom with me. But now they twined around my ankles.

I was glad to see Mozart on his feet, at least until he looked up at me and I saw that his eyes were filled with orange spell light. King was really agitated, circling around the smaller cat protectively like he'd hem him in.

No luck on that front. To my horror, Mozart slipped between my ankles and raced into the night. On the street, he rubbed his back against the golden ribbon of the spell at the bottom of the stairs. I snatched at King, guessing what he'd do, but was two seconds too late. My fingers slid through his fur as he yowled and peeled off after Mozart.

No! I leapt down the steps, just as the pair of them ran down the street. They disappeared like shadows into the night.

No, they disappeared into a new barrage of spell light. It was headed right for me, like an orange tsunami.

I fled into the house, slammed the door, and locked it, my heart pounding. The music got louder and I watched in horror as tendrils of spell light rushed under the door.

They reached for my ankles.

No! I ran back up the stairs, the snake of light in hot pursuit. I slammed the door to Meagan's room and leapt back into bed, hoping against hope that this was all a bad dream.

Just a dream.

Just a nightmare.

Nothing really to fear.

No music in my ears.

I was nearly convinced when I felt something slither around my ankle.

Like a snake.

Or the tendril of a plant, one that was growing really fast.

It was cold and wet and moving up my leg.

Not real, not real, not real.

Heart pounding, I looked. I could see a golden spiral of spell light twining around my leg, making its way from my foot to my knee. It was like watching a plant growing, some kind of jungle plant that takes over the world in leaps and bounds.

And it was taking me over.

Or claiming me.

I sat up in terror and jerked my leg back. The spell tendril tightened around me convulsively, nearly eliminating circulation to my toes. Definitely real. I yelped and ripped at it, to no effect. I couldn't get a good grip on its slimy surface. It kept growing, too, capturing more and more of my leg.

I called to the shimmer and tried to change shape but failed completely. Just like the spell light in the lot, this spell had the ability to short-circuit my shifter powers. The tendril of spell held on fast and kept getting longer. It was past my knee and up to my thigh.

And then it tugged, as if it would haul me outside.

I freaked.

I struggled.

It made no difference. It was just like being in that vacant lot, just like being bound by the spell light and powerless to do anything about it. I thrashed but it made no difference. I screamed but no sound came out.

I was already silenced.

Was this what it was like to become extinct?

I thought I could hear the sound of smacking lips and was terrified that the ShadowEaters would devour my shadow. I panicked at the prospect.

That outer wall disappeared again, just as it had when the *Wakiya* elder shredded it.

A heartbeat later, I was in that vacant lot again, still bound and helpless. I had to believe that the ShadowEaters had sent the spell to get me.

Because I was surrounded by them. There were hungry ShadowEaters on every side, slithering and salivating, their golden eyes gleaming with anticipation.

I felt the first lick, the first nibble, the first nip. It was nauseating. The spell kept tightening around me, trapping me and holding me captive. Struggling only made it worse, but I couldn't help it. I fought with all my might but it made no difference. I heard their dark laughter and smelled their anticipation. If they wanted to mess with my mind, they were doing a great job.

I screamed.

I still made no sound.

And there was a blinding flash, like lightning had struck me.

I WAS BACK IN MEAGAN'S bedroom, sitting up in bed with sweat running down my back. I was panting, but I couldn't see any spell light anywhere.

Believe me, I looked.

While I hyperventilated and my heart pounded so fast that I thought it might explode from the exertion. I had been sure that flash had been the result of my shadow being cut away, but I checked and it was intact.

Whoa.

Okay, so maybe that had been a dream. Or a Wyvern vision. Could it have been foresight?

More importantly, where was I?

I still had to be in some dream realm—Meagan's bedroom was piled with snow, and the exterior wall melted into endless tundra. As in my typical Wyvern dreams—at least the ones I'd had in the past year—I could see a bough of that enormous tree bending over the room, its leaves young and green and rustling in a wind I couldn't feel.

I knew this place.

And it was—comparatively—safe.

Even if the old ladies were missing.

Wolves howled in the distance, and it says something for my state of mind that the sound of a hungry wolf pack was reassuring.

Then I saw that Skuld was crouched on the windowsill, watching me avidly. She was almost swallowed by the shadows, motionless, her eyes shining in the darkness. She looked like an action hero, ready to spring to duty and slaughter the unworthy. Her eyes brightened, not unlike the eyes of a raven, and there was something sinister about her smile. I realized that her ponytail was bound with something that looked like sinew. I seriously didn't want to know what kind of sinew it was.

Or whose. She was spinning her scissors around one index finger, like a gunslinger playing with his revolver, as she watched me.

"Bad dream?" she asked, then started to laugh.

Her laughter was no better than that of the ShadowEaters. It was dark and malicious. If this was my ally, I had some kind of lousy company.

Maybe insanity would be a better choice. I could make friends with teddy bears and jelly beans.

"You could have helped," I said, hearing the accusation in my tone.

Skuld sobered and considered me. "How do you think you got back here?"

"*You* helped *me*?" Skuld might have looked like a warrior who got things done, but I wasn't at all sure that we were on the same side. I did not expect that she would do me any favors.

She rolled her eyes. "You didn't think you managed it yourself, did you?" There was nothing I could say to that because, you know, I had thought that.

And she knew it.

Worse, she thought it was funny. "Careful what you wish for," she said.

I blinked. "You mean that was my fault? Because I asked him to tear the veil?"

She nodded slowly, and I was horrified. "Tearing the veil opened a portal." She gave me a hard look. "One that maybe should have stayed shut."

Oops.

"I thought it just removed the glamours."

"That, too." She turned her shears so that the moonlight illuminated one sharp edge. "Many weapons cut both ways."

Okay, I should have anticipated that a *Wakiya* person—like Kohana—might not have presented all of the truth. Or that a dead shifter—like my brother, Sigmund—might have left out some important details.

"Is this the part where the Wyvern goes crazy?"

Skuld smiled. "Not all minds can bear to see the array of possibilities all at once. Fewer yet can choose wisely among them."

Another test. Another riddle. Okay, I was on this like peanut butter on toast.

"What kind of portal?" I asked Skuld.

"A portal in dreams. They can find you in your dreams now, Wyvern, because you created the portal." She arched a brow. "And they can attack you there."

"I thought they already could influence my dreams."

She smiled. "Now they can kill you."

Shit. That was not great news.

"Good thing you have friends in high places." Skuld spun those scissors into her grip. She made an elaborate snip with them, then winked at me.

So that was how she'd done it.

I asked the obvious question. "That was the flash of light? You can cut spells with those things?"

She smiled. "You *are* paying attention, after all."

"I didn't know spells could be cut with anything other than the NightBlade."

Skuld arched a brow. "There are a lot of things you don't know."

True. And if Kohana could slice binding spells with the NightBlade, it made sense that there were other weapons that could slash those nasty spells to bits.

Seemed like I needed a tool like this.

I knew Skuld wouldn't just give the scissors to me. I'd have to earn any gift she gave me. Or fight for it.

She turned the shears again, letting the moonlight gleam along the edge, just as she had done before, then gave me a hard look.

A clue.

I remembered what she'd said earlier, the other time she'd made that gesture.

"If it cuts both ways, there has to be something good about tearing the veil," I guessed. "Maybe something more than eliminating the glamours?"

She smiled at me and nodded approval. "They are still weak, but if the portal is open, they can be destroyed. Forever."

"The elder told me to hurry."

"They gain power with every shadow they devour." Skuld widened her eyes and said something I'd never have expected her to say. "Ticktock."

On impulse, I put out my hand, palm up. A silent request for the surrender of the shears.

I thought she'd say no.

Or laugh.

Instead, Skuld's smile broadened, as if I didn't know what I was asking for or the price it would ultimately demand. She was that kind of a person, I could already see that, one who liked to test you by giving you what you thought you wanted. (Maybe all these dream people were like that.) I might have pulled back my hand then, but she dropped the scissors into my palm before I could.

I knew I couldn't just give them back.

For better or for worse, they were mine, along with the responsibility for eliminating the ShadowEaters. (Okay, maybe that had been on my plate all along.)

They were huge shears and heavy. The blades were wickedly sharp, gleaming silver. The handle looked ornate and was covered with symbols. By the time I studied them, then looked back at Skuld to thank her, she was gone.

There was no more snow.

No tree.

Just Meagan's room.

No dead people.

But, yes, wolves howling at the moon.

That they had to be real was just icing on the cake.

THE MOON WAS FULL, hanging round and silver in the night sky. It was almost morning but not quite, the sky getting a bit lighter at the horizon. My dream hadn't been all dream: Mozart and King were still gone from Meagan's bed. And I still had Skuld's scissors in my hand. The cats could have been downstairs, but the scissors were too heavy to be a figment of my imagination.

In fact, it occurred to me that these babies could get me into serious trouble. The blades glinted, ferociously sharp steel polished to perfection, and when I touched them with a fingertip, I drew my own blood.

"*Save me a liver,*" Skuld whispered in my thoughts.

It was like old-speak, the ancient language of the *Pyr*, so I answered her in old-speak. "*I thought you preferred souls.*"

She laughed that dark cackle of a laugh. "*There won't be any of those where you're going.*"

It was not the most reassuring thing she could have said. After all, she was the sister who held the keys to the future. I got up and peered into the park across the street from the Jamesons' town house.

Was there a glitter of golden eyes in the shadows? Maybe the ShadowEaters were the ones howling at the moon.

That was when I remembered that Nick was sitting vigil on the roof. He was a shifter and he had a shadow.

I was out of bed in a flash.

THERE WAS NO EASY ACCESS to the roof from inside the town house. There might have been one from the attic, but the trapdoor to the attic was in the ceiling of the linen closet, and Meagan had told me once that her dad had to take out all the stuff and the shelves in order to open the trapdoor. Her parents didn't go in the attic, ever.

I wasn't ready to go out the front door, not after I'd seen the spell light there, even thought I was worried about King and Mozart. I was more worried about Nick. I called to him in old-speak but he didn't answer, which did nothing to make me feel better.

I had to go out there. I took Skuld's shears with me and went into the bathroom, moving as quietly as I could.

I'd have to use my ability to spontaneously manifest else-where. I could have used a chocolate bar for the energy surge but was afraid to make noise by going down into the kitchen. Mrs. Jameson always got up really early. Plus she'd already been up to chastise me over the cigarette. For all I knew, she was still awake.

I shut the bathroom door, turned out the light, and took a deep breath. I didn't know what I'd find on the roof, but I doubted it would be anything good. I tried to prepare myself for anything, to come out fighting if necessary.

Then I closed my eyes and wished myself on the roof.

It worked, worked so quickly that I staggered dizzily on the rooftop. The town house had a mansard roof, so the middle of it was flat. I was hoping to manifest right in the middle, to better ensure that no one would suddenly see me there. I was hoping to come out of the manifestation in dragon form, but tradition—or maybe exhaustion—prevailed.

I was a white salamander, as was usually the result when I manifested elsewhere. Of course, I couldn't hold on to the shears, which were bigger than me, so they dropped to the roof and skidded across the dusting of snow there, coming to a halt with a clatter against the metal lip.

I hunkered low instinctively, half expecting Meagan's parents to come out and check what the noise was.

The bonus of the newt form is that I can skulk without anyone much noticing, especially when my little white salamander body falls in snow. The snow was deeper than I was tall, but I followed the trail through the snow left by the shears and got my newty fingers on them again.

Then I looked around.

The snow was perfectly untouched in every direction.

Nick wasn't there.

In fact, Nick had never been there. I couldn't detect his scent at all. There was no tingle of dragonsmoke, except the faint vestige that still lingered from November's adventures. I heard nothing from the house or the neighboring houses.

I summoned the shift and changed to my human form, grabbing Skuld's shears.

I was alone.

Except for the faint echo of a spell. It was the same tune as in my dream, the one that beckoned the listener to follow it. I remembered Nick being tempted by the Mage spell on Halloween and had a very bad feeling. I strained my eyes and saw the tendril of spell light wafting over the little park opposite.

Then it snapped like a whip, cracking over the park. The pack of wolves that I'd heard earlier were gathered in the park. The spell dove among them like a spear. I heard them bark.

I saw the silhouettes of the ShadowEaters riding that spell right down into the pack. It looked like a comet, an orange projectile followed by a cluster of ShadowEaters, hanging on tight.

It was true. By asking the elder to tear the veil, I'd made it possible for them to enter my dreams, attack me there, then follow me into the here and now when I awakened. They could harm shifters on earth without requiring an invocation from the Mages. Their glamours were destroyed, so I could see them—but they could see me, too. And chances were pretty good that there would be shifters in my company, no matter where I was.

Great job, Zoë.

While I stood there, grappling with my own responsibility, the spell whipped around the leg of a wolf. The wolf pivoted, snarling as the spell wound more tightly.

Just as it had in my dream.

The ShadowEaters fell on the pack of wolves, snatching and biting at their shadows.

Which told me exactly what kind of wolves they were, even before one of them turned to look at me with eyes of pale silver blue.

This was a colossal fuckup on my part and I had to try to make it right.

I shifted to dragon form with a roar, leapt off the roof, and dove into the fray with Skuld's shears held high.

Wyvern time.

THAT ONE WOLF WAS BOUND by the spell, the light moving at lightning speed. I realized that the wolves could see the ShadowEaters but not the spell light. They leapt at the shapes of the ShadowEaters, snapping and snarling, ready to rip off a shadowed limb. Two of them were down already, Shadow-Eaters surrounding them and demolishing their shadows.

Meanwhile, the snared one struggled against a tether he couldn't see.

I bellowed and breathed fire, slashing at ShadowEaters with my talons and clearing space with my tail. I couldn't manage Skuld's scissors in my dragon form, though, and it was all I could do to hang on to them. Had Skuld been honest with me about them? I doubted it. What was the repercussion of using them? I couldn't guess, not without giving it a try.

As I hesitated, the spell wound around the wolf, choking the life from him. I figured he must be a leader if they wanted him so badly. The ShadowEaters clustered closer, making their nauseating noises, and I had no choice but to shift back to human form.

To get to the wolf I had to push through the ShadowEaters, brushing against their slippery, slimy forms, hearing their smacking lips. I felt one or two take a nip at me, and my terror rose. It was way too easy to remember my dream. I lunged through them and slashed at the spell that held the wolf captive, as if cutting a leash.

It severed instantly, but the loose end flipped around like a snake.

Looking for another victim.

It quickly targeted me as the ShadowEaters pushed closer, chanting encouragement to their spell. I cut at it again and again, hacking it into bits in a frenzy, even as the other wolves snapped at the silhouettes of the ShadowEaters. The wolves leapt and bit, ferocious in their defense of their fellow. When the cut spell fell to the ground, like a dead thing, I turned Skuld's shears on the ShadowEaters.

The first one fell back with a howl. I saw the frisson of fear run through them, and wondered anew at the power of the shears. For the moment I just kept on cutting and slashing. The ShadowEaters abruptly leapt into the sky and scattered once more, leaving me alone in the park, surrounded by a circle of wolves.

And two badly wounded wolves. They shifted between their forms as human guys and as silvery wolves. That meant they were badly hurt. Several other wolves clustered around them; one shifted to become a man with a leather pouch on his belt. He acted like a doctor, and I assumed he was the healer of their kind.

The other wolves watched, their concern tangible.

It started to snow again.

Then he nodded, and that one gesture sent a ripple of relief through the pack. The two injured shifters became wolves again and I saw one open his eyes. I was shaking with the aftermath of the fight and my relief.

The wolves turned as one to watch me, silent and wary.

I straightened, the shears hanging at my side. I realized a bit late that there were thirty wolves surrounding me.

Thirty predators.

The wolves watched me, motionless. I sensed that I was being judged, that an assessment was being made in a trial I couldn't hear, and I couldn't tell from the cold steadiness of their stares how the decision would fall.

It didn't look good, I have to say.

And I didn't blame them.

Then the one who had been bound by the spell approached me. He moved as if he was older, and I saw that his snout was silvery. He shook thoroughly, as if ridding his coat of a bad smell, then bent and sniffed the dead spell. He could either see it or smell it now that it was broken. To me, it looked like a line of ash lying in the snow.

Until he peed on it, his disdain clear.

He watched me all the while, his eyes a clear blue. I had the sense that something had changed within the pack. Their eyes seemed to glitter more avidly and their attention seemed to have sharpened. I couldn't tell what they had decided, though.

I knew it was best to hold my ground.

The leader wolf came directly to me, his gaze locked on

mine. He didn't blink. He stretched out and sniffed the shears, then folded his ears back. He gave me one more sizzling look, then lay down in front of me and put his snout between his paws. He kept his ears folded back and closed his eyes.

I knew enough about dogs to recognize that I was being acknowledged as his superior.

Alpha girl.

I smiled and bent down beside him, reaching to touch the paw that had been spellbound with my free hand. The fur was singed from the spell. His eyes opened and he stared at me, unblinking. I knew he would understand me. "I'm sorry. I will do my best to defend the alliance and ensure the survival of all of us."

There was a brilliant flash of light, and then an older man was crouched before me. His eyes were the same steady blue and his hand was in mine. We stood as one, then shook hands.

"As will we," he said, his voice a low grumble.

"I'm sorry."

"Much is unpredictable when the stars stand still. This is our teaching. What matters is your intent."

I swallowed, relieved that I had been forgiven.

I eyed the town house, so close behind us, and had to ask. "Why were you gathered here at all?"

His eyes narrowed. "We felt a threat. We came to investigate and possibly defend the dragon, to keep our pledge. When we were attacked, there were those who feared we had been betrayed." He smiled. "I thank you, Wyvern. We had doubt, but you have proven yourself." He gave my hand one last pump, his grip resolute and strong, and the wolves tipped their heads back to howl in unison.

The sound made the hair stand up on the back of my neck.

He gave a whistle, and the wolves fell silent once more. I

bowed my head at the telltale shimmer of blue, averting my gaze as he shifted shape. The healer and one other man were the only ones in human form, and they carried the two injured shifters out of the park. I glimpsed the shadows of the other wolves slipping into the last of the darkness, fading from the park as surely as if they had never been there, and felt honored by their trust.

That was when I realized there was one wolf left, standing by my side.

The one with silvery blue eyes.

He shimmered blue, and Derek was standing beside me.

"Something else is wrong," he said, his gaze dancing over my features. I knew he could smell my emotions, but his powers of observation still surprised me. "Tell me."

"Nick was going to sit vigil on the roof, but he's gone."

"Where?"

I shrugged. "I can't sense him. I—"

Derek's eyes flashed and he muttered a curse about Shadow-Eaters. He tipped his head back to sample the wind, and his nostrils flared slightly. I saw his eyes narrow, and appreciated that his sense of smell was even keener than mine.

He flicked a look at me, one that I couldn't read. "Remember that you were afraid for him."

I was confused by his tone. "What do you mean? The ShadowEaters must have taken him first. . . ."

Derek shook his head. "He's with Isabelle."

I couldn't believe it, but Derek was so confident.

Had Nick broken his promise? I had to know for sure. I shifted shape to my dragon form and took flight, reaching down to snatch Derek out of the park. I saw the flash of his smile as I soared into the sky, Skuld's shears hanging from my other claw.

"Awesome!" Derek breathed.

But I wasn't feeling celebratory or even enjoying the marvel of being able to fly. If Nick was alive and well, if Nick had decided not to bother guarding Meagan and me because he didn't believe me, I might very well make him wish he were dead. I flew straight to Isabelle's dorm, probably setting a speed record on the way.

You know that I wanted with all my heart for Derek to be wrong.

You can probably guess that he wasn't.

Chapter 7

Whenhen I landed and set Derek down outside the dorm filled with sleeping students, his face was alight. I'd never seen him look so excited.

"Wow, Zoë!" he said. "That was incredible!"

Derek is not an exclamatory kind of guy. But he was exultant. He enthused away for a couple of minutes about the wind and the feeling of freedom, and said more in three minutes than probably the whole sum of everything he had ever said to me.

And I am such a toad that all I could do was look at him and think how this was almost, but not quite exactly, what I wanted most in the world.

Yup. I still owed Jared that ride and I still wanted to see his face after I flew him somewhere. I wanted it to be Jared who was standing in front of me, looking expectant and in dire need of a kiss, and that made me feel like the lowest worm alive.

So, I turned to the door. "Let's go find them," I said, and opened it.

I heard Derek exhale slowly. I smelled his disappointment. I felt his sense of having been cheated.

And the worst part of it was that I knew he was totally justified.

I trudged through the hallways of the dorm, knowing the way to Isabelle's room, disliking that Nick's scent got stronger with every step. That made me mad. He was here all right. They'd probably come into the building by the same door we'd used. And why? What was his excuse? Why hadn't he kept his promise? It was outrageous that I'd been worried about him but he'd just been goofing off.

Never mind that goofing off had saved his butt.

Was his promise to protect Meagan and me worth as little as that?

I was glad that Nick was safe from the ShadowEaters, but I was still pretty pissed by the time I rapped on Isabelle's door.

I didn't do it very quietly, either.

I heard voices whispering inside, and, sure enough, one of them was Nick's.

The other—no surprise—was Isabelle's.

Derek and I exchanged a look. Derek had a glint of mischief in his eyes, and that was when I understood what Nick had probably been doing here.

Oh. Too late. I wished I'd just messaged him or chewed him out in old-speak.

There was the sound of rustling and whispered warnings—sometimes dragon hearing provides way too much information—the tread of feet, then the silence of someone looking through the peephole.

"Zoë!" Isabelle said, and opened the door just a crack. "What are you doing here?"

"That's what we came to ask Nick," Derek said.

Isabelle jumped a bit—she hadn't realized Derek was there—then glanced over her shoulder. She was gorgeous, her hair tumbling loose over her shoulders and her silk kimono held shut with one hand. Her feet were bare. She looked, if you must know, even more like a lingerie model than usual, given that she was wearing—right—lingerie.

But she blushed.

So did Nick—as he tried to scramble to his feet with some of his dignity intact, stammering as he struggled to think of an excuse.

He failed completely. The back of his neck was brick red.

He wasn't naked, at least. Maybe they were doing that talk-all-night thing again. Under any other circumstance I would have been glad that he and Isabelle were making it work. Not now, though.

Nick took one look at my face and tried to bluster his way out of the situation. "Z, do you know what time it is? What are you thinking, coming around here at this hour of the morning? It's not even five! People are trying to sleep."

"Sleep," Derek echoed, and both Nick and Isabelle turned redder.

"Only the ones who aren't fighting ShadowEaters," I said.

Nick rolled his eyes. "We went through that last night, Z. You just had a vision. . . ."

"Then I had it, too, and so did my pack leader and two others in my pack when the ShadowEaters tried to consume their shadows," Derek interjected.

"What?" Nick said in alarm.

"When?" Isabelle asked, looking just as shocked.

"Not even half an hour ago." Derek shoved his hands in his

pockets, looking big and formidable and pissed off. "We're here because Zoë was afraid that they might have gotten you. Kind of ironic that she wanted to save you, don't you think?"

Nick looked between us with astonishment. "But I thought . . ."

"And you thought wrong." Derek eased past Isabelle and marched into her room, poking Nick hard in the chest. "You made a *mistake*. You broke your word, and Zoë could have been hurt over it. Where would we be if she'd gotten killed?"

"Hey, now. Wait a minute. I didn't mean—"

"It doesn't matter what you thought you meant." Derek said, his tone hard. "It matters what you said you would do and what you *did* do."

"But there was no proof that Zoë's vision had come true," Isabelle interjected.

"Proof?" Derek repeated. He was furious enough to be shaken free from his usual near silence. I was in awe. "You don't need *proof*. You pledge to follow a leader and you do what that leader says. You believe what that leader tells you to believe. The effectiveness of the team relies on you doing what you're told to do." He scoffed. "You don't go changing plans for yourself and screwing it all up because you don't have all the information."

"But—" Nick tried to protest.

"But nothing! You left Zoë undefended when you had promised to stand guard." Derek looked Nick up and down, his disdain clear. "With friends like you, she doesn't need enemies."

"That's harsh," Nick retorted, his eyes flashing. "We agreed last night that she was wrong about the ShadowEaters, because nobody else had seen them."

"Nobody else but me and Kohana." Derek pulled out his messenger and waved it in front of Nick. "Funny, I don't see a message from you asking for my input." He shoved it back in his pocket and approached Nick. Nick took a step back. "You've got an interesting way of playing on a team. I'll have to make sure you're not the one who gets the job of watching my back."

Nick looked completely flummoxed by this.

Isabelle stepped between them. "But the Bastian Oracle said the ShadowEaters couldn't come into this realm."

Derek glared at her. "I guess she lied. Or maybe she's wrong. Are you going to believe a story or what Zoë and I just survived?"

Nick and Isabelle looked at each other, so obviously surprised that I felt bad for them. Never mind the part I'd played in the proceedings. None of this would have happened without my choice.

Guilt pang there. I opened my mouth to talk to Nick, but Derek pivoted and walked back toward me. He grabbed my hand as he headed for the stairs. "Don't forgive him yet," he growled, and I shouldn't have been surprised that he'd known what I was going to say.

I was astounded, astonished, and a bit disoriented that Derek had defended me so thoroughly. I'm a dragon girl. I can fight my own battles.

Although it was nice to have someone take my side.

And be so articulate about it.

Especially when I wasn't innocent, either.

"Zoë!" Isabelle called after me. "Don't be so hard on Nick. You know why he's really here."

I did know. I was glad that they were together and that Isabelle's dream was coming true, even if Nick hadn't done what he'd said he would do. The fact that Derek was treating us like a team and acting like he was in charge also threw my game.

It was nice, but . . .

Derek flashed me a grin as we stepped outside, and the sight of his pleasure mixed me up even more. He held my hand tightly, his thumb doing that slow caress, and my heart started to thump.

I was amazed by the way Derek had defended me. He'd been so absolutely, totally in my corner. My own indecision seemed like loser thinking in comparison. In fact, his defense made me aware of how unfair I'd been to him. He was holding my hand so tightly—even though I'd just rolled out of bed to fight ShadowEaters and probably looked like it. He was loyal and strong and he had my back, better even than the guys I called my best friends.

Derek deserved better than what I'd given him.

A lot better.

By the time we stepped outside, I knew how I could start to fix that imbalance.

DEREK WALKED ME BACK TO the Jamesons' town house. It was a bit after five in the morning and just getting light. There were delivery trucks and a few buses out on the roads, and not much else going on. I felt as if we were alone in the world.

And it was kind of nice.

Let's just understand here that I am not a morning person. Having spent the whole night racing around—fighting spells, kicking butt, and taking names—meant that I was exhausted right to my marrow. I could have curled up and slept through the weekend.

But for the moment, I was running on adrenaline.

And something else. Something that made me tingle when Derek took my hand in his.

I did see the occasional flicker of gray in the shadows and imagined that the wolf shifters were keeping close tabs on their wildcard. I liked the way they all protected one another, and I liked that I had won them to my side, especially as it was a result of my doing what came naturally. I couldn't have stood by and watched those wolves lose their shadows, not for any price.

And that made me think about dragons. Specifically one dragon: my dad. Should I tell him about the ShadowEaters? I knew he'd have lots to say about my making a bad choice, but maybe he'd have some advice on making it come right.

On the other hand, all the rules had changed.

"What?" Derek asked.

"Your pack is following us, standing guard." I glanced at him and he nodded, unsurprised. "I'm wondering whether we should get some dragon backup, whether I should tell my dad what's going on."

Derek considered this. "What would he do?"

I smiled. "Charge in and breathe fire. Take command."

"Against an opponent he has never faced. You've already thwarted the ShadowEaters twice."

Well, there was that.

Derek gave me a look. "We are committed to following you, not your dad. If telling your dad would compromise your leadership of the alliance, maybe the news should wait."

I instinctively agreed with him, but decided I'd confer with Nick, Liam, and Garrett just to be sure. I squeezed his hand a bit, liking that we'd been able to talk about a question of strategy, and he squeezed my hand back.

It was snowing again, snowing more vigorously than it had before. The city looked magical with all that white snow swirling across it. It was cold but not bitterly so. The snowflakes landed on my cheeks and the wind tossed my hair.

We walked along together in silence, just a hand's width of space between us. I could feel the heat of him beside me, which made my toes curl in my boots. I could smell his skin, the clean soap scent of him, and when I glanced up, his silvery blue gaze was fixed on me. He can be so still, as if he doesn't need to blink or to breathe, as if he doesn't miss one single thing.

My heart began to beat more quickly. I heard his pulse, courtesy of my dragon powers, and my heart did that dizzy-crazy thing of matching its pace to his. It's weird when that happens. It seems as if my pulse is redoubled, resonating throughout my body, overwhelming me with awareness of him.

Derek didn't say anything. He just studied me in that steady, unblinking way of his. It was as if he didn't want to affect the moment, maybe by saying the wrong thing.

In reality, I was the one who had said a lot of wrong things.

"Thanks for taking my side," I said, giving his hand a little squeeze.

"That's what I signed up for," he said, but didn't squeeze my fingers back. He looked ahead of us then, frowning a bit.

I had more work to do.

"I think it was my fault," I admitted. "I had this dream last night and was offered the chance to have the veil torn."

Derek turned to look at me, a question in his eyes.

"So everyone could see the truth of what the ShadowEaters are doing." I grimaced. "But that also seems to have given them more powers."

"Like?"

"Invading my dreams. Casting spells that snare us. Maybe even being able to target shifters through me."

"Then maybe it needed to happen," he said, stoic in his defense. "Maybe we needed to flush them out so we could defeat them."

"I'm sorry your leader almost got hurt."

"You saved him. It's square."

"Look, I wouldn't blame you if you were mad at me," I

said. "But I'm kind of caught between what I want to do and what I'm supposed to do. I have to choose all the time, right in the heat of the moment, and I'm not even sure that I'm always making the right choice. All I can do is try my best."

He flicked me a look, his eyes gleaming. "You're not the only one, you know. It comes with the territory."

"Really?" Derek had to choose duty over desire? That surprised me.

But he nodded, smiling crookedly. "Something else we have in common."

"I'm glad."

His gaze dropped to the necklace he'd given me, the silver hand of Fatima on a chain, the one I was still wearing. His eyes seemed to shimmer the way heat shimmers above the pavement on a hot summer day.

I know I caught my breath at the sight.

He stopped on the sidewalk, then turned to face me.

"I know what you're supposed to do," he said, his voice all low and growly. I shivered at the sound of it, feeling my body respond to every word. He studied me, probably seeing every secret I ever had and—given his ability to see two minutes into the future—a good many of the ones I might have soon. "But I'm never sure what it is that you *want* to do."

And I saw how much I had hurt him. I knew I hadn't been as kind as I could have been, and I knew he didn't deserve my indecision, but I wanted to be straight with him. And that meant not pretending to feel something I didn't feel, even if it was inconvenient.

"What I want is to be honest with you," I said because it was true.

He dropped his gaze, shielding his thoughts from me. He touched the back of my hand with another fingertip, the heat of his caress awakening an answering heat within me. "You never ask what I want," he murmured, then flicked me a hot look.

"Because I think I know," I said. He lifted one dark brow, inviting me to explain. "You want to go out together, to go to the dance, and—and, stuff."

The corner of his mouth lifted in a little smile. He flattened his hand over mine, his palm closing over the back of my hand. His hand was a lot bigger, big enough to engulf mine, warm and solid and strong. "What kind of *stuff*, Zoë?"

I swallowed. My thoughts were churning, descending into incoherence thanks to the press of his hand on mine. "Make an alliance?" I guessed.

"Secure an alliance," he corrected. He looked me right in the eye. "How are alliances secured, Zoë?"

I might have thought straight then, but he spread his fingers, spearing them between mine and locking his hand over mine. His grip was firm but not tight. "With treaties?" I suggested, hearing that my voice was higher than usual.

Derek shook his head. "That's for countries, not ancient species like us," he murmured, and my mouth went dry. His gaze dropped to my lips and his voice dropped even lower. "Maybe we should call it a union instead."

A hot flush rolled through my body at his intensity.

He was talking about sex.

"Eventually," he said quietly. "For now, we could go steady."

I thought I could probably manage that.

He looked down at our interlocked hands for a long moment. "Wolves are patient, Zoë, and we are loyal. I can wait. I just need to know whether it's even a possibility."

He wanted a commitment. Right here and right now.

I glanced across the deserted street, thinking as furiously as I could.

How much was I prepared to do to ensure the alliance

between shifters, to ensure that all four remaining kinds had a future?

How long would Derek be patient?

And how could I know, without any real ability to see the future, whether there really was no possibility of that union occurring? I didn't know what I was going to want on Monday; how could I know what I wanted for the rest of my life? Especially since I was probably going to live for centuries? How could I know when I'd have a firestorm—the mark of a destined union for the *Pyr*—or with whom?

Maybe unions and alliances should be made where they could be made.

Maybe securing the future for four different species was more important than my own personal yearnings, given that my particular desire was unlikely to ever come true.

Maybe I'd been right that it would be smarter to like guys who liked me, rather than yearning after the elusive ones who never would like me.

"All right, I get it," Derek said, pulling his hand away. I reached out and stopped him, putting my hand on his arm.

He looked at me, all stillness and intensity.

"No. No, you don't." I swallowed and took a breath, knowing that in this moment, what I had to do and what I wanted to do were exactly the same. "I want to see the future. I want to know how everything is going to work out. I want to make the right choice every time."

"Nobody does that, Zoë."

"Wyverns are supposed to."

"Maybe that's just the myth. What you have is the reality."

He was right. All I could do was make the most reasonable choice in the moment and hope for the best. I looked into the shades of silver and blue and gray in his eyes and doubted I would ever know anyone more steadfast and true.

My heart clenched.

I remembered my resolution.

And I knew it was absolutely right.

"This is what I want," I said, and reached up to kiss Derek on the mouth.

I tasted his surprise and felt him jump a bit. His heart skipped as it never had before and mine matched that crazy pace. Although I made a clumsy start, the kiss rapidly improved from there. We melted against each other, and he angled his head so our mouths fit together better. I felt the weight and heat of his hand on my shoulder, the touch of snowflakes melting on my face, the press of his body.

And then his tongue met mine. I felt as if I'd touched an electrical wire and pulled back, my breath coming in gasps. I felt flushed and shivery at the same time.

That was only half of what I felt when Derek smiled at me. "Okay," he said, and his voice was uneven, too. He visibly took a breath. "Okay."

I swallowed. "Okay," I said, and his eyes lit.

He smiled at me, a sweet smile that made my heart ache. "Do I get another ride?"

"Not just yet. I need some sleep." I was exhausted—not surprising given that I'd been dreaming and adventuring most of the night. I yawned, unable to help myself.

Derek grinned and flung his arm across my shoulders, turning to walk me back to the Jamesons'. It felt good to have the weight of his arm around me, the heat of him nudging against my side. I felt all squishy inside, warm from his kiss and stirred up, too.

And it was good.

IT SAYS SOMETHING ABOUT MY energy level that I did sleep. Hard. Despite everything I had to do and think about.

It seemed that I'd only just snuck back into Meagan's room and put my head down on the pillow when the alarm clock started ringing. I opened my eyes to find the sky was lighter and Mrs. Jameson was making coffee in the kitchen. Meagan went to the bathroom first, and I dozed off again.

The ring of Meagan's messenger woke me up, because she didn't answer it as quickly as usual. She came running from the bathroom and scooped it off the nightstand. "It's from Jessica," she said, then sat down on the edge of my bed to read the message. She made a face. "Mozart and King were at her door this morning. Mozart is even worse, so she's waiting for the Oracle to come, but then she wants to talk to you."

I was wide-awake then. "I hope they'll be okay."

Meagan made a face. "Maybe two gems are better than one."

More fallout from my mistake. I had a feeling the day would only get worse.

By the time I was ready, Meagan was still making up her mind over what to wear—she was hoping that Garrett might turn up today, even though it was only Thursday—so I ended up leaving the bedroom first. It was knee-deep in discarded possibilities.

I could hear the television in the kitchen when I came down the stairs and could sense that Meagan's parents were riveted by the news. Something big was going on for them to be so attentive. There was a potent silence coming from the kitchen, as if neither of them dared to breathe.

"Any persons with information are requested to contact the police. . . ."

I rounded the corner and Mrs. Jameson saw me right away. Her eyes were wide and she was pale. She gestured to Mr. Jameson, and he killed the video feed before I could hear more.

"Good morning, Zoë," Mrs. Jameson said brightly—a little too brightly, if you must know. Her smile was definitely forced. "Did you sleep well after our little incident?"

"Yes, fine, thanks," I lied.

She fixed me with a stern look. "And we will not have a repeat of that incident, right?"

"No. Not a chance. I just had the one and wanted to try it." I hung my head in shame. "I'm sorry."

"Everybody tries it once," Mr. Jameson said. "At least it wasn't dope." His wife shot him a glance that might have turned another man to stone. Mr. Jameson got interested in his breakfast.

The air practically crackled in the kitchen, and it wasn't about the cigarette.

"Something going on in the world?" I asked, nodding toward the television. The Jamesons exchanged a quick glance—which I didn't miss—then Mr. Jameson made a fuss about leaving the table.

"Nothing important," Mrs. Jameson said. "Yogurt this morning?"

You know, I've always thought I was the lousiest liar on the planet, but clearly I was going to have to surrender my number-one status to Meagan's mom. She was a completely crap liar. I'd have to have been kicked in the head by a team of mules to not realize that something *was* going on and that she didn't want me to know about it.

Which just meant that I would find out ASAP.

I agreed, she headed to the fridge, and I pulled out my messenger. I logged in and looked for headline news, and there it was.

Local Teen Murdered.

And the picture was of that kid, the one I'd seen with Trevor and Adrian, the one who the ShadowEaters had attacked. Beneath his picture, it said his name was Steve Ford.

Here was the proof that I hadn't been making up that story yesterday, but it wasn't proof that I wanted to see. Even if this Steve Ford had been an apprentice Mage, I thought it was awful that he was dead.

Had his body been found because I'd asked to have the veil torn?

I read the article quickly, and it seemed as it he'd been found just as I'd seen him in my vision.

Pool of blood—check.

Slit throat—check.

Vacant lot—check.

Missing liver—check.

The article didn't mention anything about his shadow being gone. But would it?

I felt a curious mix of responsibility and relief—because how awful would it be to be dead and have no one realize you were gone? I could easily imagine that Steve had had a horrible death. I remembered the feeling of the ShadowEaters nibbling at my own shadow and shuddered. What an awful way to die.

Mrs. Jameson turned around and nearly dropped the yogurt tub in her shock. "Zoë! No messengers before school! You have a test today."

But it was too late and we both knew it.

I shut off my messenger and put it away. "I don't know him," I lied, then added a bit of truth. "He didn't go to our school."

Mrs. Jameson sat down opposite me. "No. He went to St. Joe's."

The Catholic school around the corner. I met her gaze and saw her fear.

"You have to be careful," she said, speaking hurriedly. "You and Meagan have to stick together and ride home together. Or maybe I'll pick you up instead of you driving yourself." She grabbed her own messenger and checked her schedule, her fingers shaking.

I reached out and took her hand, and she looked up at me.

I knew what I had to do. I summoned the flames of beguiling in my eyes and looked straight at Mrs. Jameson, willing her to believe me. She wanted to believe that Meagan and I were safe, so it should be easy to persuade her. "I'm sure it was a fluke," I said, dropping my voice to that low hypnotic tone.

"The police are afraid there's a killer," she said, licking her lips.

"He was probably just coming home late," I said, willing her to agree. "Breaking the rules."

"Breaking the rules," she agreed warily, then nodded. I could feel that I was losing her.

But then I was, after all, apparently a girl who knew a lot about breaking the rules. Maybe that hadn't been the most reassuring angle.

I went for simplicity on the next try. "Meagan and I are fine."

"Meagan and you are fine."

"We'll look out for each other and come home safely."

She smiled at me in relief. "You'll look out for each other and come home safely."

"We always look out for each other."

"You always look out for each other," she said, totally convinced of that.

"You don't need to pick us up. We're perfectly safe."

"Perfectly safe."

Our gazes held for a long moment and I sent her as many reassuring vibes as I could.

The thing was, I wouldn't be able to fix this, to figure out what to do and banish the ShadowEaters, if I got grounded. I needed Mrs. Jameson to be calm and confident.

"Everything will be fine," I told her, trying to believe it myself.

"Everything will be fine," she agreed; then Meagan came into the kitchen.

"I seriously need contacts," she complained, making yet another play to ditch her glasses. "The bow of my glasses is broken again. . . ."

"I'll fix it," Mrs. Jameson said, leaping up and breaking the connection between us. She fussed over Meagan's glasses, Meagan impatient with the whole exercise. Her mother remained adamant that there would be no contacts in Meagan's immediate future.

That was when my mom called. Fortunately, it wasn't my dad, because he would have heard all the unspoken nuances in my news update, and I still had to confer with the guys about involving the older *Pyr*. Even my mom clearly had her suspicions—I could tell by her tone—and I thought she'd probably call Mrs. Jameson back later.

So she'd hear about Steve Ford and about me cutting class.

I felt bad about not sharing the news with my dad, but I knew that Derek was right. I knew this was our test to prove ourselves. We were the ones who had fought these enemies before. We had the data and I had the responsibility. We had to get rid of those ShadowEaters ourselves and we had to do it ASAP.

When I sat down to finish my breakfast, there was a news update on my messenger. Another kid had been found dead, throat slit, similar to Steve Ford. (He still had his liver, so Skuld must have missed out.) I didn't know him, either, but he'd gone to Central and played in the band.

Band. Was he another apprentice Mage?

One thing was for certain: the ShadowEaters were wielding the NightBlade in our realm—in a very icky and effective way.

FIVE THINGS I KNOW ABOUT THE NIGHTBLADE:

1. It's an ancient ceremonial knife, supposedly made from a meteorite, used by Mages to cut the shadows away from the spellbound bodies of shifters.
2. Kohana seized the NightBlade intending to destroy it, but couldn't even scratch it.
3. The NightBlade appears to have a mind of its own, or a power of its own, at least under certain circumstances. Kohana believed the NightBlade turned the Thunderbird elders against one another, poisoning their thoughts with its own desires. I'd seen it leap out of Kohana's grip to cut the ShadowEaters free.
4. The NightBlade can cut spells like butter.
5. King had known immediately that Kohana wouldn't be able to destroy the NightBlade before he even tried.

I tapped the lip of my messenger, considering the list.

I didn't know where the NightBlade actually was at this point in time. I had to assume that the ShadowEaters had it, wherever they were.

Kohana might know more, but I didn't know where Kohana had gone. In my experience, I never could find him; he found me when it suited him. He also told me very little unless it suited him.

Where was Trevor and what did he know? Could I read

his memory again? I'd done that in the fall. He was still functioning, so his memory hadn't fused with the Mage hive memory before its destruction. Still, it seemed like a long shot that I could poke around in his thoughts twice. He'd be on guard against me after the day before.

I considered number five again. Was the Bastians' knowledge of the NightBlade part of the reason Mozart had been attacked?

Talking to Jessica became much more important.

Updating Meagan would help, too. I'd tell her everything as we drove to school. You never knew—she might figure it all out before I could.

CHECKLIST FOR A TYPICAL DAY IN THE LIFE OF A TEENAGE WYVERN

1. Breakfast well. You never know what the day will bring or when you'll get to eat next.
2. Pinch an extra chocolate-covered granola bar from the kitchen, just in case you have to spontaneously manifest elsewhere and need a sugar hit to recover. Put it in your pocket: you might not have your backpack in the crisis du jour.
3. Ensure that Skuld's weapon is well wrapped and disguised. Under no circumstances reveal possession of said shears. Expulsion attracts parental attention and disciplinary measures, both of which interfere with the successful completion of all Wyvern missions.
4. Check in regularly with Muriel and smile frequently in these encounters.
5. Find out from Jessica whatever the Bastians know about the NightBlade.

6. In the quest to figure out how to banish Shadow-Eaters forever, begin by hunting down Trevor and getting the truth out of him. (Alternatively, score his liver for Skuld.)
7. Cram for math test, despite no real hope of getting more than a C.

JESSICA WAS WAITING AT THE entry to school, and I could see from her expression that something was wrong.

"Aren't King and Mozart okay?" Meagan asked right away.

Jessica nodded. "The Oracle is treating them. She thinks they'll recover." That wasn't all of it, though. Her gaze kept flicking to me. Jessica peered at me from under the visor of her baseball cap, her eyes seeming darker than usual. "Did you have a dream last night?"

I had an idea why she was asking, but had to know. "Why?"

She shuddered. "Because I had an awful one. I was bound, helpless, just the way I was in the fall." She met my gaze with horror. "But worse, I couldn't shift."

"The ShadowEater spells block my shifter powers. I couldn't shift in my dream, either, but it was okay when I woke up."

Jessica shook her head. "I can't shift anymore."

Meagan and I exchanged a glance.

"Then how'd you get free?" I asked Jessica.

She licked her lips, glanced to the left, then the right before she answered me. "Kohana came into my dream with his thunderbolts," she admitted in a whisper. "I don't know how he did it."

"He can move in dreams. He's done it before."

"Well, he says I owe him." I could see that she was worried about what or when he might collect.

I tried to sound cheerful. "I owe him, too. We're in it together."

"He's always keeping score," Meagan muttered. "I wouldn't be surprised if he set this up, just so you would owe him." She opened her locker and slammed the door hard. "I don't trust him."

"He's still part of the alliance," I reminded her. Meagan rolled her eyes, but I turned to Jessica. "Are you sure you can't shift?"

"Positive."

"There must be a spell bound to you still." I looked her over but couldn't see it. Would it be visible in her cat form? Visible to me in my dragon form? If it was there—and it must be there if she couldn't shift—I had to be able to see it some-how. "Good thing Skuld gave me her scissors. We'll cut you free."

Jessica looked confused, so I explained to her, even gave her a peek. "Let's find a place where you can try to shift."

"It's still early," Jessica said. "We could go to the gym right now and get it over with before class starts."

"No," I said. "The gym's too big. Anyone could walk in. Let's use a bathroom."

Meagan nodded. "Let's go down to the other end of the hall to that one no one uses much."

As we walked down the hallway, I was struck by an unex-pected sense of foreboding. Theoretically and intuitively, our plan made perfect sense. I knew it was the right thing to do. But the idea of Jessica deliberately attempting to shift at school made me squirm. I rationalized that I was still spooked from the day before.

How was I supposed to know that my foresight had finally arrived on the scene?

You'd think I could have gotten a formal announcement or something.

Chapter 8

The girls' bathroom we'd chosen was deserted, just as expected.

It smelled strongly of bleach and faintly of both cigarettes and perfume, which was also as expected. They'd removed all the dead bolts from the doors after my shifting incident in the fall, which didn't exactly inspire confidence in our long-term privacy.

"Just be quick," Meagan said. "I'll be the lookout."

Jessica took off her baseball cap and shook her hair out of her ponytail. It's funny, but I forgot how gorgeous she looked at Halloween in that costume that emphasized her curves. It almost seems like she's a different person, or one who lives in her brother's discarded baggy clothes. But just that act of shaking her hair free made her look sensual and feminine. It seemed that the curve of her lips was riper and more sultry and that her gaze turned knowing. She unzipped her hoodie and I saw the gold necklace lying against her skin like the precious and ancient relic it was.

She was suddenly exotic and beautiful, at ease with a femininity that she kept hidden away. I thought of her at the birthing the day before and felt young and awkward in her presence. I was pretty sure she could sense it.

I pulled the shears out of my backpack and unwrapped them carefully. We exchanged a look, Meagan confirmed that the coast was clear, then Jessica flung out her hands and tipped back her head.

I knew she was summoning the change.

I knew what to expect.

But nothing happened.

Her eyes widened and she swallowed, and I heard the nervous skip of her heart.

"Don't think about it too much," I said. "Breathe deeply; don't question or doubt your powers. I'm sure you can do it."

She nodded and brushed her fingertips across that necklace. I saw her lashes flutter and heard her murmur something in another language. Maybe it was a prayer.

Then she tried again.

And this time, I saw the golden silhouettes of a hundred cats swirling around her ankles. They took form out of nothing, just long enough that I caught glimpses of them, then faded from view so quickly that I thought I was imagining them.

I saw that faint electric shimmer of blue dance over Jessica's skin, like she'd been touched by lightning. I narrowed my eyes as it grew brighter, wanting to see the moment that her shape changed.

But the blue light was suddenly extinguished. It fizzled and died in a way that I knew wasn't natural.

Jessica blinked.

She frowned.

Our gazes met for one instant and I knew what she was thinking.

Just like in the nightmare.

Just like the moment of being spellbound.

"Holy shit," she whispered, her fear obvious. "Can you see the spell that's blocking me?"

"Not yet. Try again." I tightened my grip on Skuld's shears, ready for action.

Jessica touched the necklace with her fingertips again and swallowed her fear, murmuring that prayer one more time. The shadowy cats grew brighter and more substantial before my eyes, and I knew they were answering a summons from her.

And this time when that blue shimmer danced over her skin, the cats rubbed against something that was locked around Jessica's ankle. It must have had a glamour on it to disguise it, but the ghostly cats pushed the glamour aside to reveal it. I saw the golden tendril of spell light clearly, thanks to them.

But I saw it only for a heartbeat before it was hidden again.

This time, the shimmer just sparked off her fingertips before it died to nothing. It didn't even travel up her hands, let alone over her whole body.

The sight was terrifying.

Would I be able to see the spell better in my dragon form? My keen *Pyr* senses were even sharper when I was a dragon. It was worth a try.

I had to hope that whatever had touched Jessica wasn't contagious.

But I knew the ShadowEaters were hungry.

My adrenaline was pumping when I flung out my hands and called to my own shimmer. I felt the power of the change slide through my body. I saw the brilliant blue light pass over my skin. I felt the tide of the shift, terrified all the while that it would stop before it was done.

But it didn't. They didn't have me yet. I felt the surge as the change was completed, raised my wings to beat them hard, and tipped my head back with joy.

Jessica hooted and applauded. Meagan did, too.

I wanted to shout. I wanted to roar. I wanted to breathe fire. I thrashed my tail, fiercely glad to still be what I am, and stretched to my full size.

Jessica tried to shift and the spell tendril glimmered more vividly on her ankle. It looked luminescent to me now. I locked my dragon gaze on the spell. Even now I could see it swelling. I could see it sucking something away from Jessica, like a parasite draining the life force from its host.

And there was a small shoot of spell vine snaking toward my own foot.

It was spreading. Finding her through the dream portal, then extending into real life to target the shifters around her.

That was enough. I lifted the shears and hacked at the spell closest to my own claw first, slashing it to oblivion. It fizzled and hissed and died, shooting little golden sparks in every direction as I consigned it to oblivion.

Then I went after the one that had claimed Jessica's ankle. It was more substantial, this one, thicker and more robust and harder to cut. I had a tough time with the shears, given my lack of dragon dexterity.

"Let me help," Meagan said, and abandoned her post. She seized the shears and started to snip, glancing to me for direction.

"Right here!" I directed. I bent and caught one end of the spell, holding it out so that she could guess where it was. "Cut harder!" I said. "Faster!"

It wriggled and writhed in my grip, like a boa constrictor that would have preferred to eat me alive. I held fast and Meagan snipped with all her might. As soon as the spell tether was severed, it spewed sparks, like a high-voltage cable severed while the power was still on.

One landed on Jessica and I saw it take root, growing a tendril that began to wind around her arm. Every spark was alive, a possible cause of our destruction.

"Stay back!" I commanded, and protected both Jessica and Meagan from the onslaught of spell chunks. I grabbed the shears and sliced with abandon, then loosed a torrent of dragonfire on the scattering spells. To my relief, that seemed to work; they fell to the ground like ash when I fried them. So Trevor hadn't lied about the power of dragonfire. That was interesting. I got busy and went after every last one.

When I turned to fry the final stray spark, I saw that the bathroom door was open.

Suzanne stood there, smirking. "I knew you losers were up to something," she said, then lifted her messenger and took a trio of shots.

"No!" I bellowed, and lunged after her. I shifted shape on the way, acting on instinct, but it was exactly what she expected me to do. The flash made me stumble and I lost precious momentum. She must have nailed images of me in transition and in human form, as well, her camera clicking like mad as she backed out of the bathroom.

My heart, just so you know, had fallen right through the floor.

I wasn't even going to survive long enough to catch hell for breaking the Covenant. My dad had chewed me out before for revealing myself in both human and dragon form—the Covenant sworn by all the *Pyr* was intended to protect our privacy, and he hated when I broke it. I had no idea what

Suzanne and her friends would do to me, armed with those images, but I knew it wouldn't be good.

I had to make sure that proof was destroyed.

ASAP.

SUZANNE BOLTED DOWN THE CORRIDOR, trying to lose herself in the crowd of kids getting to class—or dawdling to not get there too soon. She kept looking back at me, and I smelled that she was surprised that I didn't give it up. She shoved the messenger into her purse, pretending she didn't have it. She dove into a cluster of her cronies—Trish, Anna, Yvonne, and Fiona—nudging Trish as if to set her on guard.

But none of them could keep me away from this.

Even the spell light that swirled around them couldn't keep me away from this.

Two of the teachers were coming down the hall together—just my luck, it was Mrs. Mulvaney and Mr. Zacharias. Mrs. Mulvaney is older than God and big on discipline. I'd had her for homeroom the year before. I swear she would have failed me in homeroom for drawing during the announcements if she could have figured out a way to do it. Mr. Zacharias is one of those people who lives in his own world. That he could walk alongside Mrs. Mulvaney, calmly sipping his coffee as she ranted about something or other, pretty much said everything about his complacent nature.

I sensed Meagan and Jessica behind me, watching, and knew that the whole school would hear about this within five minutes. Mrs. Mulvaney would happily have my hide as a souvenir if I broke any rules, too.

But the stakes were high. I needed to erase those images.

I shoved past Trish easily and caught Suzanne's elbow as kids milled all around us.

Just two girls not getting along.

"Girls!" Mrs. Mulvaney shouted, and I heard her heels clicking faster. "What's this about, girls?"

Of course, everyone ignored her.

Suzanne's pack started to taunt me as they surrounded me, and if I'd been anything other than a dragon girl, I might have worried about my own welfare. Right then and there, I didn't care. I'd shift if I had to—although that would defeat the purpose. Suzanne must have guessed how intent I was because I could feel her shaking. I let my fingers dig into her arm and smiled, letting her think about talons and fire and big sharp teeth.

It was tempting to beguile her into believing she was being fried alive.

She caught her breath.

"You have something that belongs to me," I said softly.

She threw back her hair. "As if I'd want anything of yours, Sorensson," she said, but there was an undercurrent of fear in her voice.

"Why don't you just give me the messenger?" It was a long shot, but I had to try.

Suzanne laughed. Her friends jostled around us, and that seemed to give her confidence. Either that, or it was Mrs. Mulvaney's proximity. "I knew you were a freak," she whispered, her eyes shining with malice. "And now I have proof."

I snatched her purse then, moving so fast that she didn't anticipate my move, and dumped its contents on the floor. Lipsticks clattered and bounced. A hairbrush fell. A notebook and four pens scattered in all directions.

The messenger never hit the floor. I grabbed it out of the air, threw aside her designer purse, then ran.

"Zoë Sorensson!" roared Mrs. Mulvaney.

"No!" Suzanne shouted, coming after me. The kids in the

hall parted before us like the Red Sea. I felt Suzanne snatch after me and miss. "That's *mine*. You can't steal it from me!"

I kept running, right to the end of the hall. I had to buy myself a bit of time.

"Zoë!" Mrs. Mulvaney shouted after me. "What's this about?"

I poked open the back of the camera and removed the memory card as I ran. I shoved it into my pocket, then pivoted at the end of the hall. I slammed my back into the lockers at the end of the hall, smiling at Suzanne.

The smile slowed her down.

She wasn't that stupid. I held the messenger behind my back while I replaced the back panel.

Mrs. Mulvaney was marching toward us, pointing her finger and lecturing about rules.

I held up the messenger between us. "Sorry. Thought it was mine." I tossed it at Suzanne.

She barely caught it, then scanned it for damage. It took her a minute to figure out what I'd done; then her eyes flashed. "Bitch!" she snarled, but I dropped the memory card on the tile and slammed the heel of my boot down to destroy it forever.

Suzanne squared her shoulders to glare at me, ignoring Mrs. Mulvaney. "You owe me, Sorensson," she said.

"Less than you owe me," I replied.

"Suzanne Moore!" Mrs. Mulvaney said. "Such language is inappropriate."

Mr. Zacharias trailed behind Mrs. Mulvaney and glanced down at the smashed memory card. He was probably assuming that Suzanne had taken nude pics of me in the bathroom. Mrs. Mulvaney had missed my move with the memory card. She was too busy organizing and ordering, shooing people this way and that. Suzanne and I simply glared at each other.

"She wrecked my messenger," Suzanne said. "She did it on purpose."

Mrs. Mulvaney looked at me.

"I didn't wreck it. I just thought it was mine."

Our excuses were so thin and so lame that even Mrs. Mulvaney knew that they were only a fraction of the truth. "You have it back, though," she said to Suzanne.

Suzanne nodded. "But she owes me." She mouthed the word then: *freak*.

I smiled my confident dragon smile, liking that she shivered just a bit.

"All right, everyone. Get to class," Mrs. Mulvaney said. She pointed at me. "You're coming down to the principal's office, Zoë." Suzanne only had time to smirk before Mrs. Mulvaney pointed at her. "And so are you, Suzanne. Let's get this argument sorted out, girls."

We were walking down the hall when Meagan came to my side. She handed me my bag, and I knew from the weight of it that she'd hidden Skuld's shears inside. "Your messenger is in the side pocket," she said, slanting a glance at Mrs. Mulvaney.

I made a show of checking, then feigned relief. "How weird. I never put it there before. Thanks, Meagan!"

"An honest mistake, then," Mrs. Mulvaney said, a triumphant conclusion, but Suzanne snorted.

And I looked back to see Derek scooping up the smashed bits of memory card. I flashed him a smile of gratitude. Jessica was standing beside him, back in her usual sloppy clothes, but looking much more serene. This was the alliance in action, each of us guarding one another's backs and succeeding as a team.

I should have known it couldn't last.

THEY SEPARATED US TO GET our stories without collaboration.

I insisted that Suzanne had bumped into me and I thought she'd taken my messenger, although, gosh, I couldn't imagine why she would play such a trick on me.

I have no idea what Suzanne told them, but the interrogation team went back and forth between us for a good twenty minutes. Then they had to confer with each other for another twenty. Then they decided to call our parents. They'd call Meagan's mom about me, since my parents were away, and I wasn't too worried about Mrs. Jameson. Worst case, I could beguile her. Suzanne pitched a fit about this decision, though. Apparently she was worried about having her freedom limited right before the Valentine's Day dance.

It took them another fifteen minutes to reason with her and explain that they were doing this for her own good. Suzanne wasn't buying it, but her attitude gave me some time alone in my designated corner: the principal's office. The office had windows on all sides, even the door, like it was command control—or a lookout tower. This worked for me, because I could see everything that was going on and, thanks to my *Pyr* senses, hear it, too.

What was the deal with the spell light surrounding Suzanne and her friends? I thought I had seen some the day before around Trish and Yvonne, then later with Trevor in the parking lot. Were they being targeted by the ShadowEaters? Or was Trevor up to something?

Suzanne and her cronies were all human, with no shifter powers and no spellsinging powers—at least not that I knew of. While they certainly thought themselves special, I couldn't see what the ShadowEaters would want with them.

I knew I wasn't imagining the spell light, though. It had to be Trevor's doing, but I couldn't figure out his scheme. It was a puzzle.

"Mr. Sorensson is waiting on two," the principal's secretary said from the reception area.

"Thank you." The principal came into her office, shut the door behind her, and picked up the desk phone. She looked pretty grim. She pushed for the second line, while I sat there with my mouth hanging open.

They'd called my parents.

In the Caribbean.

Why hadn't I guessed that would happen?

And welcome to the inner circle of hell. Remember that my dad is a dragon shifter—he can supply the fire, if not the brimstone, on demand.

I doubted this exchange would end well.

I OFFICIALLY LISTENED TO ONE side of the conversation, eavesdropping shamelessly and secretly on the other side.

The principal's tone had that mix of honeyed sweetness and iron will that characterized all of my dealings with her. (Probably everyone's dealings with her, come to think of it. She is not someone you would ask for a hug.) "I'm very sorry to trouble you on your vacation, Mr. Sorensson, but there has been an incident at the school and I knew you'd want to know about it."

My father made conciliatory noises.

She discussed the incident in question, distaste in every syllable she uttered.

My father made sympathetic and faintly outraged comments, which only encouraged her. He didn't defend me, not one iota. Between the two of them, I was judged and convicted in a matter of moments. The principal repeated most of her points, seeming to enjoy her moral triumph, then handed me the phone.

I stared at the receiver and gulped. All I had to do was ace a math test, check in at regular intervals with Muriel, find the NightBlade, banish the ShadowEaters, and persuade my dad that I shouldn't be on his Incinerate Now list.

No pressure.

IT IS SOME KIND OF cosmic joke that when everything seems to be going to hell, the most unlikely things come easily.

My dad doesn't like me drawing attention to myself for any reason. It makes him think of dragons being nearly hunted to extinction in the Middle Ages, and generally moves him into high-octane, take-no-prisoners, Protective Parent mode.

This is much worse with a dragon dad. Just so you know. I know because we've been there and done that.

Would I be grounded?

Exiled?

Roasted?

The principal's eyes narrowed as she watched me.

I decided to take the initiative and grovel for mercy. "I'm really sorry, Dad. I didn't mean to get into trouble. . . ."

"We shall have to talk about this when your mother and I get home!" he shouted sharply, and I winced. "You had better behave yourself for the next week, Zoë. Frankly, I expected better of you, and if one more thing happens while your mother and I are away, you will be . . ."

The principal smiled with satisfaction, then left me in the office alone.

My dad stopped in midtirade. "Is she gone?" he asked, his voice low and silky. Conspiratorial.

"Yes," I said carefully.

"You were caught," my father said easily, as if we were talking about my sneaking a granola bar before dinner. His tone had changed completely and I didn't trust it one bit. He was softening me up, faking me out before he went for the kill. I had broken the Covenant again, after all.

I nodded, then remembered he couldn't see me. "Yes." I swallowed.

"Excellent choice," he said. "Almost intuitive in its speed, which is always the key to containing any incident in which you are revealed. Did you destroy the memory card in the messenger?"

I straightened. "Yes."

"Very good. I assume that you had a good reason for shifting as you did, and that it was unavoidable?"

"Yes."

"Also that you cannot tell me about the details now?"

I glanced at the principal hovering outside her office door. "Not really, no."

My dad mused for a minute while I sat blinking in astonishment that he wasn't roaring at me. "It's entirely possible that no one will believe this Suzanne person this time, either, but for the sake of insurance, if you can be alone with her, it might be wise to beguile her. As soon as possible."

I had to fight my smile of triumph. The principal was still lurking. "Yes, Dad. As soon as possible."

"And I think a reward is in order for your deft handling of an unavoidable breach of the Covenant. What do you say to having your own car?"

"What?" I asked, barely daring to breathe.

"Your mom wants a new car. You can have the Toyota. I'll pay the insurance, but all other costs will be yours to cover. Deal?"

I was being rewarded.

I slanted a glance toward the principal, who was talking to her secretary and suitably distracted. If goodies were being distributed, I knew which one I wanted—and it wasn't the Toyota.

"You could give me the Lamborghini," I suggested softly.

My dad laughed, a throaty dragon chuckle. "That insurance I'm not going to pay. Besides, it's sold."

I was shocked. "Sold?"

"A collector of vintage cars. He's going to pick it up after we get home, which will make room for your mom's new car in the garage."

Sold? Before I even sat in the driver's seat?

Sold?

"Can I drive it just once?"

"No." He was succinct and firm. There was no wiggle room on this. "It has been sold in its current pristine condition and will be delivered the same way."

Rebellion rose hot in my chest. I wanted to choose my reward, and it wasn't the bashed-up red Toyota. "But . . ."

"Have you been maintaining the dragonsmoke boundary at the loft?" he asked crisply. "It may be starting to wear down already, and I don't want anything to happen to that car."

"I'll go after school to check."

"Excellent." His voice dropped to a warmer timbre. "Well done, Zoë," he added; then he was gone.

It says something about my state of mind that I stared at the receiver for a minute before putting it back in the cradle.

My dad was proud of me.

I had a car of my very own.

And, you know, I was thinking the Toyota wouldn't be so bad.

Suzanne's call wasn't going nearly so well, from the sound

of it. I was excused, and headed off to math class late and without having managed to spare a minute to cram for the test.

But the math test was easy.

So easy that I was sure there was a mistake. Had I gotten a different one? The wrong one? Like maybe the one I should have gotten a year ago? No one else seemed to be surprised by it, so maybe I was channeling some Meagan and Jessica brilliance.

Speaking of which, Meagan wasn't in class. Her seat at the front of the room was empty. I might have been more worried about this if Jessica hadn't been there, acting as if nothing was wrong at all.

You will be less surprised than me to realize that no one noticed Meagan was gone.

I saw a teensy shimmer of purple spell light dancing around Mrs. Dawson's head. It swirled around her head like a glittery blindfold. Apparently, Meagan *was* learning more about spellsinging—and her spell ensured that Mrs. Dawson didn't notice the empty seat in the prime A-student zone.

I could have used a bit of that for Muriel.

I had to wonder, though, how exactly Meagan was going to conjure up the test she wasn't taking.

Never mind where she was.

I surreptitiously checked my messenger and saw that there was a message from her. I might have gone for it, even against school rules, but I saw Trish watching me. There was venom in her eyes—as well as that twinkle of golden spell light—and I understood that she would be more than happy to rat on me in vengeance for Suzanne.

Who was not in class.

I smiled at Trish, dropped my messenger back in my bag, and focused on my test.

Even having started ten minutes late, I was done fifteen minutes early and itching to accomplish something before art class. When I finally got out of there, I had a plan.

First things first. I needed backup.

Dragon backup.

I sat down by my locker and tugged out my messenger again. The message from Meagan was pretty enigmatic—she just said she had something to do and would see me at lunch. I decided on a meeting at my fave tofu-burger place and sent her an update. I composed messages to the guys, my fingers and thumbs moving in a blur as I brought them up-to-date and asked them to come to the restaurant.

I was sure that if we all put our heads together over lunch, we could come up with a ShadowEater Elimination Plan.

Of course, I wasn't counting on the fact that Meagan already had one.

THE RED TOYOTA HAD IMPROVED remarkably in its appeal during the morning.

The news that it was mine, all mine, made it look infinitely better.

I walked around it in the school parking lot, admiring its color and its signs of experience. It started right away when I turned the key, as if it, too, liked that we were going to be a team.

"Nice of your dad to let you use the car," Derek said when he got in.

"It's mine now," I said with a thrill of pride. I'd already told him that Jessica had said she was going to meet us at the restaurant. I was assuming that she was with Meagan.

He looked impressed. "What are you going to do to it?"

"What do you mean?"

"You could repaint it. Black."

"Purple," I said. "Lime green."

"Or install a better stereo," he added a minute later. We skidded a little bit on a corner. "Get bigger tires for the snow."

His suggestions got me excited about the possibilities. Just because my mom had liked the car being minimal in terms of luxury didn't mean I had to keep it the same way.

It was mine and I could change it. I felt the power.

"Paint a dragon on the side," Derek said with a grin. "That would get attention."

"That would get it taken back!" I argued with a laugh.

He grinned. "Let me look under the hood later. Maybe we can soup it up a bit."

"Really?"

"Oh yeah. Engines can always get a bit of a nudge."

I was really excited about the car by the time we got to the restaurant. I parked it with new pride and couldn't help looking at it, imagining the possibilities.

It turned out that Derek and I got there first. We ordered and claimed a big group of tables in anticipation of the others arriving. Derek sat right beside me, doing this proprietary thing that made me blush. Then Nick and Isabelle arrived and gave the nonexistent gap between us a significant look.

Before I could comment—or think of how to do it—and before things got awkward (again) between the four of us, Liam arrived, as good-natured and easygoing as a ray of sunshine. He gave me a big tight hug, and it was only after he stepped away that I saw he was growing a mustache.

Or trying to.

At least, I assume that was the plan. There was a weedy little auburn thing on his upper lip.

I wasn't going to say anything, but I looked at it too long and he noticed.

"What is that thing on your face?" Nick demanded, then began to tease Liam about it.

Liam blushed. "Forget about it," he said to Nick, who (of course) did not.

"Let me help you wash it off," Nick razzed him. "A little dirt like that will just take a wipe. We've got napkins right here."

"Leave it!"

Nick and Liam started to mock box over it, the two of them becoming so rowdy that I thought they'd get us tossed out.

Then Garrett sauntered in, his gaze dancing over the people gathered at the table already. The other two dragon guys straightened up at the sight of him, maybe because Garrett always seems so serious.

Although he tried to hide it, I saw his disappointment. "Meagan said she had something to do. She'll be here in a couple of minutes, and I think Jessica must be coming with her." He smiled then and ruffled my hair as if I were six instead of sixteen, so I poked him in the gut to get even.

So, they ordered and we all sat down, leaning over the center of the table to talk in (comparatively) hushed voices about what had happened so far. The guys had some questions and I answered them, Derek nodding periodically.

"What about these kids in the news today?" Nick said.

"That Steve Ford guy is the one I saw in my dream—and again yesterday." They nodded, not surprised now. "I wonder if the other one was an apprentice Mage. It said he was in band."

Isabelle pulled out her messenger. "I saw on the way here that there were two more bodies found this morning. These were two homeless people with mental problems."

She frowned. "They had jobs until November. As music teachers."

"Let me guess," I said. "They had no history of mental problems before November, either."

"Mages," Liam said, and we all nodded. "They couldn't function after the hive memory was destroyed."

"That's what must have happened to the survivors," Nick said.

"So the ShadowEaters must be targeting surviving Mages and apprentice Mages," Isabelle said.

"Well, that's not a bad thing." Nick shrugged. "Saves us the trouble of hunting them all down."

I shook my head. "That's how they're building their power. They must be taking on the spellcasting power of every Mage or apprentice Mage they kill." I told them about tearing the veil and how the *Wakiya* elder had told me that I had to act quickly.

"But do what quickly?" Liam asked.

"That's the million-dollar question," Derek said.

Jessica arrived then. Alone. She looked flustered and a bit annoyed. Liam stood up and smiled at her, making space for her beside him. She smiled warmly at him, holding eye contact longer than I might have expected.

And Liam blushed a bit. Hmm.

"I thought you were coming with Meagan."

"No. The Oracle wanted to talk to me." She made a face and that surprised me. I thought she revered that woman.

What had changed?

"There's a problem," she said. "I can't stay."

"You've got to eat," Liam protested. "Let me get you something."

We sat in restless silence while he was at the counter, impatient to find out what was going on but not wanting him to miss anything. When Liam came back, we leaned forward for Jessica's story.

She took a bite first, nodding approval at Liam over his choice. "So, this morning, when I told the Oracle about my dream, I thought she was going to lose it completely. She said that was proof that someone tore the veil, eliminating the barrier between the ShadowEaters and us. She says it's proof of meddling." She looked me right in the eye. "*Your* meddling."

Yeah, well, there wasn't a lot I could say to defend myself there.

"Is it true, Z?" Nick asked.

I had to nod. "I told him to tear the veil."

"There has to be an upside to it," Isabelle murmured.

"Are King and Mozart okay?" I asked.

Jessica grimaced. "They're not better, just about the same."

That wasn't good news.

"But that's not the worst of it," she continued. "There were more Bastians hurt during the night and three of them aren't going to survive. Their shadows are completely gone."

Derek caught his breath and took my hand. I knew he was thinking of those two wolves.

"The Oracle says you're dangerous company. I'm not allowed to be in the alliance with you anymore or even talk to you. She's monitoring my messenger and my mom's covering the phone." She frowned at her burger. "I don't know how else she learns things, but she always does. I can explain being here by saying I had to tell you."

"But then you have to go," Isabelle said, grimacing.

"But we have to stick together," Liam said.

"Why wouldn't she ask Zoë to explain her actions?" Derek said, with some annoyance. "Why do the Bastians always have to pull away like this?"

Jessica shot him a look. "I tried to change her mind. I told her about Zoë destroying the spell that was keeping me from shifting. She said it wasn't enough."

"But there has to be something good about tearing the veil," Isabelle said again, looking at me.

"It destroyed their glamours," I said. "And it means we can destroy them."

"We just have to figure out how," Nick said with a nod.

"And fast," Liam agreed.

"I've got to go." Jessica looked at me again, and there was a mutinous glint in her eyes. "But Derek's right. The Bastians can't pull back on this issue. I think you're right. The Oracle doesn't have to know that I'm still on your side."

"Really?"

She nodded at me. "You cut me free. They would have had me otherwise. I'm in and I'm staying in."

Derek grinned approval of that.

"Do you want me to pass messages between you two?" Liam asked.

Jessica touched his arm briefly, then shook her head. "Thanks, but it won't work. They're expecting something like that." She smiled, and there was a gleam in her eyes. "But what they're forgetting is that Zoë can send me messages telepathically. Like she did yesterday. And they can't monitor that."

"No way!" Nick said. "Sending messages! That's full-power Wyvern stuff." He gave me a high five across the table. We all grinned at one another, and I was glad I had given it a try.

"You'll have to be sure you don't seem distracted," I warned Jessica. "The Oracle picked up on your concern yesterday."

"Only because she was so focused on my needing to concentrate. If I'm not with her, I don't think she'll notice."

Jessica's lips set. "Especially if I try to hide my feelings from her." Then she stood up. "But I have to go now, before she decides I've been here too long and gets suspicious." She gave me a look. "Let me know where I have to be when, and I'll be there."

"I'll tag along," Liam suggested, but Jessica shook her head. He kept talking. "I'll keep watch over you or fight Shadow-Eaters if necessary. She can't have a problem with you being defended." He held Jessica's gaze, and something about his expression—pure puppy dog with muck on his lip—must have changed her mind.

"You just want the rest of my lunch," she teased, and he grinned.

"Well, if you're not going to eat it . . ."

Jessica smiled and handed him the last of her fries.

I didn't like our group separating, but the idea of Jessica being with Liam was better than her being alone. "But what else do you Bastians know about the NightBlade?" I asked Jessica, and she shrugged. "Because King knew that Kohana wouldn't be able to break it right from the start."

"I didn't," Jessica said. "But I'll tell Liam our story about the origin of the ShadowEaters."

"She called them failed Mages."

"I'm not sure if it's important or not, but it might give you a clue." Jessica nodded, then tugged on her coat, Liam close beside her. The others started to discuss ShadowEaters as Isabelle's messenger rang with more updates on the murders.

I heard a motorcycle engine, and the bottom dropped out of my universe.

I had a sudden idea what Meagan had needed to do.

The motorcycle engine grew louder as the bike came closer.

There was no way it could be a vintage Ducati.

Ridden by the hottest guy on the planet.

The spellsinger who was corresponding with Meagan, teaching her how to develop her innate skill, and ducking me big-time.

The oh-so-sexy rocker rebel who got my dragon drawing tattooed on his back for my birthday when I couldn't get a tattoo myself.

Jared Madison.

No. It couldn't be him.

It *wouldn't* be him.

Jared had bailed on me.

I was never going to see him again and I knew it.

But that bike was pulling into the lot. . . .

And Meagan had insisted that she had a plan. Was it this one? I turned to look out the window, unable to stop myself. Derek inhaled sharply. Nick was fighting a grin. Isabelle covered her mouth to hide her smile. Garrett looked between Derek and me. Jessica and Liam glanced up on their way out of the restaurant.

Jared roared into the parking lot, looking leaner and sexier and roughly ten zillion times better than ever, with Meagan hanging on to the back of his bike.

My heart stopped.

Then it fell through the floor, popped out in China, did a gleeful somersault, and charged back through the earth's core to slam into my chest again. No wonder I couldn't breathe.

Jared parked, then helped Meagan off the back. Just the way he'd helped me off his bike a couple of times. My knight in black leather.

I was sure my mouth had to be hanging open. Smooth— that's me.

No. He was not *my* knight in black leather. I reminded

myself of his silences and unresponsiveness. Assuming he was here for me was just plain dumb.

Had he come to help Meagan? I had to consider the possibility, given that she'd been in contact with him, and I hadn't.

Meagan tugged off her helmet, revealing her jubilant expression. She waved at me, racing toward the restaurant as Jared parked the bike to his satisfaction. He took a lot of care with it, just the way I remembered.

"Hey, Zoë!" Meagan shouted as she entered the restaurant. "I thought we needed a secret weapon! What do you think?"

I could not say one word.

I watched Jared saunter toward the restaurant, his eyes gleaming as he smiled at me. He knew his effect on me so precisely that he could have measured it out. I doubt anyone else missed it, either. My gaze was locked on him, as if he were the only person in the universe.

In that moment he was.

Me, I couldn't say a single word. I couldn't even *think* of a single coherent word. Even *hi* would have been a stretch.

Instead I thought about the way Jared had teased me, the fact that I owed him a ride, the way he kissed, the way he provoked me and challenged me, the way he made me feel simultaneously excited and confused.

Like I was feeling right then and there.

It would have been nice if time had diminished his effect on me. Or if absence had made the heart forget. No luck. Mine was beating double time while I thought about the song I was sure he'd written for me last year and the tattoo—my dragon drawing—he had on his back.

I itched to see it.

Or maybe just to see him half naked.

Of course, he had bailed on me. He hadn't been in contact at all. And I was sitting right beside the most loyal and helpful guy ever. I slapped my impulses down and fought them, hard.

I believed I'd made the right choice.

I'd believed it more five minutes earlier, but I'd work with what I had.

Isabelle moved and Jared eased into the seat beside me, pressed the length of his thigh against mine, and leaned closer to steal one of my fries. His eyes were glinting with mischief and still appeared ten thousand shades of green. He bit the fry, so obviously enjoying my awareness of him that I thought I would spontaneously combust.

"Hey, dragon girl," he murmured in that low sultry voice of his, the one that gives me palpitations. "Miss me?"

Then he winked at me, and I was a goner.

Again.

Or maybe still.

I barely noticed Derek shoving out of his seat to leave. In fact, I wouldn't have noticed at all if he hadn't sworn under his breath and slammed the door.

Even so, it didn't seem important.

Which was a very big problem.

Sadly, it wasn't my only one.

Chapter 9

Garrett smiled at Meagan and moved to make a place for her to sit. Meagan blushed and sat down beside him, looking radiant and happy.

So at least something was going right.

"You want something to eat?" Garrett asked her quietly.

Meagan looked at me, grinned at my reaction to Jared's presence, then stole the other half of my tofu burger. It wasn't as if I was going to manage to eat it, not while I was sitting there gobsmacked. She and Garrett shared a smile and he sat back down beside her.

I tried to focus on job number one, which was keeping the alliance together.

One member of which was walking away. "We have to stick together," I reminded them all, looking at Derek's retreating figure.

Yet not wanting to leave Jared.

Now I needed to be in more than one place at a time. I wanted to be here. I should go with Derek. I should stick with Jessica and Liam. I needed to check in with Muriel in sixteen minutes. All the while, I was keenly aware of Jared close beside me, listening and watching as my carefully built alliance shattered into shards.

Isabelle took a napkin and started to write on it. "Okay, we have a bunch of issues," she said, starting a list. "It might make sense to split up to solve them. We need to locate the NightBlade to destroy it. We need to figure out how to destroy the ShadowEaters and why we need to hurry. It would be good if we could find Kohana and learn what he knows." She glanced up with concern. "You don't think they've captured him, do you?"

"We never know what side that guy is on," Nick said, eyeing the menu as if he wanted another round.

"Nick and I will look for the NightBlade and Kohana," Isabelle said firmly. "I'll bet one will lead us straight to the other."

"Don't you have class, Zoë?" Garrett asked.

I nodded. "And a detention afterward." I snapped my fingers as I remembered something. "Which happens at the same time as Trevor's jazz-band practice."

"Good," Jared said. "You can show me where, and I'll corner him, see what I can learn."

"He's not going to want to talk to you," I protested.

Jared grinned. "Don't underestimate my charm."

His confidence annoyed me. "You're not part of the alliance," I said. It sounded rude the way I blurted it out, but it was true.

"So maybe I'm joining up." Jared glanced pointedly over the table. "Doesn't look like you have much of a team left, anyway."

It was too much.

First he ignored me.

Then he showed up and confused me.

Then he implied criticism of what I was doing, even though he wasn't doing anything. In fact, if he hadn't arrived, Derek would still be at the table.

"And whose fault is that?" I demanded of Jared. "You just show up, out of the blue, and screw up everything. Why? Because you like to mess with me?" I pushed to my feet, really angry. "It's not funny. Jessica and I were nearly claimed by ShadowEaters in our dreams last night. They're free, and the veil between their realm and ours is destroyed. We have some kind of limited-time offer to destroy them but I'm not sure what it is. I know in my gut that it's going to take every one of us to pull it off. We don't have time for screwing with people's feelings just for fun." I hauled on my coat and zipped it up with a savage gesture.

To Jared's credit, his cocky smile was gone, but I was too mad to let it go.

"Did you see the news?" I demanded. "That kid, that apprentice Mage, is dead. They sacrificed him. This isn't a game!"

"He was an apprentice Mage, Z," Nick said.

"So what? Maybe he didn't know what he was getting into. I doubt he knew that he was going to be sacrificed before it was too late to save himself. I understand what he must have felt in his last minutes, and it's not funny."

I turned on Jared before I lost my nerve. "I'm glad you think it's entertaining to mess with people's lives," I said to him, my tone snarky. "Thanks for your help. I'll have to put you in my will."

Then I pivoted and marched out of there. I might not have been breathing fire, but I was pretty sure there was steam coming out of my ears.

Nobody came after me.

Big surprise.

TREVOR FELL INTO STEP WITH me as I was walking back into the school. I spared him a look and kept walking. He seemed nervous—again—but I was pretty sure he was putting it on. There was a shimmer of spell light around him, but it wasn't very bright. It was just enough to ensure I didn't forget what he was.

"Zoë, I need your help."

I glared at him. "Be serious. We've been there and done that."

He shook his head. "No, this is different! Didn't you see the news?" He dropped his voice to a horrified whisper. "They're hunting apprentice Mages!"

I stopped and turned to face him. "So you invoked them, but the ceremony went wrong. If they were eating shifters and I came to you for help, what would you say?"

His gaze locked with mine, then danced away.

"If I ask you now to tell me what they want and how they can be stopped, will you tell me?"

"Zoë, I just need some help. . . ."

"Bullshit. Clean up your own mess." And I marched into the school, leaving him staring after me.

I had my locker open before I thought of it. The Shadow-Eaters were hunting Mages and apprentice Mages, eating their shadows and taking on their power. They were building their strength with spell power from their own kind.

But what had traditionally given Mages a burst of energy was the elimination of a species of shifter. And what was supposed to give them the big final surge was the elimination of all remaining shifter species. I'd asked the *Wakiya* elder what they wanted, and he'd said they wanted what they'd always wanted.

To become pure spirit and poison the universe with the strength of their malice.

The ShadowEaters would stop only when they destroyed all of us—unless we destroyed them first.

The question was how.

I GOT THROUGH THE REST of the day somehow, even though Meagan and Jessica didn't come back to school, nobody sent me a message, and Derek had disappeared without a trace. I even survived my stupid detention.

I was feeling like a total loser at my locker afterward when I packed my books up for another riveting night of homework and nightmares. I could not solve this riddle, and it was the most important one ever.

Then I saw denim in my peripheral vision. Dark jeans and biker boots.

I knew who was wearing those jeans.

"Still pissed?" Jared asked. His eyes were glinting, as if he were on the verge of laughter.

That annoyed me. I'm not funny when I'm mad.

"Didn't anyone stop you from coming into the school?"

"Some woman. She was intense."

"Muriel."

"Perfect name for her." His grin widened. "You probably didn't even know that I'm your cousin from Philadelphia."

I straightened and didn't look at him. "Shouldn't I be pissed with you, *cuz*?"

He leaned against Meagan's locker, apparently thinking, and folded his arms across his chest. "It wasn't quite the reaction I'd hoped for."

"Then you shouldn't have screwed up everything when you got here."

I saw the flash of his irreverent smile. "True."

I made the mistake of looking at him when he made that concession and the warm glint in his eyes confused me all over again.

"Maybe I just didn't think it all through, dragon girl."

"Maybe you just like to make an entrance." I slammed my locker.

He fought a smile. "I do." Then he leaned closer, his proximity making me dizzy. "But maybe, dragon girl, you mess me up just about as much as I mess you up."

What?

That made me look at him. The notion of me having an effect on any guy, especially a guy like Jared, was radical enough to stop me cold.

He must have seen how it surprised me, but he just held my gaze steadily.

Willing me to believe him.

It took me a minute to find anything resembling coherence.

I glanced down the hall and saw Muriel watching.

Was Jared just telling me what I'd longed to hear?

"But notice that I haven't screwed up your life over it," I said, although my tone wasn't as frosty as planned.

He laughed. "Haven't you? I just bailed on my band again to come here and help you fix this *issue*. Trust me, they are not happy. There was some manager coming to hear us play tonight, and Angie nearly ripped my heart out when I said I wouldn't be there." He grimaced. "It's entirely possible that they are no longer *my* band."

I stared at him in shock. He'd trashed a chance for his band just to be here. I could understand Angie's frustration in a big way, but in a bigger way, I was impressed that he'd done that to help me. I shouldered my pack, well aware that my resistance was melting pronto. "You did that to come here?"

"I did that to help you, Zoë."

Why did he have to use my name? It was easier to keep my guard up when he called me dragon girl.

Okay, everything is relative. I still can't keep my guard up completely, but it's at least in the vicinity.

"I thought you didn't answer to anybody."

"I don't." He glanced up and down the hallway and I swear he looked surprised by what he was going to confess. "But I help the people I care about." He looked me in the eye, dead serious. "Like you."

I opened my mouth to argue, but the astonishing thing was that he was right. He had helped me solve the riddle, each and every time. He'd prompted me to try harder when we'd first met, then returned to help me fight the Mages. He'd sent me that book the second time, leaving a note in it to guide me to the answer.

Maybe he'd help me with this one.

I watched him warily. "That could be true only if you know the way to destroy the ShadowEaters."

His grin lit his features. "Bingo, dragon girl. I think I know how get rid of them for good." His eyes glinted with satisfaction at my evident surprise; then he turned and strode down the corridor.

I ran after him like some besotted fan. "When exactly is it that you plan to start helping me?"

"Now."

"Are you going to tell me what you know?"

"No," he said, and I could have swatted him. "I'm going to *show* you."

"What about the NightBlade? Do you know how to break that?"

"First things first." He held the door for me, and stepping into the cold air made me catch my breath. It had nothing to do with my elbow brushing against his chest. "Let's go for a ride."

RIDING WITH JARED ON HIS motorcycle was every bit as exhilarating as I remembered. If anything, it was more exciting in the city, as he cut in and out of traffic with elegant ease. I halfway didn't want to bother him with questions, but there was so much I needed to know.

"How do you know this?" I asked finally, taking advantage of the fact that there were microphones and headsets in the helmets.

"There has to be some benefit of having been courted by the Mages for an apprenticeship."

Right. Jared was a natural spellsinger, like Meagan, and the Mages had tried to recruit him. That's why Derek didn't trust him at all. He said it wasn't clear how far Jared had progressed in the training and that we only had Jared's word on the fact that he'd declined to continue. And Jared had acknowledged that the Mages had been using him to get to me, even without his agreement.

I had a funny feeling then that maybe coming with Jared hadn't been the smartest choice.

That feeling redoubled when he parked the bike in front of that vacant lot.

It was the very same one. Same streetlight, trash can, locksmith, convenience store. I thought back to being trapped here by Trevor and Adrian, of the ShadowEaters biting my shadow, and shuddered in recollection.

"Not here," I said.

"Here," Jared insisted, and turned off the engine.

Before I could ask more, Jared marched to the edge of the sidewalk. He looked up, as if he was looking up the stairs of that library glamour I'd seen before. Then he propped his hands on his hips and began to hum.

It was a coaxing melody, like he was enticing something to come out of the shadows, to reveal itself to him when it would have preferred otherwise. I could see the silvery light of his spell, like fireflies dancing amid the falling snowflakes, winking and glinting, tempting something to follow them.

And when I looked back up, the library was there again, just as substantial as it had appeared before.

"You summoned the glamour again," I said, astounded that he'd been able to do this. "How?"

"Spellsinging 201." He reached back and grabbed my hand, then started for the stairs.

I halted, fighting his grip. "Where are you going?"

"Inside the glamour."

"You can't do that. It'll ripple and disappear. It's not real." I pointed. "And what's behind it is dangerous. I nearly was consumed back there. . . ."

Jared looked pointedly between me and the glamour. "Don't you want my help?"

I was way out of my depth, no matter which way you measured the distance to the shore. It wasn't much consolation that I knew it. "Yes, but not like this."

He tilted his head to study me. "I thought you trusted me. That's what you said before." His words were soft, and I sensed his surprise.

As if my not trusting him could change everything.

I was torn. I did trust Jared. I had told him that I trusted him, and I wanted that to still be true. But he wanted me to do something that I knew was dangerous.

And I wasn't nearly ready to attack the ShadowEaters. I had no plan. No understanding of their weakness. It was dumb to just leap in and hope for the best.

I extricated my hand from his and took another step back. "I do trust you," I said. "But you don't have all the information here. I've been in that glamour and I nearly died, and I'm not going to go in there willingly again."

His eyes narrowed. "Even if it might be the only way to accomplish what you seek to do?"

"Even then."

"Even if you didn't have all the weapons you needed last time, but you do now?"

I sighed. I swallowed.

I took a step back.

He half smiled and glanced away, then looked back at me, his eyes bright. "A dragon girl shouldn't be afraid."

"I'm not afraid. I'm learning from experience."

He lifted a brow, skeptical, and I knew we'd never agree on this. Probably because it wasn't strictly true. I *was* afraid. No, I was terrified. I had learned that from experience and I didn't think it was a bad thing to recognize when a choice could cost me my life.

But Jared was daring. Jared was reckless.

Maybe Jared had less to lose.

Or less to live for.

I felt that we were on opposite sides of an abyss, that there could be no middle ground. There was only one thing I could say.

"I'm sorry." I turned and walked away from him, past the bike and down the street, feeling the weight of his gaze as he watched me.

And when he finally started the bike again, its sound faded from earshot.

He rode in the opposite direction.

That was that.

But this time, I'd sent him out of my life.

Funny, but it didn't feel like much of an accomplishment.

I FEARED I COULDN'T GO into that glamour and survive, not without a better plan, and I resented that Jared had expected me to do it at his request. On the other hand, I had a niggling sense that I'd made a big mistake by turning him down. I walked back to school to get my car, arguing both sides of it in my mind until I was sick of myself.

Eventually I heard the faint hum of a motorcycle cutting in and out. I was sure it was the Ducati and I suspected that it was trailing behind me, even though I never caught a glimpse of Jared. The engine was throaty, maybe a bit unhappy to remain in a low gear. It both irritated me that Jared was following me and pleased me that he was sticking with me.

As usual, he was mixing me up in a very big way.

It was getting dark, though, and I was starting to glimpse the golden glint of the eyes of ShadowEaters in the periphery of my vision. When I looked straight at them, they faded from view, as if they'd never been.

As if they were figments of my imagination.

But I could feel them.

And I could hear spellsong.

Faintly.

Hauntingly.

How many apprentice Mages did they have to divest of their shadows before they could attack me outright? Were they mustering power? Or waiting for an opportunity?

It took me a while to realize there was another song on the wind, mingling with the throaty purr of the Ducati's engine.

It was Jared. He was humming that song of his, the one called "Snow Goddess," the one I thought was about me.

That's what he was doing: trailing behind me and defending me with his spellsong. Keeping the ShadowEaters at bay.

Maybe I hadn't ditched him after all.

My heart did that stupid lurch thing where it leaps and practically sticks in my throat.

I finally reached the school, only to discover that the little red Toyota was parked all by its lonesome in the lot. It seemed to look particularly ill used, battered, and sad. But it was mine. I was feeling a bit bashed up myself. Maybe we belonged together.

I got in and started it, turning up the heater to full blast. My fingers were too frozen to even compose anything on my messenger. I sat there, letting the ice in my veins thaw, and watched the spellsong swirl around the car. Orange, viney Mage spell light, interspersed with flickering purple Jared spell light. Jared's spells looked like barbed wire, with big nasty spikes. I had to like that.

I was so busy looking that I didn't see Suzanne, not until she rapped on the passenger's-door window. I nearly jumped out of my skin at the sound.

What she said astonished me even more.

"Hey, freak. Give me a ride." She yanked open the door and flung herself into the passenger's seat, treating me to a vicious glare. This made me wish I had locked the doors as soon as I'd gotten in. "Let's go already."

"Excuse me? I never offered you a ride."

"But Trevor is a no-show and I'm freezing my ass off, and you owe me big-time."

I didn't move. "I don't owe you anything."

"Oh no? I could make your life miserable in so many ways,

and you would deserve it. But give me a ride and we'll be friends."

I laughed. "With a friend like you, I wouldn't need enemies."

"Listen, bitch," she began, and pivoted to face me.

But I had had enough of Suzanne for one day. I turned on the beguiling flames pronto and she forgot whatever she was going to say.

Her mouth dropped open a little bit. "What's wrong with your eyes?" she asked, her voice already a bit dreamy. She was pretty suggestible, which worked for me.

"There's nothing wrong with my eyes," I said in my beguiling voice.

"Nothing wrong," she echoed, then shook her head and looked away. "This is some kind of freaky dragon trick you're trying to pull on me and it isn't going to work."

She reached for the door handle but I hit the power locks, glad yet again that my dad loves his toys. This car had nothing on the new sedan he'd parked at the airport.

Even with all its gadgetry, I didn't lust for the sedan, though. It was the ancient gas-powered Lamborghini that snared my heart and held fast.

"Hey!" Suzanne shouted, then turned to look at me again. I had the flames in my eyes turned up, ready for her, and smiled when she stared.

Caught.

"You didn't see anything in the bathroom today," I said, low and enticing.

Suzanne licked her lips, fighting the notion.

I tried another tack. "You got a shot of me naked."

"Naked," she echoed with satisfaction.

"Just to humiliate me."

Her eyes shone. "Just to humiliate you."

"But there was nothing strange about it."

"Nothing strange," she echoed softly.

"Just a skinny butt."

"Just a skinny butt." She said that with malice, savoring her advantage in the curve department over me.

I was tempted, you know, to shift shape in the car when she was trapped with me, to compel her to watch me make the change, just to find out whether some humans really could be driven insane by the sight of the transformation. I'd never done it really slowly, never lingered in it so there could be no doubt of what was happening, but I wanted to now. Just for the sake of gathering evidence. Proving theories. For the benefit of *Pyr* and mankind.

But I stuck with beguiling.

Who says I'm not a good kid?

I dropped my voice an increment lower and made it softer. "There are no dragon shifters in our school."

She closed her eyes and I thought I'd lost her. Then she shuddered from head to toe and I saw how much that lie relieved her. "No dragon shifters in our school," she said, as if the weight of the world had slipped from her shoulders.

"Arty kids, losers, math whizzes, jocks. The usual variety."

She smiled. "The usual variety."

"Nothing special at Ridgemont High."

Her lip curled and she glanced at the school. "Nothing special at Ridgemont High."

I let my voice become normal again. "So, you want a ride?"

Suzanne started, as if awakened from a long sleep, then glanced at me. "Well, there's no one else around, is there? Beggars can't be choosers." She gave me an address on Riverside Drive.

"You live there?"

"No, freak. Trevor does. I'm going to find out who he thinks he is, leaving me standing in a snowstorm."

I had to razz her a bit, make our exchange seem authentic. "Does he usually forget about you?"

Suzanne was annoyed with me and with him. "He was supposed to meet me after his jazz session and give me a ride home, but there's no sign of him."

"Funny he'd do that. Maybe he's got another girlfriend."

"Be serious. I'm the best thing that ever happened to him." She punched savagely at her messenger. "He'd better have a good excuse. I left my car at home today because of him, and passed on a ride from Trish in her new car." She flicked me a look. "It's not like I'd volunteer to be seen in this heap."

"You have an interesting way of saying thanks," I noted as I made to turn down Riverside Drive.

"Don't go all the way to the house!" she instructed. "The last thing I need after this day is for Trevor to see me in this car with you."

"You're welcome," I said tartly after I stopped at the corner.

She got out of the car, leaning down for one last taunt through the open door. "You should be thanking me," she said. "I'm probably the most popular person you've ever had in your car."

"So what?"

"So I have the Midas touch. This could change your social fortunes, Sorensson."

"Not if no one sees you," I smiled. "But it's okay. Let's keep both of our reputations intact."

She slammed the door then, content that she'd won a round. Meanwhile, I was feeling triumphant that I'd secured my cover according to the Covenant.

One more item off my To Do list.

Too bad there were still so many more.

There was no chance of that depressing me. I watched Suzanne walk down the street, swinging her backpack onto her shoulder. To my surprise, a wraithlike shadow separated itself from the shadow beside a house. Suzanne started; then I overheard her greet Yvonne.

They walked together, and I had time to think that they deserved each other before Yvonne glanced back at me. Her eyes shone gold as she smiled.

Then I blinked and she looked normal again.

I looked in my rearview mirror and caught a glimpse of a guy on a bike tagging behind me. I saw the gleam of Jared's protective spell and the sight of both made my heart skip a beat.

It was true that he didn't have all of the information, but neither did I. I knew just about nothing about spellsingers.

Maybe if we pooled our data, we could find a solution.

Maybe it was just an excuse to talk to him again.

Maybe I didn't care.

I WALKED INTO THE LITTLE park opposite the Jamesons' town house after I'd parked the car, relieved to be within shouting distance of dinner. I wasn't quite ready to go in, not when I had questions for Jared. I could hear the thrum of the bike trailing behind me still and see the wispy tendrils of Jared's spell wafting around me. It was like a gossamer net, spun out of sapphires and amethysts, protecting me but not confining me.

There was so much I didn't know about spellsong, so much I would probably never understand. His spells could be so many different colors and shapes. All I knew for sure was that Mage binding spells were orange.

I turned to face him, staring at the silhouette of his figure on the motorcycle at the end of the block. He didn't move closer, just braced his heels on the ground. Waiting. Giving me space. Not expecting me to answer to him, either.

Could he read my thoughts, even at this distance?

"What are they?" I asked. "The ShadowEaters?"

He took that as encouragement to ride the bike closer, then turned off the engine when he was beside me. He didn't get off the bike, and he didn't have his helmet on.

"They're Mages who took the last rite."

So the Bastians had it right. "Their book calls it metamorphosis."

He nodded, scanning our surroundings even as he listened to me, humming when he wasn't talking. He hummed a little harder before he answered me, buttressing his spell, then spoke quickly. "By eliminating species of shifters, they assume the powers of the shifters that are no more. They also strengthen their own ability to shift between forms." He glanced around us, looking worried, so I tried to fill in the gaps.

"I've seen Adrian rotate between forms," I said, and Jared hummed some more. "He can take the shapes of all the eliminated shifters. Or he could until he became a ShadowEater."

"But he couldn't hold any of those forms for long. It was a fleeting transformation."

I nodded. "He held the other human form for a while at boot camp."

"A sign of his prowess. The more proficient the Mage, the longer he or she can hold a form. They all max out around a week, and it completely wears them out."

"And the metamorphosis?"

"Is an advanced rite for full Mages to move to the next stage. They were supposed to become immortal and move beyond the constraints of the physical realm."

"But that's not what happened."

He shook his head. "They did it too soon, I think, before they had mastered all the necessary skills. Instead they got stuck halfway between human and immortals."

"Can they take other shapes?"

"No. They have only their former human skins, filled with spell light." He grimaced, hummed a bit more. "I don't think they understood fully what it meant to fulfill the rite. The ritual talks about joining the divine and becoming divine."

"But it's not very divine. They're predators, always hungry for more shadows, at least from what I've seen."

Jared smiled. "It wouldn't be the first time that the advance publicity oversold the attraction."

I smiled back, unable to help myself. "But was there just one group who did it? Is that where they all came from?"

"The story is that there was a mass rite several hundred years ago. All of the full Mages participated, thinking they were going to change the world. And all of them transformed into ShadowEaters."

"You never told me that part."

"I thought it was a bullshit story—you know, the kind of thing they'd made up to make being a Mage sound cool. I never really believed that ShadowEaters had been created from human Mages."

"But I saw Adrian do it."

He nodded ruefully. "So it was true. Which explains why all you shifters thought they weren't an issue. Essentially they would have disappeared, all at once."

I nodded. That made sense to me. "So, the power surge from eliminating all shifters would catapult the newer Mages into that divine immortality, as well as the Mages already trapped as ShadowEaters. So what happens if they succeed in becoming pure spirit?"

He exhaled. "A universe filled with powerful malice, instead of striving toward goodwill and peace." He met my gaze. "Probably one without shifters."

Right.

He frowned at the bike. "Not a place I want to visit, much less live."

It didn't sound as if I'd have a chance to live there.

Jared's expression was grim. "There has to be a way to beat them, dragon girl."

It would have been nice to know how.

The glint of golden eyes was clearer now in the shrubbery at the perimeter of the park, and even with Jared's spell enfolding me like butterfly wings, I shivered at the sight of them. It seemed to me that I could hear them salivating, and felt them drawing closer. I could see tendrils of spell light inching toward me, easing along the ground like thick vines. One dared to breach Jared's spell, and sparks flew from the point of contact. The Mage spell fell back, singed, but three more tendrils took its place, edging closer.

I knew I would dream of them enfolding me, snaring me, squeezing me, sucking the life out of me, and offering my shadow to the ShadowEaters.

"I should go in," I said.

"No lock can protect you from them." Jared was serious. "Should dragons be afraid of what needs to be done?"

"I'm not afraid," I insisted, but we both knew it was a lie. "I just need more information before I risk my life. I need to have a plan."

He watched me, humming, cutting me no slack.

I threw out my hands. "I'd built a team. I had everyone working together. Then you came along and scared Derek away, made it sound like I have to do everything myself. That's not leading. That's sacrificing."

"Don't Wyverns sacrifice their self-interest for the good of everyone else?"

"That's what the last Wyvern did," I said, my tone bitter. "I'm not quite ready to die."

Jared said nothing. He held my gaze for a long moment, then bent to start the bike. "Suit yourself," he said quietly. "You don't have to answer to me."

I knew I'd disappointed him, but it wasn't as if he hadn't disappointed me a few times. I stood there and watched him ride away, knowing I was safe—for the moment—within his spell.

But as soon as he rounded the corner, I ran for the house. I was sure there were Mage spells pursuing me, but when I locked the door and looked through the peephole, all I saw was a cloud of golden eyes gleaming in the darkness.

MEAGAN AND GARRETT AND LIAM were at the dining room table. Mrs. Jameson was in the kitchen, and dinner smelled good. Vegetarian lasagna, maybe. Even though I hadn't thought I was hungry, I realized I hadn't eaten much all day. The looks of relief on their faces reminded me that I hadn't checked my messenger, either.

"You okay?" Liam asked, getting up when I appeared. "We were worried about you."

"I know. I'm sorry."

"You're late," Meagan said, her expression filled with concern.

"I was with Jared," I admitted, shedding my coat and taking a seat.

"I knew we had to trust you," Garrett said. "That you'd let us know if you needed help."

"But the thing is, we've found something," Meagan said. "We broke the code on that book!"

"Not we—Meagan broke the code," Garrett corrected.

"You mean the book about Mages and their spells that you found in the fall?" I asked. "The one that was in Latin and in code, too?"

"Right. We'd translated the Latin, but never broke the code. Until today." Garrett nodded and nudged Meagan, his expression filled with admiration. "Tell her."

Meagan blushed, pushed her glasses up her nose, flicked a look at Garrett, then back at me. "It's about music, just like we thought, but it's specifically about *musica universalis*."

"Should I know what that means?"

"The music of the spheres," Liam contributed. "Pythagoras wrote about it originally. For him, the harmony of the spheres was about celestial sounds emitted by the planets, each one harmonic with the others because their orbits were in proportion."

"You know that?" I asked him, surprised.

He grinned. "I've learned it today."

Garrett continued. "The idea is that there's perfect harmony in the heavens and that we should emulate that here on earth."

"Okay. But I don't understand the harmony."

"Pythagoras is the one who discovered the mathematical relationship between pitch and the length of the string on a stringed instrument, which led him to conclude that harmonious sounds can be mathematically calculated."

I was lost and it must have shown on my face.

Garrett grabbed a sheet of paper and drew a sine wave. I remembered that from math class. Then he drew vertical lines, one at the beginning of the wave and a second where it started to repeat. "That's one interval," he said, and I nodded. Then he drew a second sine wave, one that had two repetitions in the same linear distance.

"That one's half as long," I said.

"If it's exactly half as long, these two notes will be in perfect harmony."

"But these are graphs," I protested.

"Which represent tones." Meagan went to the piano. She played a note, then a second one. When she played them together, I could hear the way they vibrated together in a very sweet kind of harmony.

"Wow. But what does this have to do with ShadowEaters?"

"The Mages figured out that if you have four harmonic tones in unison, it invokes power," Garrett said. "Their book is all about those four perfect notes, how to sing them purely, how to add them together, then what to do once you have that chorus."

Liam leaned closer. "Even better, it's how they made the NightBlade out of the stone from a meteorite."

"It's the weakness Kohana was looking for. It's how we can break the NightBlade," I guessed.

They all nodded. "As long as the power we summon isn't stolen by the ShadowEaters for their own purpose," Meagan added.

Cheerful thought.

"Do you know what the notes are?"

Meagan shook her head. "It's obviously a secret passed down orally through the generations. It's never defined in the book."

"Or at least we haven't found it yet," Garrett added.

Meagan frowned. "It'd be hard to get pure harmonic notes with the human voice and to hold them for long enough to achieve anything. I'd think they'd each train for one note."

"We'll figure it out," Garrett said.

I had a thought and leaned across the table. "Isn't your mom surprised to have the guys here?"

They all clearly thought this was funny, because their eyes danced with mischief. Meagan grinned. "Garrett told her that we had an assignment together, that he and Liam were new here and needed extra tutoring."

"You beguiled her," I accused Garrett, and saw the truth in his quick smile.

"Just a little. For the greater good."

"But what about later?"

"We'll guard from the roof," Liam said.

I shook my head. "You'd better ask Jared for some spell protection. They're out there and they took other shifters last night. I don't want to lose you guys."

"I'll ask him," Meagan said, and pulled out her messenger to do it. "He can teach me the spell and we'll weave it together."

"Does Jared know the four notes?" I asked. "Or one of them?"

Meagan shook her head as she kept tapping. "I already asked."

"That part is up to us," Garrett said.

It was like a riddle, but one I had very little chance of solving on my own.

There was an optimistic thought to end the day.

"Has anyone heard from Derek?" I asked, ever hopeful, but they shook their heads as one. Everyone had messaged him, so now I tried, too.

I seriously hoped I hadn't offered up the next sacrificial victim.

I SLEPT WITH SKULD'S SHEARS under my pillow, one hand locked around them.

Just in case.

Chapter 10

I shivered in the night, feeling the cold chill of snow slip down the back of my shirt. I tugged the comforter up higher, trying to block the icy fingers of the wind, and squeezed my eyes shut. I held on tight to the shears. I really didn't want to visit Skuld and her sisters. I thought maybe I could ignore the whole dream interlude.

No luck. A finger poked me in the shoulder. Hard.

"You think I can't tell when you're awake?" There was a thread of humor in Skuld's tone. "Come on, Wyvern. You have work to do. No ShadowEaters will get you on my watch."

I felt her move away, obviously expecting me to follow. The absence of her presence was as formidable as the weight of her gaze on me. I felt a huge yawning void behind me, dared to be relieved that she was gone, then caught a whiff of carrion.

It wasn't her absence that made the air seem still.

It was that the wind had completely stopped. I sat up and looked.

Skuld *was* gone.

I think. The thing was that I couldn't see very much clearly. I was surrounded by a blanket of white fog, fog that glistened slightly, as if illuminated by a source I couldn't see. I stood up with reluctance, the hairs standing up on the back of my neck. That smell of rot was pervasive and troubling. I recalled Skuld's affection for battlefields and had an idea where I might be.

I looked down and yelped. I was standing on a pile of corpses. There was blood staining the ground, the smell of putrefaction in my nostrils, gaping wounds and spilled guts and eyes staring at nothing everywhere I looked.

Suddenly, being without Skuld didn't seem like such a good idea. I thought I heard something ahead of me and to the right, so I ran that way. I winced as bits crunched under my feet, knowing they were bones and teeth and skulls.

For my once in my life, I wished I'd worn boots to bed.

My bile rose along with my panic. My state was such that spotting Skuld, striding through the detritus as if she were going to pick up the mail, was a relief. I raced after her, and she must have heard me coming, because she paused and turned to watch me approach. There was humor in her eyes, as if I were the crazy one.

I gagged when I saw the eyeball impaled on the end of her knife.

She laughed at me, then ate it off the tip of the blade, chewing with gusto. "Thought you were too tired after your day of doing nothing," she said, arching a brow.

I had to look away, look anywhere but at her with her gleaming eyes and those squishy pink eye bits between her teeth as she smiled.

"I didn't do nothing today," I protested, trying to defend myself. "I fought the ShadowEaters even before the sun was up."

"But not when you could have beaten them," Skuld said, giving me a significant glance.

"They could have captured me with their spells if I'd gone into that glamour. It would have been reckless and stupid."

"Bold," she said, bending to examine a corpse. The person had been decapitated, and Skuld showed a keen interest in the severed head. She slit the rotting skin, poked her knife into a fissure between the bones, and used it to widen the gap. I nearly retched.

"It would have been stupid," I said.

"It's stupid to forget your assets." She gave me a steady glance, munching on a treat from the decapitated body. The corpse's staring eyes seemed to look at me, too. "I'm going to stop giving you gifts if you forget to use them."

"Where are they now?"

"Hovering." She peered into the distance, chewing. "They prefer to hunt when you're all asleep, but that will change as they get stronger." She finished her snack and tossed the head like a baseball before turning to stride on. I glanced after the discarded head and caught my breath.

Because it had landed beside a corpse that looked just like Derek.

I charged through the debris with purpose, needing to know for sure. I dropped to my knees in front of the body, not caring about the muck anymore.

It *was* Derek, and that truth made me whimper. His pale blue eyes were wide open, staring up at the sky. His heart was silenced. I touched his shoulder, unable to believe my eyes, but his skin was cold. His hoodie was torn and I looked down to see that his chest had been ripped open and his guts were spilled on the ground.

Then I did puke.

"You'll know this one, too," Skuld said with an ease I wasn't nearly feeling. She seized my shoulder when I didn't move and dragged me through blood and bodies to another corpse.

Garrett, frozen forever in a grimace of pain. As still as a sculpture. His body was shredded, just like Derek's. I saw with horror that he cast no shadow.

"No," I whispered.

"Sure," Skuld corrected me easily. "Take a good look at the future, Wyvern." She strode away then, content to leave me to take it all in.

They were all there. It didn't take me long to find them. King and Mozart and Jessica, Liam and Garrett and Nick, Derek and Kohana. They were all mixed up, their bodies tangled with one another and various parts torn away. There were other corpses mingled with them and I guessed that these were the shifters of their kinds, the ones I didn't know. I saw the kid brothers of Liam and Garrett and Nick, too, the *Pyr* who were just coming into their powers. I saw all of the older *Pyr* I knew and loved, every single one of them slaughtered and dead.

So many dead shifters. The future was a battlefield covered with fallen shifters. It had to be all of them, really, except for me. I had to put my head between my knees for a minute at the prospect of being all alone.

When I opened my eyes, I saw a dragon talon severed from the claw. It was so covered in blood that I couldn't even identify the original color.

I pushed to my feet and shouted after Skuld. "Why? Why are you showing me this?"

My cry echoed and I realized that the air was ridiculously still. There was destruction in every direction, fog obscuring the distance, but the only movement came from me and Skuld.

The only life.

She turned to peruse me, still chewing. "Because you let it happen, of course. Do you think I show you these things for my own amusement?"

"I wouldn't put it past you. There are a lot of livers here."

She smiled and sighed, nudging a body with her boot. "And more than one good soul." She gave me an intent look, as if I were missing something important.

That was when I saw that the corpse she poked was me.

Impossible!

I marched to her side in terror and denial, forcing my way through the fallen, needing a closer look. It *was* me, wearing my fave black jacket and boots, silver rings on my fingers and my earlobes, my body ripped open and my guts spilled on the ground.

Utterly still.

One hand was missing.

That had been *my* dragon claw I'd found twenty feet away.

"What did I do?"

She shook her head. "No, Wyvern. The question is what *didn't* you do." With one last searing look, she spun on her heel and walked away. She moved really fast, covering distance in a major way with her long strides, but I tried to run after her.

"But what was that?" I shouted. "Does this have to happen? What can I do to prevent it? You have to tell me!"

Skuld was a hundred feet away, on the verge of being swallowed by the fog. "I don't have to tell you anything," she said softly, her words carrying to my ears with a ghostly echo. "But let me ask you this: What would you die for? What would you die to save, Wyvern? Is there anything that matters that much to you?"

Then she was gone, her marching figure swallowed by the fog. I yelled and raced after her, squinting my eyes shut as the fog took on a brilliant radiance. It shone on all sides of me with fierce white light and turned hot, as if I had stepped into the middle of the sun.

And with the heat, the ground beneath my feet softened. I sank down, knee-deep in corpses and blood. I tried to shift shape but my shimmer was AWOL. I tried to manifest elsewhere but no luck.

Meanwhile, the muck was pulling me down. It was like quicksand, sucking at me, dragging me deeper. The more I struggled, the faster I sank. Everything I could reach to grab for support was part of a body, soft and putrid.

The smell of rot assailed me. I fought as I sank deeper and deeper, to my waist, to my shoulders. In no time, the sickly soup of corpses was right beneath my nose, and I knew my next breath would be disgusting.

How long could I hold my breath?

How could I escape?

Why couldn't I shift shape?

I shouted for Skuld, fearing she wouldn't help me.

I was right.

I WOKE UP, PANTING AND terrified in Meagan's room, my fists clutching the sheets.

I was safe, but that was by no means a permanent situation or a guarantee, given what Skuld had shown me. Meagan was sleeping soundly. I looked out the window and I saw the glimmer of purple spell light spun by Meagan and Jared, wound around the house.

I thought I could see zillions of ShadowEater eyes gleaming in the darkness behind it.

I got up, shut the drapes, and perched on the side of the bed. What would I die for? I thought of my afternoon adventure with Jared and knew that I had chosen wrong. I hadn't entered the glamour because I'd been afraid, afraid for my own survival. I'd been more worried about myself than for my friends and the world around me.

Yet Meagan and Jared had spun spell light to protect me while I slept.

Thanks to Skuld, I now knew what I'd die for.

I could only hope I hadn't missed my last chance to get it right.

MEAGAN'S MOM WAS FREAKING BY the morning. The body count was up—four more bodies had been found. Meagan was surreptitiously checking her messenger, trying to determine whether they were all Mages and apprentice Mages, or whether the ShadowEaters had gotten any shifters, too. Nick and Liam were okay, and headed off to guard Isabelle for the day.

I didn't want to send Jared a message in the morning, even though I was determined to see him. Actually, it was because I was determined to see him that I didn't ping him. Experience had taught me that Jared blew me off when I sent him a message. I didn't want to warn him that I was looking for him and have him disappear.

Again.

It was entirely possible that this time would be different, that this time he would hold his ground and wait for me, but there was too much at stake for me to bet on that. Jared came to me when it suited him, or he disappeared. I needed to find him before he could take off.

So I asked Meagan where he was staying and she told me that he was crashing at a hostel popular with musicians. It wasn't that far away, so I decided to go there first thing.

I'd chosen my acid-green wrap, the one I'd been wearing the first time I'd met Jared, and knotted it around my neck. I told myself that I'd grabbed it because it was warm, but I also knew it makes my eyes look greener.

Black jeans, black jacket, black sweater, black boots, black eyeliner, purple gloves, lots of silver jewelry, and I was ready for anything. Pretty much. At the last minute, I rummaged in the bottom of my overnight bag and got the red rune stone Granny had given me in a dream almost a year before. Who knew if I might need it again? Skuld's shears had a place of pride in my backpack.

Meagan nodded when I met her at the door, and I knew she knew what I was up to. We drove in silence together.

At least until Sigmund showed up.

"Message for you," he said, suddenly leaning over the seat from the back. His head was right between us, and I was so surprised that the car swerved.

"What's wrong?" Meagan asked, reaching for the wheel.

"You need to stop doing that," I complained.

"What do you mean?" Meagan asked. "We'll end up on the sidewalk!"

"Not you. Him."

Sigmund chuckled.

Meagan shrank back, leaning against the car door as she stared at me. "Who?"

"Sigmund."

Then she took such a careful survey of our surroundings that I knew she couldn't see Sigmund. "And where exactly is Sigmund?"

"In the backseat." I had to lean around his head to make eye contact with her. Meagan flicked a glance at the road, and I focused on driving.

"There's nobody else in the car, Zoë," Meagan said with care.

As if she were talking to a crazy person.

Sigmund chuckled. "Told you," he said, gloating.

I could have slugged him, but I spoke to Meagan. "I'm not

losing it. My dead brother, Sigmund, is here, in the backseat, trying to make me think I'm going nuts."

Meagan looked pointedly at the backseat. "Did you get enough sleep last night?"

"No. But that doesn't change the fact that he's here."

Sigmund was killing himself laughing by this point—no pun intended.

"Do you often talk to dead people?" Meagan asked.

"Just Sigmund. He's kind of irritating like that." I thought for a minute. "And the *Wakiya* elder."

Meagan nodded, considered it, and clearly decided to go with it. "So, is there a point to his being here?"

"He has a message, apparently." I stopped at a red light, then turned to Sigmund, ignoring the triumphant glint in his eyes. "You'll notice that she doesn't think I'm crazy."

"Yet," he acknowledged with a grin.

"Who's the message from? And what is it?" We were about a block from school, at the corner where I'd have to turn left to go to the hostel. Meagan would go right to the school, which we could see. Kids were arriving slowly, some being dropped off at the curb by their parents, others driving their own cars into the student lot.

I stopped at the curb, parking there for Meagan to get out, then turned to look at Sigmund. Meagan watched me, expectant.

"This is so good," Sigmund said. He winked, then got all gooey. Really, he could have been melting. His hair and his eyes and his face softened, like wax from a burning candle. I couldn't help but stare. Everything about him dripped and morphed and slid into something else.

Right before my eyes, he became Kohana.

"Well, if you're not going to tell me, I'm going to class," Meagan said, and opened the car door.

I kept staring into the backseat, fascinated and horrified. Sigmund-Kohana grinned, that provocative grin so characteristic of Kohana, his dark eyes glinting. "Hey, *Unktehila*," he said, and waved two fingers at me.

Was this another glamour? Was I talking to Sigmund or Kohana?

If it was a glamour, who had created it?

Or was Kohana dead, too?

I must have looked shocked at the idea, as shocked as I felt.

"Zoë?" Meagan asked, concern in her tone as she leaned back into the car. "Are you okay?" I didn't know what to say, not until Sigmund-Kohana delivered his message.

To my astonishment, he tipped his head back and sang a single note with all his might.

It vibrated in my ears, so resonant and clear that I knew I'd never forget it. The glass globe on the exterior light of the apartment building next to us exploded suddenly, and Kohana's singing stopped.

He winked and disappeared.

Just like he'd never been there.

"Oh, my God!" Meagan cried. "How did you do that?"

"I didn't." In fact, I couldn't believe it had even happened. I turned off the car and got out, going to the lamp. The glass was broken, all right, shards all over the concrete walk. I looked at the matching light on the other side of the apartment building doors. It was still vibrating slightly. When I leaned close, I could even hear it moving in the fixture.

"Is that cool or what?" Sigmund whispered in my ear. There was no sign of him or of Kohana, and Meagan was looking at me as if I were bonkers.

Maybe I was. I was a bit freaked myself by the way Sigmund had changed into Kohana.

No. Meagan had heard it, too.

"But you heard it, right?" I asked Meagan. She nodded, then looked determined. She pushed up her glasses, eyed the broken light fixture, then emitted a perfect echo of the note Kohana had sung. She held that note as I watched the globe on the second fixture vibrate with greater and greater intensity.

Then the light shattered just as the first had done.

I was no less shocked the second time.

"It's mathematics," Meagan said matter-of-factly. "The result of creating a sine wave that induces a vibration. The oscillation can be too much for the physical item that is echoing the frequency, like that old bridge video we saw in physics class. The wind set up a resonance that vibrated the bridge apart."

I did remember that vaguely. I'd thought it was faked.

She smiled, seeing that I didn't entirely follow her explanation. "What happened?" she asked. "What didn't I see?"

I told her and was relieved—if surprised—that she believed me.

"Don't be ridiculous, Zoë," she said, noting my surprise. "I heard it, too, and I know you can't sing, let alone hold a note like that. Do you think it was really Kohana?"

"I don't know what to think. Sigmund tends to be enigmatic, but pretty much everything he has told me has proven to be true." I frowned and made the inevitable observation. "I'm wondering whether Kohana is dead."

"Why? Because Sigmund is dead and Sigmund brought him along?"

I nodded.

Meagan frowned at the ground for a moment and I could almost hear her thinking. "But you've dreamed of Kohana before. You said before that he could move in dreams."

"Maybe he's in trouble. He was trying to trick the apprentice Mages and he was determined to get the NightBlade back. Maybe they caught him."

Meagan pursed her lips. "Maybe Kohana's giving us one note of the harmonic sequence to destroy the NightBlade."

"Maybe. But there has to be more to it than that," I said. "Just playing or singing those notes can't be enough, or Kohana would have done it himself." I squared my shoulders and looked back at the car. "I need a spellsinger. Wish me luck."

"Luck," Meagan said with a smile. "Let me know if you need help. I'll keep working on this and see what I can come up with. Maybe I can figure out the other notes."

We parted ways. She headed on to school and I took my detour to the hostel.

I wouldn't think about Muriel or what might result from my choice to cut class. I wouldn't think about what my dad might have to say about me choosing to seek out Jared. I wasn't going to think about how I'd blown it with Derek, or fret about the plans that the ShadowEaters had for destroying us.

I had to save the world instead.

IT WASN'T SNOWING FOR ONCE, and the sky was a clear crisp blue. The air was cold enough to freeze your lungs in one breath, making me glad to have the car. (*My* car.) Once I got off the main streets, the snow squeaked under the tires. When I parked and got out of the car, I saw that the driveway to the hostel hadn't been shoveled. I was glad to have my black boots with the serious treads, not just because they look awesome but because they give great traction.

The hostel was in an old house, what had once been the grande dame of the block but was now showing some neglect. It had three stories and stood apart from its neighbors. There was a driveway down one side and a carriage house at the back of the lot. The carriage house had a definite lean to the right.

It was so quiet that the house itself might have been slumbering.

I realized a bit late that Jared was probably a night person and might still be asleep. My imagination busily conjured images of Jared bare-chested, my dragon tattooed on his back. From there it was easy to imagine more, but I'll spare you the details. Suffice it to say that I didn't find it that chilly any longer.

I had climbed the ancient steps to the front door and raised my hand to the bell when I heard the sputter of a motorcycle engine. Then there was a clanking sound, a definite obscenity, and the clatter of tools. I could smell oil mingled with Jared's scent.

You know my heart skipped at that.

The sounds were coming from behind the house.

I peered around the house, down the driveway, noting that there was a single line of bike tracks in the snow as well as a trodden-down footpath. It looked like people used the back door, which was why I'd had to break a trail up the steps. As I walked down the driveway, the smell of oil grew stronger, as did the sound of muttering.

I rounded the corner to find Jared there with his bike, glaring at it. He had a wrench in one hand, and his hair was standing up in spikes. He was wearing jeans and a long-sleeved T-shirt, despite the cold, and he looked mad enough to spit. There was a cloth spread across the snow and lots of what must have been engine parts spread across it.

"Mechanical problems?" I asked, savoring the way he jumped.

It's easy to forget when you hang with shifters that humans don't have such sharp senses as we do. We're harder to surprise or sneak up on—although Derek manages to do it to me—and I found it pretty satisfying to have surprised Jared.

For once.

Then he surprised me with the warmth that lit his eyes.

"You changed your mind," he said, admiration in his voice. It had to be a guess, but there was no doubt in his manner. "I knew you would, dragon girl."

"How'd you know?" I came around the back porch of the house, sizzling as I stepped closer to him, pretending to be fascinated by his bike. It was safer than meeting his gaze, especially if he was going to be saying nice things to me.

"You have more strength than you realize, but sometimes you spook when I surprise you. I thought you'd come around with a bit of time." He flicked a glance at me. "Took less than expected." I caught his grin, saw pride in it, and got interested in my boots.

"Thanks for the spell light."

He nodded once in acknowledgment, then crouched beside the bike, his expression rueful. "I hate gears. I've had problems with third ever since I got this bike. Doesn't matter how many times I replace the parts or reassemble them."

I crouched down beside him, relieved to be talking about something else. "Have you asked Donovan?" I asked. Nick's dad had sold the bike to Jared. "I mean, it was his bike before. Maybe he knows the trick."

Jared grinned. "He said he wondered whether it would give me trouble, too. He said it had always been that way, as long as he'd had the bike, and he'd been starting to think it had something personal against him."

I laughed. "That doesn't make sense."

"No. Especially as it has the same grudge against me." He surveyed the array of parts and chose one.

"So, you know how to put all this back together?"

"It's like a jigsaw puzzle, Zoë. And now I've done it so often I could do it in my sleep. I keep hoping the next time will be the trick."

Who would have guessed he was so persistent?

Jared started to work then, frowning in concentration as he fitted the parts together. I sat down on the back steps of the house, brushing off some of the snow first. From the look of them, the wooden steps had been painted a couple of hundred times, but all the layers were peeling. It was strangely peaceful in the backyard, only power lines and telephone poles breaking the view of the backs of other houses, their windows blank.

I propped my chin on my hands and watched Jared work. He moved decisively and worked quickly, so certain of each choice. He had clearly done it a lot, because the reassembly was almost choreographed.

"What changed your mind?" he asked softly.

"I had a dream of what the future might be if I didn't act."

He flashed me a smile. "Hey, Wyvern."

I smiled back, but only for a second. "Well, I almost died there on Wednesday."

"What?" He pivoted to look at me, his work forgotten.

"Trevor lured me there, saying he wanted my help to stop Adrian from performing a ceremony he didn't understand. But they did perform it, and they needed a sacrifice, and . . ."

"They tried to make it you."

I shivered and nodded, then told him the rest. He was thinking more about the story than his gears; I could see that.

"How'd you get away?"

"Manifesting elsewhere."

He nodded slowly, although I wasn't sure whether he was thinking about what I'd said or the gear box. "That's uncommon among shifters, you know. I think you might be the only one who can do it. The other species must have forgotten."

"Maybe they didn't ever know. We wildcards seem to have different powers, both from our own kind and from each other."

He bent down beside the bike again, and it wasn't my imagination that his brow was even more furrowed. "That has to be important," he murmured. "No wonder you didn't want to go in."

I told him what had happened the next night, and he asked to see Skuld's shears. Jared surveyed the shears. He didn't touch them, just had a good look, then went back to the bike.

"The answer has to be something about us wildcards," I mused, drumming my fingers on my knees. "They seem to be targeting us but waiting for something."

"Maybe all of you to be together. Maybe the effect is even greater if you're all finished off simultaneously."

I stared at Jared, hearing the resonance of truth in his words. "Do you know that?"

"Just a guess."

But it was a good one.

"There's a lot of old lore about the entrapment of shifters," he said quietly. "I should have paid more attention to it when they were trying to recruit me."

"Why didn't you?"

He shrugged. "I like my own freedom too much to ever want to snare anybody." He turned and looked at me, his eyes filled with invitation. "I like it better when shifters come to me."

Our gazes locked and held then, and I felt the temperature rise in that yard. I could have fallen into his eyes forever, with all their umpty-gazillion shades of green. My heart started to do that wild dragon thing of matching its beat to his, and I felt our breath synchronize, too. It makes me dizzy when that happens, although I realized then that it wasn't a sign of kismet as much as it reflected my own attraction.

And I could—apparently—be attracted to more than one guy at a time.

The feeling was more powerful with Jared, though, and I wondered whether it was just that I didn't know him as well or whether we really did have a stronger connection. I wondered whether I was ever going to know, and sighed as I deliberately looked away.

"What's bothering you?" he asked, focused on his bike again.

"What do you mean?"

"Something's bugging you. I noticed it yesterday. Come on, spill it. The bike won't be fixed for a few minutes yet."

"We could go in my car."

"It'll wait a few minutes."

"Are you afraid, too?" I asked on impulse.

His gaze flicked to me and back to the bike, so quickly that another person might have missed it. I heard his quick intake of breath, too, and felt the jump in his pulse.

He wasn't certain of what would happen.

Maybe this was an opportunity to learn more. To go in armed with more data. I watched Jared for a minute and remembered that he was the one who seemed to know the most about dragon lore—well, other than my dead brother, Sigmund. That was probably because he'd had Sigmund's book on the *Pyr* for a while and read it repeatedly.

Maybe he knew something more about Wyvern stuff.

"It's this Wyvern thing," I admitted, shamelessly fishing.

"Sounds like you've been working at it."

"It's the future part that isn't happening. Plus Sigmund says that this part of a Wyvern's evolution or development can drive a Wyvern insane."

"That's not very encouraging."

"No. It's not. But he's like that."

"Wait a minute. Sigmund who?"

"Guthrie. My older brother." Jared glanced up, surprised.

"Yes, the dead one who turned *Slayer* and wrote that book you had, mostly to piss off our dad."

"Probably worked, given what I know of Erik."

I nodded.

"So, you're talking to dead people, then?"

"Only Sigmund. And only when he feels like it." I left out the bits about the *Wakiya* elder and Kohana's appearance this morning. I'd noticed before that there was something electric between Kohana and Jared. No need to spoil the moment.

He straightened and flashed me a grin. "That's reassuring."

"Is it?"

"It's got to be better to talk to a limited group of dead people, in terms of your sanity, than all the dead people ever."

I threw a snowball at him. Jared laughed and ducked.

I stretched out my legs, trying to explain my frustration to him. "The thing is that I'm supposed to be able to see the past, the present, and the future simultaneously, but I never really know what's going to happen."

He cast me a glance. "Never?"

I blushed then and looked down. "Well, not about important stuff."

Jared smiled. "So you're in good company. Nobody else can see the future, either."

"But I'm supposed to be able to! I'm the Wyvern."

"I don't understand why you'd want to see it," he countered, surprising me a bit.

"Doesn't everybody want to know what's going to happen?"

"Only superficially." He straightened and faced me, gesturing with a greasy motorcycle part in one hand. "I mean, if you could see your whole future, every choice and its consequence, every seemingly random event, every single thing that was going to happen to you before you die, then what would be the point of living? You could just look at it all, like watching a movie, then say, 'Oh, that's that,' and die."

"Not funny."

"I'm not joking." He bent down beside the bike again. "What if you can't see the future because it's filled with a thousand possibilities? What if it's a network of choices influencing events? What if choosing one path closes off another? What if it's not a fixed destination but a realm of possibilities?" He glanced up. "What if the only way to see the future is to live it?"

"Then what about this Wyvern ability?"

"Maybe what the Wyvern sees is the array of possibilities that can result from a single choice." He shrugged. "Maybe she can see where this decision will lead, based maybe on the other decisions being made simultaneously. Maybe it's a very short-term thing, this vision of the future."

"Two minutes' warning, max," I said, thinking of Derek.

Jared glanced up, apparently recognizing my reference. "That's the wolf's gig, isn't it?" I nodded, and there was suddenly a bit of tension between us.

"So, are you dating him?" Jared was trying to sound indifferent, but he blew it completely. He was deeply interested. I heard it in his voice, which was thrilling.

Once again, I felt a strange sense of personal power, an inkling that my choices were part of whatever resulted from this discussion. Was Jared right? I stretched out my legs, acting casual about it, knowing I was anything but. "Sort of." I took a deep breath. "He's a good friend and a nice guy. He's here, and he's intense, and there are no games."

Jared smiled. "That future is clear?"

I bristled at his tone, thinking—rightly—that he was criticizing Derek for being predictable. And that irritated me because Derek was predictable and it wasn't one of the things that attracted me to him. I did like Jared's adventurousness.

"He's direct," I said, hearing my own defensiveness. "I like that."

Jared straightened then and turned to confront me. His eyes flashed with unexpected annoyance. "Direct? That's what you like now?"

"It's better than not having a clue what someone is thinking. It's better than never hearing anything at all!"

"I told you about Donovan's warning!"

"I don't believe that you would change your mind about anything you really wanted to do, regardless of who told you not to do it. Even Donovan." I stood up. "I believe that you didn't call me because you didn't want to see me."

Jared didn't like that. He didn't like it one bit.

His lips tightened for a moment; then he pointed at me. "You want direct? Here's direct. You're sixteen. I haven't been for a while. That makes you jailbait, and I'm not going to have any more dealings with cops ever again. And if you don't think that changes my choices, then you can think again." He pivoted to crouch down beside the bike, his body vibrating with anger.

Why hadn't I thought of that?

I watched him for a few minutes, the silence charged between us, and knew he wasn't going to speak first. "You never told me what you did."

"Because it doesn't matter." He spoke quickly and with heat. "I was full of hell when I was sixteen. Nothing major, but I got the attention I wanted—then found out it wasn't worth having. They sealed the records, so I'm not going to be the one to spill the whole sordid story."

It bothered him. I could see that.

I could have been graceful and let the conversation die.

Instead I pushed him. Call it making the future.

I went to his side and crouched down beside him. He didn't look at me. "So, what does this jailbait comment really mean? Since you're being direct?"

"You want me to tell you the future? The one you can't see?"

"Give me your version of it."

I didn't think he would, not in a million years, but Jared surprised me one more time.

"That I'll be turning up for the next two years. Just checking in, keeping in touch, helping you out when I can." Jared stepped closer and his eyes brightened as he turned to face me. We were almost nose to nose. He arched a brow, his expression completely intense, and I knew I never wanted him to be any other way. "But once you're legal, the only way you'll get rid of me, dragon girl, is to tell me to go away forever." He smiled crookedly, smiled enough that that deep dimple made an appearance. "I'm hoping that by then, you won't do that."

My heart thumped.

My breath caught.

He'd said exactly what I'd wanted to hear, and even better, I knew that wasn't why he'd said it. Jared had said it because he meant it.

And this was my chance to push my future in a specific direction.

So I leaned forward, eliminating that little sliver of space, and kissed him.

It felt, just so you know, every bit as good as it had the other times.

Plus it just felt right.

Chapter 11

My messenger rang, and I was so absorbed that I almost didn't realize it was mine. It was in the pocket of my jacket, the sound muffled a bit. It was Jared who pulled back, then caught his breath.

"For you, I think," he said, and his voice was rough.

He straightened and cleared his throat and turned his attention back to his bike.

It was Meagan and she was freaking out. "Derek's gone," she said as soon as I answered. "Trevor's not here today and neither is Suzanne. I can feel spell light in this place like crazy. It's like the school is filled with spellsong. It's enough to make me feel sick, and I can't even make a dent in it."

"Where's Jessica?"

"She's right here and really worried about you."

"I'm okay. I'm with Jared. We're going after them."

He glanced up at me, and I saw that there were no more bike bits on the cloth. He tightened a nut, threw his leg over the bike, and started the engine. It caught and ran with a throaty throb, and he grinned in triumph. He fiddled with the gears, nodded with satisfaction, then revved the engine for emphasis.

"Keep us posted," Meagan said.

"I will. Take care of Jessica. You're the spellsinger."

"Got it," Meagan said. "And, Zoë, be careful."

Right. I was, after all, getting on Jared's bike.

WE GOT TO THE VACANT lot, and the glamour of the library that Jared had summoned was still there.

I slanted a glance at him, wondering at the power of the spells.

This time, though, it was swirling with orange Mage light. I could see the spell pressing against the windows from the inside, as if it were full of the chaotic power of spells, spells so potent and vibrant that they couldn't stay still for a moment. They couldn't just glow—they had to zoom around like manic fireflies.

"Can you see the spell light?" I asked Jared quietly.

"I can feel it." Even though we were both wearing helmets, I could hear how grim he was through the microphone. "It's only going to get worse," he added, which was probably true.

I got off the bike, liking that he offered me his hand, and tugged off my helmet. I watched with some amusement as he parked the motorcycle carefully.

He glanced up and caught my smile, took offense a little. "What's so funny?"

"I'm not sure you're going to ever need it again." I glanced at that spell light and knew it would be some kind of miracle if we went in there and returned alive.

On the other hand, we didn't have a lot of choice.

"Think positive," he said.

I nodded and tried to do just that.

Even though I'd never seen spell light so vivid or frantic.

"Is it true that they mostly hunt at night?"

"Until they get stronger."

"Can we tell how strong they are yet?"

He gave me a look, and I got it. Not without going in.

Jared fastened the helmets to the back of the bike and came to stand beside me. We were just looking at the glamour of the building. He reached out and took my hand, gave my fingers a squeeze.

"What did you get busted for?" I asked, and felt his surprise.

He glanced my way. "What difference does it make?"

"Probably not much, but I'm thinking I might not ever have the chance to ask again." I shrugged, my gaze compelled to watch that orange spell light. "Do me a favor and get rid of one distraction."

"Just one?" I heard the smile in his voice before I saw it.

I squeezed his hand back. "Just one."

He heaved a sigh and considered the glamour. I knew he wasn't really looking at it. "It was a guitar. I really wanted it. My dad could have bought it for me, but he'd never buy me a guitar."

"Why not?"

"He thinks music is a waste of time." Jared pursed his lips. "My dad is really successful. He makes a lot of money and he buys a lot of stuff. That's important to him. The stuff and the way other people admire his stuff." He shook his head. "It was never very important to me. He thinks that because we don't want the same things, I'm just not ambitious. He thinks the music is an excuse, a way to be lazy." He turned to look at me, his eyes glinting. "I asked him about the guitar. We had a huge fight, not just about the guitar, but about everything. He had a lot to say about my being a disappointment and not being worthy of being his son."

"Ouch."

"I was mad and I was done. I went and took what I wanted. The owner knew me, though, because I'd been in to admire that guitar so many times. It didn't take a brilliant cop to follow the bread crumbs to me." He grimaced. "I was stupid."

"Why didn't you just get a job or do something to earn the money to pay for it?"

"Impatience. I wanted to impress some people, some people who didn't deserve to be impressed."

He wasn't looking at me, but his words made me remember my own act of theft. I'd stolen the carrier for a pizza to impress Adrian, the apprentice Mage. I'd returned it, but still.

That gave me an idea. "Were the Mages trying to recruit you then?"

"What difference does it make?"

"Well, their spells can make people do things they wouldn't do otherwise. They can make you think things and act in ways you wouldn't usually. . . ."

Jared squeezed my fingers. "Thanks, dragon girl, but you don't need to find an excuse for me." He released my hand, then held up his right hand. "This is the hand that broke the store window." He looked at his left hand. "And this is the hand that took the guitar from the display." He met my gaze, his expression resolute. "It doesn't really matter what influenced me to do what I did. I did it. I had to answer for it. And I can never change the fact that I did it."

"Did you go to jail?"

"No. My dad knows people. He tried to fix it, the deal

being that he'd be rid of me forever in exchange. I had to work in that store for six months for free, and give back the guitar. It turned out to be the best thing that ever happened to me. The owner was really cool and encouraged me to learn to play better. That's where I met my bandmates and where I realized what I wanted to do with my life."

"Did you tell your dad?"

"No point. He'll always think I'm a loser with no ambition." He shrugged and glanced at me, cautious. "Besides, he doesn't have a son anymore."

"I don't think you're a loser."

He considered me and I saw the glint of hope in his eyes. He spoke softly then, his words making me shiver. "Maybe dragons do see beyond the surface."

"Maybe."

"Donovan was the only one who stood by me. He sold me the Ducati cheap, because he knew I loved it and would take care of it. Dragons have always been there for me. Which is why I wanted to meet you, to meet the only dragon girl there is." He turned to face the glamour while I tried to deal with the lump in my throat, and he took my hand in his once more. "Maybe this is what it's all about, Zoë. Maybe finishing these ShadowEaters—and by extension the Mages—is why we met and why we connect."

"I don't think so. I don't think that's good enough."

He smiled at me. "Saving the last four kinds of shifters isn't enough for you?"

"Not nearly."

"Maybe that's what I like about you, dragon girl. You're not one to go with the easy choice."

"I'm a dragon," I said with pride. "We don't do subtle."

"No, I guess not." He looked at me and my heart nearly broke with yearning. But that spell light was dancing and tugging at my attention, so strong that it drew my gaze even from Jared.

"So, what do you say?" I said, acting all cavalier. "Shall we kick some butt and save the world?"

"It's too early for lunch," Jared said with a grin. "We might as well do it."

And we marched up the steps, hand in hand.

This time, the glamour didn't waver.

It glowed.

I refused to think that it was a glow of anticipation.

THE WINDOWS WERE SO FILLED with golden spell light, it appeared as if the interior of the building was on fire. Even though it was an illusion, it felt foolish to be walking closer. Once again, the street was completely vacant. We could have been the last two people left on the planet.

Maybe that was the effect of the spell. My heart was pounding, not just because Jared was holding my hand so tightly and his shoulder was brushing against mine. I could feel a beat, one that resonated through my whole body and shook my bones.

Jared started to hum. I saw a purple and blue spell unfurl from his lips, sweeping around us. It was small, a gossamer net, and I wondered whether he was trying to fake them out by pretending to be a less powerful spellsinger than he was. I had to assume that he could buttress that filigree net and be quick if necessary.

I hoped he was quick enough.

We reached the double doors. I took a shaking breath, uncertain what we'd find inside. Jared gave my fingers one last squeeze, then released my hand and opened the door.

At his touch on the door handle, the glamour collapsed into nothing.

We were falling—right at the same moment that the ShadowEaters swarmed us. There were thousands of them, snapping and licking and biting, pressing against us on all sides. They were more powerful than I'd expected—they'd let me underestimate them until it was too late.

Jared shouted, losing the rhythm of his spell, and I couldn't tell whether he could see them or just sense them. It didn't matter. They were blinding in their brilliance and their sheer quantity. They snatched at us as we tumbled, and I felt the graze of teeth. The spell light danced around us like a web, and there was only one thing I could do.

I called to the shimmer and, in a flash of pale blue, I shifted to my dragon form. I snatched Jared up and leapt into the darkness, soaring high in the air. A wind erupted, swirling around us like an angry hurricane, and the ShadowEaters shouted. Jared began to sing, brilliant purple spell light spilling from his mouth to surround us like a cocoon.

Jared gave a shout of triumph as I flew higher and I cleared both the turbulence and the ShadowEaters. I turned then, looking down at the ground. They were there, their golden eyes gleaming in the darkness, and I wasn't really surprised when the first one leapt to snatch at us.

"The first guard," Jared said.

He was right. They were a distraction.

I peered into the shadows beyond them. With my sharper sight, I could see a nexus of spell light far below. It was leaping and sparking like a bonfire lit in a trash can.

If I wasn't completely disoriented, it was at the same spot where Trevor and Adrian had summoned the ShadowEaters.

There was a spellbound figure beside the bonfire.

Was it Kohana?

"Sing," I said to Jared, then dove toward the flickering golden light. He sang with vigor, throwing out his hands as he conjured an impressive shell of purple and blue spell light. He wove it around us, shaping the spell with such dexterity that I knew he'd been practicing for this moment. We were inside a mesh cocoon of his spell light that repelled the assault of the orange spells. Jared's spell wove and sheltered, like a gleaming net. Theirs were all spikes and points and lightning bolts intended to cause as much damage as possible.

The ShadowEaters howled in anticipation of a feast, leaping toward me and snatching at my claws and wings. I soared through them like a fighter jet, protected by Jared's counterspell and targeting the bonfire. It might be a lure, but it was where the prize could be found. Those spells seemed to respond to my proximity, and the flames leapt higher as I dove toward them.

I saw Trevor. I saw the book that he was consulting, reading it like a songbook. I saw Kohana bound on the ground before the bonfire, shifting shape rapidly between human and Thunderbird form.

I chose to believe that this wasn't a trick, that Kohana really was in danger. It was a risk, given his history, but I couldn't do otherwise.

As I dove toward them, the ShadowEaters pressed behind us, pushing us closer in a way that did nothing for my confidence. Trevor suddenly and triumphantly pulled the Night-Blade from his sleeve. They hooted and clustered near him, anticipation making them vibrate in the air. I raced toward him, talons outstretched. That was when I saw two more figures spellbound on the ground.

Nick and Isabelle.

Motionless.

And Suzanne was sitting beside them, as if she had been frozen in stone.

"The sacrifice," Jared whispered, and I knew he was right. Trevor intended to join the ShadowEaters, too. "Put me down," he instructed tersely.

"But . . ."

"I need to brace my feet to sing properly, and you don't need the deadweight."

I chose not to think about the literal meaning of what he'd said. I set him down as easily as I could without slowing down very much, and he gave me a thumbs-up.

Just as he'd said, his spellsong became suddenly brighter, swirling up to surround me like a protective cloak.

Trevor continued his invocation, then pivoted with a flourish. "Shadow and blood!" he cried, and reached for Suzanne. I watched in horror as he slit her throat and she tumbled to the ground, like a doll. He laughed, turning toward Nick and Isabelle with glee. I plummeted toward the earth and snatched the NightBlade out of his hand, the sharp edge still dripping with blood.

"No!" Trevor shouted, not releasing his grasp on the handle. His eyes were radiant gold, as filled with spell light as those of the ShadowEaters.

I soared high, but he hung on with superhuman strength.

I had the NightBlade but wasn't sure what to do with it. I didn't want to use it, because I was afraid it would twist my impulse to its own purposes. I wanted to ruin it. But I had no idea how—and there was no guarantee that any plans I made with it in my grasp would be my own.

They might be the will of the NightBlade.

I tried to sing the note that Sigmund had delivered in that message, well aware that I am officially tone-deaf. It couldn't have been the right note, or maybe it didn't matter, because it made no difference to anything.

Then Trevor began to snap at my shadow. His features dissolved as I watched, his clothes disappearing and his body becoming an anonymous skin filled with light.

I thrashed, flying haphazardly in an attempt to shake him off. He finally locked his teeth on my shadow and ripped a bite free with such savage force that I felt as if my soul were being torn. He laughed again, exultant, then threw himself into the air to join his fellows. I was stunned that he left me in possession of the NightBlade, as if it didn't matter.

I looked down to see a ShadowEater taking a bite from Kohana's shadow, delighting in ripping it away from his body. I heard Kohana cry out; then the ShadowEater joined its fellows. They swirled in the sky, mingling and whirling, potent and disgusting.

Then they circled and prepared to dive toward the bonfire to finish what they'd begun.

They were going to have a feast.

On Nick and Isabelle.

Over my dead body.

Jared had taken advantage of their momentary absence. He sang with all his might, widening the cocoon of spell light to protect the three captives. He could have been weaving a bubble over them, one that defended them from the ShadowEaters' assault. I felt their indecision like a tangible force, then knew their choice a heartbeat before they made it.

They turned on me, thousands of hungry beings, and lunged toward me. They were intent on ensuring that I was surrounded and trapped, their spell light flying through the air like ropes and grappling hooks cast at the walls of a medieval fortress.

I held the NightBlade high and shouted a taunt, then dove through them. It was my best impression of a football play. I flew toward my pals without thinking about landing, just descending as fast as I could. I burst through Jared's bubble of spell light, almost certainly because he let me, then shifted shape.

In human form, I skidded to a halt. I put my hand down to brace myself, and felt something sticky and warm.

I chose not to look at Suzanne just yet.

I was glad that I still had my backpack. I hauled out Skuld's shears and cut Nick free with a savage slice. He shifted shape, leaping skyward in dragon form to rage dragonfire at an approaching golden tendril of spell light. I cut it away, as well, chopping it into tiny chunks. It writhed as I did so, like a snake that simply would not die.

When it was still and blackening to ash, I would have gone to Isabelle and Kohana. But I felt heat and I turned just as the bonfire leapt suddenly high. I thought the ShadowEaters were calling to it, because it fired straight up in the air, making a tall plume of flame.

Which burned right through Jared's carefully constructed spell wall, the way a flamethrower might incinerate a piece of tissue paper.

I pivoted to see that Jared was ashen from his efforts. All the same, he taunted them. "Can't even take out a novice Mage? What a useless bunch of spellsingers!"

I cried out when the ShadowEaters surrounded him, their spell light wrapping around him like a thousand heavy ropes. Jared sang a defensive spell, but he was ferociously outnumbered. He cast me a hot look, one that told me he'd drawn their fire on purpose.

For me.

"No!" I shouted, and would have gone after him, but Nick shouted a warning.

"Now, Z!" I looked up to see the net of spell light closing around us, as it had once before.

Nick soared down and snatched up spellbound Isabelle, grimacing as the spell light tried to wind its way around him, too. I reached with Skuld's shears to cut it back and heard Jared's song become louder.

"Go!" he roared, just before they surrounded him and took him down.

"No!" I screamed, and would have gone after him.

But Nick snatched me up, letting me cut Isabelle free as he shot into the sky. He flew straight toward the closing wall of spell light, holding fast to both Isabelle and me. She was unconscious in his grasp, and I could feel his tension.

I was crying for Jared, knowing they'd finished him off. Grief gave me power, though. I held the shears open and used them like a sword, slashing at the rapidly closing net of spell light. Nick slipped through like he was greased, then raged ever higher in the night sky.

Isabelle didn't stir.

Jared was lost far, far behind us.

And the air was brilliant gold with the frenzy of ShadowEaters at their feast. I was tempted to lean my head on Nick's powerful shoulder once we had escaped and cry my heart out.

I'd failed.

Miserably.

But I felt his anxiety and fear for Isabelle, and knew that showing my terror wouldn't help him at all. It was my job as leader to give him hope and inspire him to go on.

I'd do my best and we'd fight right to the end.

Even if the chances of winning seemed more slim by the minute.

Jared was dead.

"*Go to the school,*" I said in old-speak. "*Meagan and Jessica might be able to help Isabelle.*"

"*Good idea,*" Nick agreed, then looked down at me. "*What about you?*"

"*Just take care of Isabelle. I've got an idea.*"

It wasn't true, at least not yet, but Nick didn't need to know it. I felt his heart skip with hope.

Then I closed my eyes, knowing exactly where I wanted to be.

Alone.

I SLAMMED INTO THE DRIVER'S seat of my car, panting and perspiring and trembling. I looked around with some trepidation, but the street outside the hostel looked just as it had earlier in the morning. There were a few pedestrians, one woman pushing a baby carriage, another walking a dog, and a couple of older kids with backpacks, maybe going to class at the college. The snow was still falling lightly.

It was astonishingly normal.

I took a deep breath and looked at the house, which also appeared to be the same. The driveway wasn't shoveled and the paint on the porch was peeling.

Had I dreamed it all? Or had it really happened?

You know what I wanted the answer to be.

I took a deep breath and opened the car door. My heart was pounding, but I had to know for sure. I went down the driveway, noting the single tread from a motorcycle and a line of footprints. Were they mine? They matched my boots perfectly, which was not a good sign.

There was silence behind the house, no tinkling with motorcycle parts, and I pretty much knew what I'd see when I came around the last corner. There was a mark in the snow where a motorcycle had been parked. The sheet where Jared had spread out the gear parts was folded and jammed under the railing of the back porch, right where he'd left it. And there was a circle of melted snow where the bike's exhaust had heated the ground.

No motorcycle.

No Jared.

Losing him hadn't been a vision or a dream. It had happened.

I tipped back my head, fighting my tears, wishing I really was going crazy, because then Jared would be safe and I wouldn't be the biggest failure of all time.

Insanity was the much better choice.

After a few moments, I pulled out my messenger. The in-box was loaded with messages, but I didn't have the heart to sit and read through all the news. Kohana and Jared were dead. Nick and Isabelle were headed to the school, and Jessica and Meagan would be there. What about everyone else? How much of a team did we have left? I sent Garrett and Liam messages to come to the school, too.

Most important, how much power had the ShadowEaters gained in that ceremony?

I might as well find out the worst of it, live and in person.

I turned around and trudged back to the car, then drove to school, my heart dragging behind the exhaust pipe. I was sure things couldn't get any worse, but, naturally, I was wrong.

ONE LOOK TOLD ME THAT the ShadowEaters had really scored.

The school could have been one of my dad's pyrotechnics displays, but an interactive one. It was surrounded by a halo of brilliant yellow and gold Mage light, so bright that I could hardly look straight at it. The building seemed to radiate golden spell light, the binding spells weaving around and above it in such frantic patterns that the sight made me sick.

I'd probably made the school more of an attraction by having everyone gather here. But I needed them all together.

Still, I had major trepidation about going into the school. I parked the car and watched the spells dance for a minute, dreading whatever I would find inside. Never mind what would happen to me when I got in there. Maybe we were all doomed. Maybe the ShadowEaters had already won.

Maybe this was it.

Maybe I wasn't going to go down easy.

I pulled out Skuld's shears and tucked them inside my coat, wanting them closer than in my backpack.

Then I got out of the car, my mouth as dry as sandpaper.

The first ShadowEater appeared beside me when I'd gone only ten steps. Its eyes glowed with that luminescence. I turned to look at it, shocked that it would be so overt about stalking me in broad daylight.

It bared its teeth and snapped in my direction.

I pulled out Skuld's shears and snapped back, chopping off its hand with one savage gesture. It howled and retreated.

Victory was fleeting. I watched in horror as spell light poured from its severed wrist. It swelled up like a cloud of animosity, a miasma of sizzling spell fury. The spell light inside the ShadowEater was spilling out of his skin, and as the orange cloud became bigger, his silhouette deflated like a balloon. In a heartbeat, there was a towering cloud of spell light before me, crackling like a bonfire, lit with interior sparks.

And a flat, dark skin on the ground, discarded.

It looked a lot like a shadow, actually.

The cloud swirled and joined the display surrounding the school. I knew it made the existing spells burn brighter and move with more agitation.

When I looked back at the ShadowEater's skin, it was gone.

So I had eliminated a ShadowEater, but its energy had strengthened the spell surrounding the school. This couldn't be a good revelation. I hid Skuld's shears beneath my coat again and walked warily toward the school.

How could the ShadowEaters be dispersed and the spell light extinguished for good? It was a riddle, and I reminded myself that I was good at solving riddles.

Even when somewhat short of sleep.

To MY RELIEF, THERE WAS a tendril of purple spell light slipping through the barrage of brilliant swirling gold. I knew that had to be coming from Meagan and followed it with purpose. There were lots of kids in the halls, so it must have been between classes. I looked at the time on my messenger, not sure what class I was missing.

I didn't even have a chance to find Meagan.

Muriel stood by my locker, a sentinel with a sour expression. "You're late," she said, scanning me with disapproval.

"I, uh, had car trouble," I lied. "It wouldn't start."

"You should have just walked."

"I thought I could fix it but I was wrong." I forced a smile. Muriel, she of the many merry smiles, did not smile back. "Sorry, Muriel. I should be in English class, right?"

"Art class," Muriel corrected.

"Bonus!" I feigned enthusiasm.

She watched me with suspicion. "You never miss art class, Zoë," she said quietly. "Would you like to tell me the real trouble?"

The real trouble. I was tempted to tell her, just to see her reaction.

I watched Trevor murder Suzanne this morning in order to convert himself to a ShadowEater, a being of spell light and malice. There wasn't anything I could do about it since I was fighting binding spells myself at the time. The worst part is that the guy I'm crazy for let himself be killed by the ShadowEaters to give me a chance to escape, and I have no idea what the point of living is with him dead.

No. The truth had no place in this discussion.

I glanced up and down the hall, relieved to see Meagan closing in fast and Jessica right beside her. Both looked freaked, but both were surrounded by a glistening blue halo of Meagan's spell light. I sent Jessica a thought about Meagan defending Garrett, Liam, Nick, and Isabelle, who should arrive soon. She nodded once and bent to whisper to Meagan.

Meagan's gaze was locked on me and her eyes were wide with horror. Best-friend radar never fails. She knew something really bad had happened, something bad enough to shake me to my marrow.

I couldn't send the news about Jared through Jessica.

And then there was Muriel. "You should know, Zoë, that the police wish to talk to you."

"The police?" I was genuinely shocked and Muriel knew it.

She beckoned with one finger and a police officer strode down the hall toward us. He was trying to look friendly and pretty much failed. He was older than Muriel, a bit stocky, and had the weary appearance of someone who had seen a lot of nasty things.

Maybe because his eyes were dancing with spell light.

Good. He was going to keep me busy while the Shadow-Eaters slurped up the last bits of Kohana and Jared. I appreciated their concern for my schedule.

I would fry them all—as soon as I figured out how.

I shot a look at Meagan and Jessica, but they were heading down the hall. Going to defend the others. At least something was going right.

"This is Detective Smith," Muriel said. She preened a little, as if she thought he was hot, which was just about the most revolting idea I'd had all day. (Which is saying something.) "He wants to ask you a few questions."

"Okay. Are you going to stay with us?"

Muriel flushed and smiled and gestured to the empty classroom adjacent to my lockers. Detective Smith got out his digital notepad, and the interrogation began.

He asked my name and address, my age and my grade, even though he must have known all of that already. I understood that these questions were supposed to help me relax.

They didn't.

He asked about my car and my parents, then gave me an intent look.

That golden spell light dancing in his pupils gave me the serious willies, but I held his gaze. I knew he'd think I was lying if I looked away.

"Suzanne is missing. I believe you know her."

"Everyone knows Suzanne."

"Someone saw her get into your car last night, but no one has apparently seen her since."

"Yeah, I gave her a ride."

He scribbled with his stylus. "Why?"

I shrugged. "She asked for one. It was snowing and she said Trevor hadn't picked her up like he was supposed to."

"And what was her destination?"

"Trevor's house."

He flicked a look at me. "And that's where you left her?"

"No. She wanted to be dropped off at the end of the block." Detective Smith arched a brow, and I smiled apologetically. "She didn't want to be seen in my car."

His attention sharpened at that. "Why not?"

"It's too old and beat-up to be cool."

He flicked through his notes with a fingertip. "But doesn't Suzanne have her own car?"

"Yeah. A new Interceptor convertible."

"Then why did she need a ride from you?"

"Her car wasn't here. Maybe because Trevor was supposed to give her a ride."

He impaled me with a brilliant yellow glance. "Isn't it true that you and Suzanne had a fight yesterday? Isn't it true that she didn't have her car because she was being punished by her parents for that fight?"

"I don't know why she didn't have a car."

"But the fight?"

"Yes, we fought. Muriel saw it."

"And what was the reason for that fight?"

"She took a picture of me in the bathroom. It was embarrassing and she was going to show it to everyone."

"So you took her messenger?"

All of this was public knowledge. I saw no point in denying it. "I asked her to delete the picture. She refused. I took the messenger and deleted it myself, then gave the messenger back to her."

"In fact, you removed the memory card and destroyed it."

"That deleted the image forever."

His nostrils flared. "Yet despite this, you gave her a ride."

I shrugged. "We had settled it. What was done was done."

"You weren't afraid she might try to get even with you?"

I looked at him. I had had enough. "No," I said, and there was a bit of dragon in my quiet tone. "I'm not afraid of Suzanne."

Our gazes locked and held. The spell light in his eyes danced with greater intensity, becoming brighter as he tried to stare me down.

I wasn't daunted.

Maybe there was more dragon in my expression than I'd realized, because Muriel became flustered.

She even forced a smile.

"And why were you in the parking lot alone last night in the first place?"

"Because I'd just gotten out of detention." It was half of the truth, anyway.

The detective glanced up at Muriel.

She nodded, ever helpful.

"Why were you late today?" the detective asked. "Didn't you have class this morning?"

"I did, but I had car trouble," I lied. I held the detective's gaze, and funnily enough, he ran out of questions then.

Muriel effectively ended the interview. She made encouraging noises about my being willing to start fresh with Suzanne.

The detective got fed up and excused himself.

But Muriel had a full head of steam. She spouted a lot of stuff about ensuring that I did what would make my parents proud, that I kept a positive attitude and kept my grades up. It was imperative that I not develop any habits that could imperil my academic record, and surely I knew that Muriel would be there for me whenever I wanted to talk more.

I nodded and even managed to conjure up a tear of heartfelt gratitude. Muriel gave me a hug, which astounded me, and promised to talk individually to my teachers about my attendance. Then she smiled at me and told me not to be late for my class right after lunch.

Lunch.

Right.

I was starving.

Meagan, the best friend in the whole world, was waiting by our lockers for me, protective blue spell light at the ready.

"*So?*" Meagan demanded as soon as Muriel was gone. "What did the police officer want?"

"Did you hear about Suzanne?" Jessica asked. "She's missing."

"No," I said. "She's dead." I heaved a sigh. "So are Kohana and Jared."

They were both shocked. "Trevor isn't here today, either," Meagan said.

"Because he's become a ShadowEater," I said grimly.

They both started to ask questions, their voices hushed, but I held up a hand. "I need food."

We headed for the cafeteria, wading through the dizzying golden cloud of spell light. I could practically feel Jessica sweat, and reached out to take her hand.

Sadly, the daily special was some mystery meat loaf that would have looked disgusting even if I wasn't vegetarian. I went straight for dessert and got myself a chocolate sundae with fudge sauce.

It might, after all, be my last meal.

We took a table in the corner and huddled over our lunches.

"Where are the guys?" I asked. "I sent them here."

"I sent them to Isabelle's place with Nick," Meagan said. "They wanted to stay, but I could see how the spell light was getting to them."

"Safer for them to not be enchanted if we have to fight for our lives," Jessica said.

I tugged out my messenger and pinged Liam and Garrett and Nick. They were all freaked, but they were together and with Isabelle.

Who was still comatose.

Like King and Mozart.

At least the guys were together.

"You can see the spell light, right?" Meagan said. "Is it really bad?"

"It feels really bad," Jessica said. "And watchful."

I glanced over my shoulder at the light swirling in the cafeteria. I could see shapes within the cloud of light and knew that there were ShadowEaters among us, choosing their prey. Meagan's light was protecting us, but I wondered how many other kids would lose their shadows before nightfall.

Never mind after that.

"They're everywhere," Derek said quietly. He'd slid into the seat on my other side when I'd been looking the other way. I jumped, like I always did, then I hugged him in my relief.

"I was afraid. . . ."

He hugged me back after a moment's hesitation, as awkward as I'd expect. "We had to convene," he said gruffly. "Vote."

I pulled back to look at him, fearing what he would say.

He held my gaze, his own expression wary. "They're with you," he said, then dug into his meat loaf special.

I couldn't help but notice that he said *they* instead of *we.* I supposed I had that coming.

As we ate, I recounted the whole sorry story of my morning, including what had happened when I took out the ShadowEater in the parking lot. Meagan hummed quietly, buttressing the protective spell that surrounded us.

"What else happened here?" I asked, eating my sundae before it completely melted.

"Suzanne's friends are missing," Jessica said, nodding at Meagan to keep humming.

Meagan beckoned to me, indicating that she wanted the notebook I always carry. I use it to sketch dragons, but Meagan turned to an empty page. She wrote quickly, without stopping her spellsinging, and Jessica read what she wrote to us.

"Meagan used that note you heard this morning as the beginning of a harmonic sequence. She says it could be the tenor part in a harmony." Jessica looked up, her eyes bright. "It's in a minor key."

"Which we know that Mages like." I nodded, feeling as if Meagan was supplying the clue we needed. Jessica frowned as Meagan drew a musical staff and sketched in the notes, her gaze dancing over Meagan's rapidly drawn notes.

"So this would be the first note," Jessica said, singing the note I'd heard from Kohana this morning in a single clear *Ah!* "The soprano part to go with it is this." She sang another, higher note, then did the same with the bass and the alto parts.

"Theoretically, if we sing them all together, that would make the harmony that might vibrate apart the NightBlade," I said, and Meagan nodded with enthusiasm. "But only two of you can sing." I had an idea then, and recorded Jessica's singing into four different music files on my messenger. It wouldn't play all four concurrently, so we shared the files and queued up our messengers to play them all at the same time.

I turned to watch the spell light as the harmony began, thinking I'd see something in the motion of the spell if this resonance was powerful to the ShadowEaters lurking in the spell light.

It made no difference at all.

I was disappointed, and so was Meagan. "That can't be it."

She frowned and scribbled that she'd look for alternatives.

Was she wrong? Or were we just missing a critical piece of the puzzle?

"What's next?" Derek asked, and I understood that he was saying that he was still following the dragon. I smiled at him with relief and saw a wary gratitude dawn in his eyes.

"I need to reinforce the dragonsmoke at our loft. I promised my dad." I shrugged. "Maybe I can find something in my dad's hoard or in that book to solve the riddle."

"I'll come with you," Derek said immediately, and got to his feet.

He looked purposeful, which didn't bode well for any discussion we might have on the way.

It said something about my day so far that I was glad to have his company, even so.

Chapter 12

*I*t was forty-seven kinds of bizarre to enter the loft where I lived with my parents, knowing they weren't home yet bringing a guy with me.

On the one hand, Derek was adamant that he had to defend me.

On the other hand, this was breaking every household rule I knew.

Plus it gave me a funny feeling.

Not only was he in my home, not only was he crossing the dragonsmoke barrier with me, but he was going to see me breathe smoke. I felt incredibly self-conscious about that.

My dad's dragonsmoke barrier had begun to erode, just as anticipated. It touched my skin like quicksilver, the chill of it making all the little hairs on my body stand up in unison. I shut the door behind us and locked it. The loft was still and echoed with its emptiness. There were no fetid smells coming from the kitchen, which was a good thing.

I gestured to the room. "You might as well come in and sit down. I don't think there's anything much to eat."

"It's okay," Derek said, and perched on the end of one of the black leather couches in the living room. "Kind of stark." The room was austere, almost monastic in its strict simplicity, which was precisely how my dad liked it. The ceilings were high in the space and the rooms uncluttered—which left lots of room for dragons to gather.

"My dad does black and white in a big way."

Derek smiled. "I like him already."

I sat down opposite him, not really settling back into the couch's squishy comfort, either. "Look. About yesterday . . ."

"There's nothing to say. I saw how you feel about Jared." He looked away from me and his throat worked a bit. "And now that you've told us the whole story, I think maybe I was wrong about him."

"What do you mean?"

Derek looked back at me, his pale eyes seeming unnaturally bright. "He let them take him this morning so that you could get away."

I nodded, sadness welling inside me again because I hadn't been able to save him.

Derek cleared his throat softly. "As much as I'd like to hate his guts, I respect what he did for you."

I looked up, astonished by this.

Derek didn't blink as he watched me. "Wyvern, lead us."

I had to walk through this with him to make sure I understood. "But you were the one who wanted to ensure the alliance, who wanted commitment from me in order to follow me."

Derek grimaced. "Didn't I tell you that I understood about having to do your duty instead of doing what you wanted?"

"But I thought you liked me."

"I do like you." Derek swallowed. "I'm not sure it's enough, though."

I stared at him.

"I know I don't like you as much as you like Jared. I understood that yesterday."

"But you left like you were mad. . . ."

"I *was* mad. I was trying to do what I was told to do, and you were messing it up." He swallowed visibly. "And when I saw the way you looked at him, I knew that you could only ever give me a fraction of that." He heaved a sigh and looked away. "If you can't look at me the way you look at him, I don't want half measures."

"Black or white," I murmured.

"All or nothing," he agreed. He almost smiled. "I said I'd follow the Wyvern, and that means that the Wyvern's agenda is my agenda."

I was glad I was sitting down. Relief would have buckled my knees. All of the wolves were in, despite my choices.

I still needed a plan. I settled onto the floor, kicked off my boots, and cracked my knuckles.

"Anything I can do?" Derek asked.

"Just be quiet. It's kind of a meditative thing."

He watched, his eyes glittering as I summoned the shimmer and let my body shift shape. The surge of power ripped through me with explosive force, compelling my body to take its alternate form. I loved the sensation of it.

In a heartbeat, I was a massive white dragon, my tail unfurled across the floor and my wings resting against my back. I opened my eyes to find that Derek had braced his elbows on his knees and was leaning forward to watch.

That did just about nothing for my self-consciousness. But I knew what I had to do. I let quiet slide through me, although the exercise was a little more difficult than usual. I breathed slowly and deeply, letting my eyes drift closed, persuading my heartbeat to slow to a fraction of its usual pace.

And I breathed smoke, a long glittering tendril of gossamer dragonsmoke. It wound from my lungs through my nostrils and into the air of the loft like a vein of silver. I directed it toward the exterior, letting it slide beneath the front door, weaving it back and forth across the doorway, entwining it with the thinning remnants of my dad's dragonsmoke barrier.

Once the interweaving began, I slipped into a familiar rhythm, focusing on the dragonsmoke and the protective barrier it made. I forgot about everything except breathing smoke in a long steady tendril.

Breathing smoke can't be fascinating to watch, especially to someone who can't see the smoke. I noticed that Derek got up and looked out the window of the loft after a while. I kept breathing, intent on my task, but a bit curious as to what he'd do.

A few moments later, he bent down and unzipped my backpack, then removed a book. His book. Herodotus. He waved it at me to show me what he'd taken, turned on the reading lamp at the end of the couch where he'd been sitting, and settled in to read a few travel tips about the ancient world.

To each his own.

I breathed smoke.

SOME TIME LATER, I HEARD a guy walking around my dragon form.

Derek and I had been alone; then suddenly there was someone else in the loft. No doors or windows had opened.

My eyes were watchful slits. Dragons never truly sleep, you know. We doze. We slumber. We might look comatose. But on some level we are always vigilant. Maybe our interior alarm systems are preset to a more sensitive level.

I heard the guy in the loft, even though his footfalls were silent.

Derek was still reading on the couch opposite me. He looked pretty engrossed and utterly unaware of the intruder. That was odd.

The loft had fallen into the shadows of early evening.

The intruder walked around my tail. I felt him looking at it, as if he'd never seen the like. He wasn't afraid—his pulse was too slow for that. He was more curious. But wary. He walked slowly around my back as I remained motionless, feigning sleep. I could practically feel the weight of his gaze as he studied my folded wings. I felt the air move as he lifted a hand, then dropped it again, deciding against an exploratory touch.

He smelled like wood smoke and the outdoors. Was he a vagrant or a street person? How had he gotten into the loft without setting off the alarm system that deterred human invaders? He could have passed through the dragonsmoke barrier easily—it didn't trouble humans—but there was no door or window open.

He took another step, coming around my left shoulder. I tingled with the awareness that he was checking me out and braced myself for whatever he might do. I was prepared to roar to life, to pivot and fry him to cinders, no questions asked. He had invaded my parents' home and my father's lair.

We dragons have no sense of humor about uninvited visitors.

My dad's hoard was here and I was in charge, left to defend our earthly possessions and personal security.

I was ready.

He took another step, and I saw his silhouette in my peripheral vision.

I smelled blood. Old blood. Dried blood. It awakened something primal within me. Who knew what this guy had done? Who knew what he planned to do next? I was ready to defend everything I cared about.

I held my breath, waiting on that next step that would bring him more clearly into my range. One more step. One leap and breath of dragonfire. There was no explanation he could give to justify his presence, nothing he could say to save himself.

He took that step, he crouched down to look into my eyes, and he whispered the one thing that evidently could stop me cold. "*Unktehila*, we need your help."

There was only one person who called me by that name, by the name the Thunderbirds had given to the dragon shifters. Kohana called me that, but Kohana was dead.

I raised my head and looked at him. It was the *Wakiya* elder from my dream, the one who had dropped his cigarette on the rug. His dark eyes glinted as he watched me, and I guessed that he had known all along that I wasn't really asleep.

And I should have known that this was another Wyvern vision of the possibilities. Both real and not real. Okay.

"I told you to hurry," he said. "And Kohana gave you the clue you need."

"It doesn't help if I don't understand it."

Derek kept reading as if I hadn't spoken.

The elder reached into the pocket of his jeans. With one hand, he withdrew a stone.

It was a piece of red rock, rounded and small enough to hold in one hand. I knew it had a rune scratched on one side and a circle etched on the other.

How had he gotten it?

How long had he been creeping around the loft?

"Hey, that's my rune stone!"

"And it holds the answer." He lifted it up so that the circle was facing me and gave me a hard look. Then he sang the same note Kohana had sung. He tugged his other hand out of his pocket and tossed a handful of what looked like snow into the air. It glistened and glittered—maybe it was a handful of starlight—and then aligned briefly into a musical staff.

I was reminded of what Meagan had drawn at lunch.

The circle on the stone looked like a note.

I still didn't get it. Meagan had already theorized that Kohana had given us the first note in a harmonic sequence, but the harmony she'd come up with hadn't made any difference to anything. "We tried that already," I said, but the elder smiled.

He tossed the rune stone in the air and caught it again. By the time I followed the trajectory of the stone and looked back at him, we were standing on the red rock that I'd visited before, snow swirling all around us.

"Here the earth speaks her secrets. Here the truth of the riddle is revealed." He bent and brushed the snow away from a section of the rock that was covered in carvings. He touched one of a bird, a figure that repeated over and over on the rock face.

"*Wakiya*," I said, remembering that this red rock was a place sacred to the Thunderbirds. *Wakiya* was the name they used for themselves and this was a drawing of one.

The elder nodded, then tipped back his head to sing. He sang that note, letting it ululate in the back of his throat. Other men stepped out of the flying snow, forming a circle around him and creating a chorus. They were ghostly, there but not there, their voices the most material sign of their presence.

It was potent, that singing. It made my body tense and my pulse quicken. It was summoning a kind of energy.

The dead elder who had brought me here stopped singing, letting his fellows carry the note as he turned to me. "Four kinds left," he said. "Four notes."

"Each one is characteristic!" I said with excitement. "Each of us has to provide our note to destroy the NightBlade."

He smiled and stood, extending his hand to me. "Let us defeat the threat together."

I shifted shape and stepped forward in human form to shake his hand. His skin was papery, just like Sigmund's. Was it progress to be shaking hands with more dead people as well as talking to them? I really didn't have time to think about it.

"You have to help," I said to him. "I can't do this alone."

"I have just offered my assistance."

I knew instinctively that this wasn't enough. "No, you have to come with me. We have to defeat them all together. You have to sing the note, live and in person, to do the *Wakiya* part, since Kohana can't."

"I am not alive, though."

"You can still sing."

He frowned and shook his head, looking back at his ghostly fellows. "My time in your world is done. I have done what I can, but I cannot go back there again. The portal is secured against me."

"Then I'll just take you with me," I said with a confidence I didn't quite feel. "I'll make a portal." He looked surprised, but I gripped his hand and smiled. "Here we go."

Worst case: he'd be right and it wouldn't work.

Best case: I'd have the fourth surviving kind of shifter present and accounted for.

You know which option I was hoping for.

I took one last look at the red rock in the snow, not at all sure I'd ever see it again. It was tranquil and powerful, a wonderful place but not one necessarily for me. It had been an intersection for our kinds to negotiate our differences, but I had a feeling that now that was achieved, the *Wakiya* would secure it for themselves.

Which meant I had to make this work.

I closed my eyes, holding fast to the elder's hand. Spontaneously manifesting out of a dream—instead of just waking up—felt like the right answer, but I wasn't at all sure it could be done. I couldn't think of another way to take the elder with me, though, and I was going to trust my gut.

I wished with all my heart and soul to be back in my parents' loft, back opposite Derek, and hoped I'd be in dragon form. I felt the tingle that always accompanied my attempts to spontaneously manifest elsewhere, felt my body begin to make the transformation, and tightened my grip on his hand.

Holy hoard. It worked.

WHEN I MANIFESTED IN THE loft, I gave a hoot of joy. I was in my dragon form, exactly the way I wanted to be. And—bonus—the elder was still with me, clutching my talon. I had time to see that he was as impressed as I was; then Derek shouted in surprise.

He sat up, his eyes wide. "Zoë, what are you doing?"

"Solving the riddle!" I cried, triumphant, and shifted to my human form in a glorious tide of shimmering blue light. The elder nodded approval. "And bringing help."

Derek looked pointedly around the loft. "What help?"

"Him." I gestured to the elder, who seemed mightily amused.

"Uh, there's no one else here, Zoë."

"Don't worry about it. Trust me." I hauled out my messenger and checked the time. It was eight thirty already. "We've got to get to the dance."

Derek was looking at me like I'd completely lost it. "I thought you didn't want to go anymore."

"We have to go. The ShadowEaters will be there. They'll have the NightBlade and will try to take out at least one wildcard. We're all supposed to be there, and the school is already filled with spell light." I was hauling on my boots as I talked, grabbing my keys and my backpack. Excellent—I still had Skuld's shears. "If Jessica's there, she's in trouble already. Let's go!"

I bolted out the door, and Derek came after me. I ran down the stairs to the parking garage, trusting the ghostly elder to keep up. Meanwhile, I messaged Meagan, my fingers flying. She'd gone to Isabelle's place with Jessica, so I told them all to come to the school together and meet us there.

I was through the door to the parking garage when she called. I quickly explained the issue, then remarked, "You said there were four parts to the harmony."

"Soprano, alto, tenor, and bass," she agreed.

"Which one was that note of Kohana's?"

"Tenor."

I got into my car, scrolling through the recorded notes stored on my messenger. Derek got in the passenger's seat, looking a bit shaken. Like he'd been startled awake to find the world shifting hard. I smiled at him and delegated a task. "I need a sound, characteristic of the Neuroi, that matches one of these notes. A powerful sound for you, or a ceremonial sound."

Derek's eyes shone with purpose as he took my messenger, scrolling through the audio files as I turned the key in the ignition. The car sputtered but didn't start. I tried again as he worked through the three remaining notes.

Nada. The engine was dead.

No, the battery was dead. It should have had enough juice for the week, but I'd taken that extra trip downtown to Jared's hostel and run it dry. Stupidly, I hadn't thought to plug it in when I got home. There was no time to charge it up because we had to get to the school before the others were hurt.

I could have shifted shape and flown there in dragon form, carrying Derek. But I was afraid that I would need every crumb of my dragon powers for the fight ahead. Plus I might end up needing to beguile a whole bunch of innocent bystanders who saw me in dragon form (don't we love the Covenant?) and I just didn't have time.

But there was another choice.

I slanted a look across the parking garage to the car carefully covered with a tarp and protected for all time. Or at least until its new buyer came to collect it in a week or two. My heart skipped a beat at the boldness of my idea.

The Lamborghini was here.

Its gas tank was full.

And I knew where the keys were.

It seemed that this was the night that some dreams could come true.

"BE RIGHT BACK," I SAID to Derek, and raced upstairs. I grabbed the Lamborghini's keys and was back in the garage in record time, moving practically at the speed of light.

Derek was gone.

My messenger was emitting one of those notes, the sound echoing around the parking garage in a decidedly eerie fashion.

I panicked for a second, certain the ShadowEaters had gotten him.

But no. Derek was in wolf form. I exhaled in relief when I saw him. His paws were braced against the pavement in the space that was usually occupied by my dad's new sedan. My messenger was on the ground beside him, holding that note.

When he saw me, he tipped back his head and loosed the howl I'd heard the wolf shifters make when we triumphed over the Mages in the fall. It was a sound that made me shiver.

And it perfectly matched the note emanating from my messenger.

The *Wakiya* elder lounged against the fender of my car, nodding approval. "That's two," he said, and I laughed.

"Help me get the tarp off," I said to Derek, snatching up my messenger on the way past him. I saw the blue shimmer of his shifting shape; then he was beside me again. In no time at all, we had the car unwrapped, and we both stopped to stare.

The car was perfect. Utterly black, polished to the gleam of a dark mirror, sleek and powerful, and apparently untouched by human hands.

My heart did a trio of backflips.

Was I out of my mind?

"Pretty much," Sigmund said, and I could have smacked him.

If I'd been able to see him.

I was not happy that he was adding the disembodied voice to his repertoire of dead-guy tricks. He would choose this moment to change his rules.

"You know, in some cultures, it's believed that people who see the dead do so because they'll soon be dead themselves," Sigmund said conversationally.

I was sure he was referring to my dad's reaction to me driving the Lamborghini.

"Thank you very much for that," I said. "I'll keep it in mind."

"Keep what in mind?" Derek asked.

"Don't worry about it." I forced a smile, feigning confidence, and hit the button to unlock the doors. The car beeped and the lights flashed. I heard the locks disengage.

"You know how to drive this thing?" Derek asked, his uncertainty clear.

"I guess I'll learn," I said, and his eyes widened. I opened the driver's-side door. I was more terrified of damaging this car than I'd been of anything ever in my life.

Which was saying something, given that I lived with dragons and fought ShadowEaters on a regular basis.

On the other hand, I was thrilled.

And I told myself I didn't have a choice.

There were, of course, really only two seats in the car, the backseat pretty much big enough for just an umbrella or a purse. I realized suddenly that I was the reason my dad had had to set aside his precious automobile.

No room for a baby seat.

I glanced at the elder, who moved his arms to pantomime flying. I gave him a thumbs-up. Derek looked between me and the place where the dead elder stood, with an expression that told me he couldn't see our companion.

I got in, was swallowed by the leather seat, and was amazed that my dad had given this up for me. It was completely deluxe, and so antique that it could have been from another planet. Slick, though.

I looked at the dashboard in awe and uncertainty.

Derek visibly swallowed and I wondered what he saw two

minutes in his future. "You think your dad will be cool with this?"

I didn't need dragon powers of perception to hear his worry.

"No," I admitted, to Derek's obvious alarm. "He'll be furious enough to spark an inferno." I smiled. "Unless we save the world tonight."

"No pressure," Derek said, gritting his teeth and fastening his seat belt.

I felt for the seat adjustment. I'm tall, but my dad is taller, and I couldn't quite reach the clutch.

"There," Sigmund said, and I felt his fingers on mine, even though I couldn't see him. The rearview mirror moved, seemingly of its own accord, and I was relieved that Derek didn't seem to notice. Ditto on the side mirrors.

Sigmund set me right up. "Act like you know what you're doing," he advised. "It'll inspire confidence, even when you're putting it on."

I turned the key and the engine roared to life. I said a quick prayer, then looked at the gearbox, mystified. I knew how to drive a standard, but the gearbox was different.

"You'll find reverse over here," Sigmund whispered in my ear, and I was really glad to be hearing dead people. He walked me through the gears in order, up to fifth and back to first. An older brother teaching me to drive. That thought made me smile. "Easy on the clutch, sis. It's pretty punchy. This baby is made to race, after all."

"Right," I said. "Thanks."

"And if you fry the clutch, neither one of us will be safe from Erik."

"I could blame you," I teased, seeing how Derek was staring at me.

Sigmund laughed. "And I'd blame you. Who would he believe? You're the only one who has a physical form."

He had a point. I put it in reverse, feeling where the clutch engaged, and backed out of the spot with care. Derek was looking at me as if I'd lost my mind, but was probably thinking it would be smarter not to distract me.

"So, what do you see two minutes in our future?" I asked.

"Nothing good."

"Skeptic." I grinned at Derek, probably looking like a maniac, and touched the gas.

The car surged forward like a cheetah let loose.

In precisely one half second, I knew that this car was made for me. I knew that driving it would be more fun than anything I'd ever done.

Me in this car was kismet.

Just like I'd always believed.

THE TIRES SQUEALED AS I rounded the corner to the exit. Derek was pale but I didn't care. Our spaces were at the back of the garage, so I had another corner to go. I took the second corner in a harder turn, thrilled by how responsive the car was.

Derek audibly gulped.

"Time is of the essence," I informed him.

I heard Jared in my thoughts. *A dragon girl should be bold.* I blinked back my tears and focused. I'd have plenty of time to mourn later.

First I had to make his sacrifice count.

The parking garage had a sensor that lifted the door. As soon as we passed it and the door mechanism clicked, I knew we were going too fast. The garage door was old and clunky and took forever to ascend.

I hit the brake. The Lamborghini squealed to a halt, skidding a bit on the pavement and sliding toward the opening door.

"Shit!" Derek shouted.

The Great Wyvern was with me. The door was no more than two inches over the hood of the car as we slid beneath it and came to a stop. The door continued to crank upward. I was so relieved that I took my foot off the clutch.

And stalled it. The cheetah lurched forward another foot and came to a choking halt.

I knew the garage door would reach the top, remain open for a timed interval, then close again. Was there a sensor to detect a car or anything beneath it? I wasn't sure and it seemed a bad time to find out. I turned the key hard in the ignition and the engine ground in complaint.

Derek swore some more and peered through the windshield at the garage door.

It hit the top and stopped.

"Easy, easy," Sigmund said. "Don't flood it."

Right. Deep breath. Stay calm. I put on the emergency brake, put the car in neutral. I could feel the seconds ticking down and the sweat rolling down my back. I squared my shoulders, ignored Derek's agitation, depressed the clutch, and tried again.

The engine started, settling into a throaty purr. I would have hit the gas, but Sigmund shouted, "The brake!" He sounded more agitated than I'd ever heard him.

Too late. I stalled it again.

The door started to descend.

Sigmund swore with enthusiasm.

Derek watched the door descend and I could hear his breath quickening. "Hurry up, Zoë."

"You'd think it was your car," I muttered. I went through

my routine again—neutral, clutch, ignition—and the car choked for only a moment before the engine started again.

"Maybe it likes abuse," Sigmund muttered, but I ignored him.

I had things to do. I could see the shadow of the garage door coming closer and knew there would be no other opportunity. I disengaged the emergency brake, put it back in first, and touched the gas.

"Move it already," Derek shouted, and I floored it.

The car shot out into the night. It is possible that the garage door scraped the roof of the car. Or touched it. I'm not sure. But I saw it ascending again in the rearview mirror. Then I saw a vivid flash of yellow light in that mirror, and a massive black bird swooped out beneath the descending door. He disappeared from my view and I knew he'd be flying above us.

I had one heartbeat to think myself a success before Derek screamed a warning.

The car bounded onto the road—I swear it took flight at the end of the driveway. It was a fast beast, faster than I expected.

Too late, I saw I'd neglected to check the road for oncoming traffic.

"Left!" Sigmund roared.

"Right!" Derek cried.

I swerved hard to the left to avoid a van that had been moving along the street, minding its own business, until I'd decided to occupy the same physical space. The other driver honked as I skidded. I realized there was a bit of ice on the road, too. There was an oncoming car and I was in the wrong lane. Sigmund reached over and jerked the wheel hard to the right.

The Lamborghini fishtailed with glorious drama. Derek swore again and tightened his seat belt.

"Steer *into* the skid," Sigmund shouted.

"I'm trying!" I shouted back.

"Try harder," Derek complained.

After about ten thousand years of sliding around, the tires found their grip. We were at the end of the block, the light was green, and I saw no reason to take it easy. Time was wasting. I rocked it into second and left the honking van in my dust.

"Help me with your foresight," I said to Sigmund.

"Do it yourself, sis," Sigmund murmured.

I might have argued with him, but something opened in my mind. I saw a network of possibilities, an array of scenes emanating from this point in time like a glorious web. It was the future, in all its myriad possibilities. I put the engine in third, accelerated through an intersection before the light changed to red. The display in my mind's eye changed, some possibilities falling by the wayside, others becoming visible.

It made me think of driving down a highway and seeing all the choices available from the next exit. If I passed on that exit, the options at the next one became visible. If I took the exit, there were more options created as a result of my choice.

Exactly as Jared had said.

The future was mutable.

And we made it ourselves.

But this vision in my mind's eye made driving the car like a game or a simulator. I could see all that was coming, and the result of all possible choices—at least in the short term. That fed my confidence in a very big way. It wasn't two minutes' warning. It was much, much more than that.

"Don't dig your nails into the upholstery," I told Derek. "It'll tick my dad off."

"There's a truck coming into the next intersection from the right," he said grimly.

"I know."

"He's not going to stop and we're going to take it head-on!"

"I don't think so," I said, and pushed the gas pedal to the floor.

I swerved hard to the left while entering that intersection. The light was green and there was no other traffic. The truck honked, leaping into the intersection from the right. Derek swore. I zoomed right around that truck, rocketing into the next block, leaving us unscathed.

I swear there were flames coming out the back of this car. We were one, dragon girl and Italian sports car, its performance an extension of my own abilities.

I got us to the school so fast that it was almost disappointing.

I DELIBERATELY SKIDDED THE CAR to a halt at the front door of the school, almost but not quite bumping the tires against the curb. I turned off the ignition with some regret and we turned to look at the school.

It was glittering with spell light like a Christmas tree.

Worse than that, it was surrounded by ShadowEaters. They milled outside the school. They mingled with the kids who were attending the dance. They were inside, too, and I suspected that any kid foolish enough to wander away from the larger group might not come back. They'd taken out apprentice Mages individually already, after all. Now the ShadowEaters pushed against the kids, exuding menace, vibrating with frenzy.

I sensed they were waiting for something.

Enough power for a full and final assault.

I had a feeling that I knew where they'd get that surge of power.

"Can you see them?" I asked Derek.

He shook his head, looking—it must be said—a bit green around the gills. "Feels really bad, but I can't see anything."

"There are ShadowEaters everywhere. I'll bet the Night-Blade is here, too."

"Big finish," he said, nodding. "What do we do?"

"Let's act as if everything's normal and see what we can learn."

He exhaled, clearly not liking my plan but not having another, and got out of the car. There were a group of cool kids approaching, drawn to the car and obviously wondering who was driving it.

Were they ever going to be surprised.

Derek bent and kissed the ground, deliberately giving me a hard time. The kids laughed, razzing him about his ride. I saw that there were ShadowEaters following the group of kids, their eyes shining with malice. They nibbled at them, pinched them, considered them as if they were choosing from a buffet. Even though the kids couldn't see them, they eased away from the ShadowEaters instinctively, sensing something they didn't like.

I got out of the car and they were suitably astounded. "It wasn't that bad," I said to Derek, blushing furiously as they encircled the car, talking about Zitty Zoë's deep secrets.

Derek gave me a look. "Next time, I'll walk."

The kids laughed aloud and I pretended to be insulted. I locked and armed the car, then came around it to Derek's side.

That was when I heard the music drifting out of the doors of the school. I had seen the golden spell light churning around the building from the moment we arrived, but now I saw a tendril of blue and green spell light winding through it. The golden spells surrounded the blue-green thread, containing it and feeding off of it but still letting it grow.

Because it was Jared singing "Snow Goddess."

I stared in shock, my heart thudding. Was it a recording?

I watched the blue and purple spell light swirl upward, knowing I'd never seen it emanate from any recording of Jared's before.

"He's alive," I whispered, my heart thudding.

Derek swore under his breath. "They saved him for this."

I nodded, my throat tight. "They baited the trap."

"That means you can win, Zoë."

I wasn't so sure of that. I thought it just meant they needed me for their ritual.

Or my shadow.

A taxi pulled in beside us and squealed to a halt; then Jessica, Meagan, Liam, and Garrett spilled out. Jessica shuddered as she looked at the school, and Meagan gasped when she obviously recognized the tune.

I whispered to Meagan about Derek's howl when I gave her a hug and felt her nod. Then she got her Einstein look and I knew she had the solution.

She immediately typed a message, and my eyes widened when I read it.

> *"The keening note the Bastians use to summon the ancestors must be the soprano."*

I looked at her and she nodded furiously. It made sense. We last four kinds held the secret to the four notes that could destroy the NightBlade. We wildcards hung out with spellsingers, which meant we could figure it out.

That explained why they wanted to finish us off so badly.

And the note had to be distinctive to our respective kinds.

That left the *Pyr* with the bass note. I played the note and couldn't think of anything we did that echoed that sound.

"What are you doing?" Liam asked in old-speak.

"Solving the riddle that can destroy the NightBlade," I said, and told them what I was looking for. Liam looked thoughtful, but Garrett frowned.

"If Jared's alive, we have to save him," Garrett added, glancing toward the stage. *"No time to mess around with games and riddles."*

Meagan's eyes lit as she looked between us. "Is that old-speak?" she asked. She grinned and tapped madly on her messenger, which then emitted a tone so low that everyone in the room looked skyward.

Thinking it was thunder.

"One octave lower!" Meagan said, triumphant. "That's it!"

"But how do we know when to make the sound?" Derek asked, turning toward the stage.

"I'll give Meagan a signal," I said. "Watch her for your cue."

We nodded at one another, exchanged looks, and I probably wasn't the only one who took a breath. I offered Derek my hand; then we marched toward the doors together.

There was no way that I could turn away from Jared, even if he was spellbound.

No matter what the consequences might be.

Chapter 13

I could see a thousand possibilities extending from this moment as we walked into the school. Very few of those options for my future ended well. I suspected that Derek was silent because he could see a subset of the same thing.

Some things were as expected. There were red streamers hanging over the doorways and signs for the dance. Red hearts were plastered on windows and walls. There was smoke in the air and it wasn't all cigarette smoke. A bunch of the teachers were on patrol, watching over us and trying desperately to look young and cool. (They failed. Every one of them.) Lots of people were dressed in red or red and white, and there were many couples holding hands. Music was playing, sending out a strong bass beat.

That the same song was being played over and over again didn't seem to bother anybody.

That it was Jared singing "Snow Goddess" sure bothered me.

There were ShadowEaters everywhere. The other kids didn't seem to see them, although they shivered periodically and glanced over their shoulders as they talked and laughed in their groups. They eased back to let Derek and me pass, growling and biting as we moved through the throng of them. I was sure one licked me, and I tried not to shudder.

They let us pass because they thought we were stepping into their trap. They thought they were going to have their big slaughter, taking all of us out at once, and get their power burst to make it to that pure spirit form.

What they were going to get was a surprise.

There was a lot of spell light, too, winding around our ankles, the tendrils so thick that they hid the floor. We waded through a maze of spells, like explorers in a hostile jungle. I felt the spell snakes slide over my boots, never really binding me but making sure I understood that they could.

I cradled the weight of Skuld's shears beneath my jacket with my free hand, glad to have them.

There was a trickle of sweat running down my back.

I saw some apprentice Mages in the hallway, although there were a lot fewer of them than other times we'd squared off. I knew which ones they were because they were flickering between the forms of the species they'd conquered. There's something about a merman becoming a basilisk, then becoming a butterfly, that catches the eye. (Trust me.) They were agitated or excited, maybe worked up in anticipation of whatever waited ahead.

That couldn't be a good sign of anything.

It was interesting that the apprentice Mages were in attendance, given that the ShadowEaters were there, too. The ShadowEaters had been hunting surviving Mages and junior apprentice Mages, after all. Did this bunch think they were the top of the class? The ones who could join the Shadow-Eaters? They might just be stupid, but the fact that they could move between forms indicated that they were at least as adept as Adrian.

They might have the same false confidence as Adrian, too. I could hope.

We stepped into the cafeteria, and I was startled by how many unfamiliar people were there. Not that we hadn't been introduced—I'd never seen most of them in my life. The dance floor was thronged with hot guys and gorgeous girls, none of whom looked familiar.

Were we at the wrong school? An alternate universe?

Then two of the guys turned to Derek and made a single nod of acknowledgment. When he nodded back once, they returned to their dancing, and I guessed.

"They're yours," I said, and he gave me a slight nod.

I was relieved and worried that the wolf shifters had come. Was this part of the ShadowEaters' plan? To ensure that as many shifters as possible were present, to improve the shadow feast?

I didn't want to look at the stage. My heart was so filled with hope that Jared was okay that I didn't want to lose that possibility. I didn't want to see him spellbound or injured or turned into some kind of zombie.

I just wanted to close my eyes and listen to him sing, in case it was the last time.

"Want to dance?" Anna asked suddenly. We all started to find her right behind us, smiling as if we all were actually buddies.

I saw the glimmer of spell light in her eyes. She smiled at Garrett.

"It's a trick," I warned him in old-speak.

"*I know, but also an opportunity,*" he said. Then he smiled at Anna, took her hand, and headed for the dance floor. I could see two of Suzanne's other cronies, Fiona and Trish, and both of them had eyes of glowing gold like Anna's. Trevor and the ShadowEaters had spellbound them.

Converted them to staff.

Like Suzanne, they were probably going to be sacrificed.

"Great idea," Liam said, feigning enthusiasm as Garrett and Anna started to dance. "Let's dance," he said to Jessica, and they followed Garrett.

"I don't like this," Meagan said, worry in her tone. "They're waiting for something."

"It's going to get worse," Derek said, folding his arms across his chest as he stood between us. Sure enough, the spell light seemed to be swirling with greater intensity, becoming brighter by the second.

Liam and Jessica took to the dance floor, and I was surprised at how smooth a dancer Liam was. He guided Jessica through the crowd with ease, following her slight nods to pause in the vicinity of one attractive girl after another. Dancing made it easy for her to spread the word.

I looked at Derek and he looked at me. There was a weight of expectation between us, a moment of what might have been; then he turned to Meagan. She looked between us but I nodded, relieved that she would have a wolf standing guard over her. They did the same thing, sliding through the throng of dancers. Derek exchanged a word with this wolf and that one, and I turned to look at the stage.

When I saw Jared, I caught my breath.

He was snared in a golden bubble of spell light and looked to be lost in his own world. He played the same song over and over again, crooning the words, making love to his guitar. As I watched him, I realized that he was trapped in a sequence of moments, doomed to repeat them over and over and over again.

Was he aware of his fate?

Did he know I was here?

Was he still in there?

I had so many questions, but two were the most important. Could I save him? And if I did, would he ever be the same?

He was surrounded by ShadowEaters, as if they were his backup band. Their eyes shone a brilliant gold as their ranks parted suddenly. They pushed forward a guy who looked like he'd rather be anywhere else in the world.

Kohana.

I gasped. He wasn't dead, either.

No, they'd saved him so they could eliminate all four wild-cards at once. They really wanted the energy boost to be as big as possible—and they were that confident that they'd win. That simultaneous execution was what was going to give them the power surge they needed.

I had to stop them!

Just as when I first met Kohana, there was a noose of spell light around his neck. His hands were bound before him. The music stopped. The dancing stopped as everyone looked around, uncertain.

I had a really bad feeling.

Then everything happened very fast.

THE SPELL LIGHT SWIRLED IN a golden frenzy, taking on a pulsing energy that was faster than the beat of Jared's music. I heard a different song become ascendant. The Shadow-Eaters converged on the cafeteria, pressing in from the perimeter with obvious hunger.

That was when I saw that the scene had frozen.

At least, all of the normal kids were frozen, trapped in a single moment of time.

Which meant that all the shifters and spellsingers were revealed, because none of us were frozen.

The ShadowEaters laughed and grabbed. They surrounded Liam and Jessica, closing around them like an ardent swarm. They isolated Garrett, and Anna helped to push him away from the group. He fought her, but the ShadowEaters had him outnumbered.

Meagan understood immediately what was happening and started to sing. Derek shifted shape when the ShadowEaters surrounded him and Meagan, with only Meagan's determined spellsinging giving those two a buffer. I could see that she was losing the battle, though, even though she was determined to keep singing.

Derek leapt and snapped, his hostility helping to keep the ShadowEaters back. They retreated, maybe acting instinctively, because his bite had no effect. His jaws closed on empty air and spell light, but he kept snarling all the same.

Meagan kept trying to ease them toward Garrett, and I knew she wanted to get him inside the influence of her spell light.

Then I heard Trevor laugh. How could that be?

There was a ShadowEater on the stage, one that burned a particularly vivid shade of gold. He was singing a spellsong, one that pulsed and caressed his silhouetted form. As the song grew louder, I saw his dark skin take on detail again, his features appear out of the shadow and brilliance.

The ShadowEater became Trevor, right before my eyes.

His eyes still shone the vivid gold that characterized ShadowEaters, but he'd moved back to the physical sphere.

How long would the spell last?

Why had he done it?

Trevor held the NightBlade high over his head, its dark knife gleaming with evil intent, and I knew exactly why he'd done it. This was it!

A ripple of excitement passed through the cafeteria. The ShadowEaters pushed Kohana closer to Trevor and the stage, moving faster although he struggled against the spell. Anna and the ShadowEaters kept Garrett at the perimeter of the room, isolated from all of us. A group of ShadowEaters pushed Liam and Jessica toward the stage.

Meanwhile, the mood in the cafeteria was turning frantic. The ShadowEaters vibrated more rapidly in anticipation. They pressed closer, gnawing on the captives they surrounded. The apprentice Mages spun more quickly through their forms, adding their voices to Trevor's song.

When I looked back toward the stage, I saw something that made me sick. Nick and Isabelle were there, surrounded by a net of spell light. Isabelle's eyes were golden and glazed, and she was completely entranced—as was Yvonne, who held their spell tethers. Nick was struggling, without success, against his spell, which had him tightly bound. I was both relieved to finally see them and terrified that they were spellbound. Meagan's protective spell had been destroyed.

Jared played and played, lost in a world of his own.

This couldn't get worse.

I saw the ShadowEater Trevor hold up the NightBlade. I saw him begin the invocation and target Nick and Isabelle.

They weren't going to be sacrificed again.

Even if they were bait for me, and even if I was going to die, I was still going to win.

Because I could see that Trevor's spells were once again feeding on Jared's music.

All I had to do was silence him.

Before anyone was sacrificed.

THE GOLDEN MAGE SPELL LIGHT became blinding in its intensity as someone's hand locked on the back of my neck. I turned to find Trish behind me, her eyes shining gold. She pushed me hard toward the stage, tripping me when I resisted her.

The spell snakes locked around my ankles, binding them together with lightning speed. I fell to the ground. I hauled out my shears and hacked at the spell snakes. I heard the others shout out and knew they were in trouble, too. The spell snakes grew faster and faster, replicating and replacing themselves, locking around my legs, binding me to the hip so fast that I knew I didn't have much time.

Trish laughed as I hacked at them in desperation.

I stabbed down a bunch of snakes, slashing with a violence I didn't know I had in me. (And I'm a dragon. Think about it.) The spell snakes obscured my vision, and the shears caught on something more substantial.

Trish.

The spell light poured from the cut, revealing her to be a ShadowEater. I didn't have time to think about when that had happened or why, because she snarled and leapt at me. Spell light spilled from her mouth, targeting me.

I ripped the shears through Trish in self-defense. She collapsed like a rag doll, spilling spell light all over the place. It rose into the air, a renewable resource, and made the Shadow-Eaters pulse with new vigor.

Her skin turned dark and empty, like a deflated black balloon.

Ick.

I shifted shape with a roar, calling to the others to do the same. Liam shifted, becoming a glittering malachite and silver dragon. I thrilled at the sight of him. I was awed when

Jessica changed into a jaguar and they fought back-to-back.

Garrett shifted into his garnet and gold dragon form with a roar and breathed dragonfire on every ShadowEater foolish enough to get between him and Meagan.

Meagan sang her heart out, and soon had both Derek and Garrett within her bubble of spell light. The trio moved with purpose, surrounded by her song, making steady progress toward the stage.

Trevor lifted the NightBlade high over Kohana. "One more species possessed for all time!" he cried.

"One more triumph!" cried the apprentice Mages. The ShadowEaters kept us from the stage through sheer numbers, their dark menace keeping us from saving Kohana.

I didn't have time to mess around.

"No way!" I shouted, and spontaneously manifested right behind Trevor.

In human form.

I had surprise on my side. I seized the NightBlade and retreated. He came after me with a snarl, but I slashed once at him with Skuld's shears. The sharp blade cut his side and spell light spilled through the gash. He shouted in rage.

I expected him to collapse, but he began to sing with fury.

I didn't have time to free Kohana, not yet. I tried Skuld's shears on the bubble that held Jared captive, but they bounced off the golden sphere without making a scratch.

How could I free him?

When I looked back, I saw that Trevor's spells were attacking and binding every note that Jared made. Trevor milked each one dry, using Jared's power to heal his own wound, twisting Jared's spells to his own purpose. I watched in horror.

Then he came after me.

I retreated around the bubble that imprisoned Jared. It looked like spun glass and I had to believe I could break it, even while dodging Trevor. The NightBlade was humming in my hand, filling my thoughts with darkness. I didn't trust it one bit, but instinct told me that it could be used against this spell.

What would be the price?

I didn't know, but I had to try. I stabbed it into the bubble of spell light, which exploded on contact into a flurry of golden stars.

Jared fell lifeless to the ground, his song silenced.

Maybe forever.

He was completely still.

I stared in horror at what I'd done; then I heard Trevor snarl behind me.

I SPUN TO FIGHT, HOPING I could fix everything else once we survived. The NightBlade wriggled in my grip, trying to get away. Who knew what it wanted to do next? I sure wasn't going to use it again.

I leapt over Jared and slashed at Kohana's bonds with Skuld's shears. He was free in a heartbeat, tossing aside the noose. He shifted shape and flew high, obviously glad to be free.

That was when the *Wakiya* elder began to sing the note from the Thunderbirds. I realized that no one could see or hear him because he was dead.

No one but me.

And the NightBlade. I saw it quiver when he started to sing. In fact, it vibrated in my hand, acting like a tuning fork.

Trevor snatched at it, but I stabbed at him with Skuld's shears again. He didn't back down, and I was soon slashing at spell snakes as fast as he could make them.

"Now!" I cried, and Jessica began to sing the keening note

that the Bastians used to summon the ancestors. The other cat shifters at the dance joined in, and soon the air was filled with the eerie cry that gave me goose bumps. I saw the golden ghostly cats appear and begin to mill through the crowd on the dance floor, their eyes glowing hot red.

The NightBlade vibrated harder.

Derek tipped back his head and howled, the signal for his fellows to join in. There was a dizzying flash of brilliant blue as a quarter of the guys on the dance floor changed shape, becoming wolves. There were big wolves and small wolves, silver ones and white ones and charcoal ones, wolves with blue eyes and wolves with eyes of pale green. Every single one of them tipped back his head and howled that same note.

"No!" Trevor shouted. They targeted me then, apprentice Mages and ShadowEaters and minions pouncing. I shifted shape to dragon form, hiding the NightBlade along with my clothes. I could feel it shaking beneath my scales, twitching as it responded to the notes being sung.

"*Old-speak, old-speak, old-speak,*" Garrett began, repeating the same words over and over again in that deep note. I saw Meagan shake her head and tap her messenger, and he changed his words to her suggestions. He let loose a long low stream of "*Ooooooooo.*"

I stumbled over the stage, cutting Isabelle and Nick free. Isabelle was out of it, but Nick shifted shape. He became a fearsome dragon of vivid orange and yellow, his scales gleaming so brightly that looking at him was like looking into the sun. He roared and breathed dragonfire, apparently in relief, then took up the note that Garrett was singing. Liam and I joined in, and the NightBlade resonated so hard that it shook itself loose of its hiding place.

It fell onto the stage.

I leapt after it.

Trevor pounced on it and held it high, triumphant that he'd caught it. He pivoted to face me, his intent clear. I breathed some fire, just to let him know I wouldn't go down easily. We squared off, and I kept singing that bass note.

Before he could do anything with the NightBlade, it shook hard. He could barely hold on to it, and I meant to snatch it from his grasp.

But it shattered, shattered into a thousand thin shards.

They scattered across the stage, a thousand thin slices of darkest night. I thought it was my imagination that they looked like shapes as they fell to the stage.

The ShadowEaters gave a horrible cry; then they faded to nothing so abruptly that they might never have been. The spell light winked out. The cafeteria, instead of being bathed in the sickening hue of spell light, was pretty much normal again.

"No!" Trevor shouted and fell to his knees, trying desperately to gather up all the broken bits.

I stepped forward like an avenging angel and changed back to my human form. I raised Skuld's shears over him, and he looked up at me in fear. "You're the one who wanted to move beyond the physical sphere," I reminded him. "Who said dreams don't come true?" I watched terror fill his golden eyes; then I slit him in half, loosing the spell light that had filled his skin.

This time, there was no spell light for him to use to save himself.

Like the others, he deflated. Unlike the others, he made a low moan as he ceased to exist. The spell light that had filled him rose into the air, seeking to join more energy of its kind. Finding none, it winked out.

Like someone had flipped a switch.

I STOOD THERE, SHAKING IN the silence that stretched afterward. I was dimly aware of the crackle of blue light, the shimmer of the wolves and Bastians changing back to human form and the dragons doing the same. I stared at the empty shell that had been Trevor, incredulous that it was finally over.

The spell that had snared the normal kids was broken, as well. I heard the music start again—although it wasn't Jared singing anymore—and the laughter of people flirting. I looked at Jared, who didn't get up or wake up.

What had I done to him?

"Those would be mine," Skuld said from beside me. She put out her hand for the shears. I was pretty astonished to be able to see her when I was awake, but she smiled and winked at me. "Good job."

So I'd passed another test. I looked between her and the shears. "Thanks. I guess I don't need them anymore."

"No, you don't." She shoved them into the holster on her belt and tossed her braid over her shoulder. She then bent to pick up the pieces of the broken NightBlade. "I hate a mess," she muttered, but I sensed there was more to it than that.

I didn't much care. I dropped to my knees beside Jared, knowing that if the cost of destroying the NightBlade and eliminating the Mages was his death, it had been too high of a price. I couldn't feel a pulse and his skin had become very pale.

I felt Nick behind me, the weight of his hand on my shoulder. I saw Isabelle kneel beside me and take my hand in hers. She was still pale and looked unsteady, and there were tears in her eyes. "It doesn't have to be this way, Zoë," she whispered.

"Maybe all Wyverns are doomed to lose at love," I said. "Or to sacrifice for it."

"No," Isabelle said with such conviction that I wanted to believe her. She reached into her purse, always prepared, and pulled out her deck of tarot cards. She shuffled it once and then offered it to me.

Our gazes met.

I didn't want to shuffle them. I didn't want to touch them. I halfway didn't believe they'd respond to me. But I reached over and I cut the deck, turning it over in my hand to show the card.

The Magician.

I looked at Isabelle. She smiled.

"Number one," she said, indicating the Roman numeral at the top. "The prime mover, the card of artists and of people who make things happen by directing energy and resources."

"People who make the future happen," I said, remembering Jared's ideas about that. "People who choose."

Isabelle nodded and put the deck away. She straightened and stood beside Nick. I saw her slip her hand into his. I glanced up to meet her gaze and realized that she was wearing the necklace he'd had made for her.

The last Wyvern had made herself a future.

I'd make myself one, too.

I eased closer to Jared, realizing that we could have been in a little bubble of privacy. The dance went on around us, a tight circle of shifters and select humans and a spell-singer hiding Jared and me from view. Liam and Garrett were there, Meagan and Jessica, Isabelle and Nick, Derek and Kohana. They were my friends and they were all on my side.

Well, except Kohana. I was never sure about him.

He smiled at me, maybe guessing the direction of my thoughts.

"This one's for you, *Unktehila*," he murmured, then sang a trio of notes.

I saw the vivid green of his spellsong. It danced like a feather on the wind, then settled over Jared's heart. I realized that Kohana was helping me, that he was repaying the debt between us.

Mostly I knew this because the dead *Wakiya* elder nodded with obvious satisfaction.

Meagan watched Kohana, listening to him with care. She then added her voice to his in a simple harmony, the two of them jamming softly together.

Meagan's spellsong was red this time, and I liked how it twined with Kohana's. The two threads of spell light wound together like plies of yarn or snakes on a caduceus or a DNA string.

Jessica improvised some scat. She didn't make spell light but it sounded pretty.

I loved that they were trying to help me.

To help Jared.

That gave me hope.

The entwined spell light wound toward Jared, making a vortex over his heart. I felt as if it were showing me something. I put my hand into the middle of the swirling spell light, touching my finger to the eye of the hurricane.

And Jared's heart pulsed hard beneath my fingertip.

He wasn't dead. He was injured.

Maybe he was lost.

Maybe he just needed someone to call him back from wherever they had banished him.

I flattened my hand, putting my palm against his chest. My mouth was dry and I was nervous, uncertain. But I'd learned to fly without a manual and I'd learned to become the Wyvern without any instruction book.

I had my instincts to guide me, and they were pretty good.

On impulse, I touched my lips to his, keeping my hand flat against his chest. It was a sweet kiss, a chaste touch of my lips to his, but I exhaled a tiny breath against Jared's mouth. I could feel it tingle as it crossed my lips, electrified by his proximity, maybe. When I sat back, it seemed that there was a glimmer of stardust sliding over his body.

Suddenly his eyes flew open, those gazillion shades of green nearly stopping my heart cold. He studied me, probably reading my thoughts, and I held his gaze, letting him look.

He must have liked whatever he saw.

"Hey, dragon girl," he murmured, and his voice sounded rough. Then he smiled crookedly at me, the sight of that dimple making my own heart skip. "Would this be the happy ending?"

"Not quite," I said with a grin. "I still owe you a ride."

"You're never going to deliver on that," he teased, his eyes dancing.

"Get it in gear, Madison," I retorted. "We're going right now."

I stood up and imperiously offered him my hand. He got to his feet under his own steam and visibly shook off something. The others hugged him or pumped his hand or thumped his back. He checked his guitar, then entrusted it to Nick, congratulated Meagan on her spellsinging, thanked Kohana.

Then he took my hand in his and smiled just for me.

"So, I was thinking, dragon girl," he said, looking down at our hands.

"Always the better choice," I teased him, and his grin widened.

"I kind of like this town."

My heart leapt in anticipation as he glanced toward my friends.

"Since I don't have a band anymore, would it cramp your style if I found a job in town?" He shrugged, avoiding my gaze. "Maybe hooked up with another band?" He looked me in the eye. "Met your dad?"

My heart stopped cold. "Wouldn't cramp my style at all."

"Good. Good." He smiled, getting that wicked glint in his eyes, the one that made the world seem full of possibilities. He slid his arm around my shoulders. "Because the way I see it, I've got a couple of years to fill and this would be a good place to do it."

This time when I smiled at him, he bent and kissed me. Hard. It was every bit as thrilling as the very first time.

And I had a feeling it always would be.

We turned as one and walked out of that cafeteria together as if we owned it.

And, you know, I think we did.

You HAD TO GUESS THAT when the evening was all over, I had a dream.

I felt the snow landing on my face and heard the click of knitting needles. I rolled over to find the three Wyrd sisters busily at work, just as usual. Granny was knitting with superhuman speed, Urd was spinning wool for her so fast that her hands were a blur. The snowdrift that Granny—also known as Verdandi—had knit swelled over their knees like a protective blanket. Skuld was leaning back against the trunk of the tree, cleaning her nails with those massive shears. The tree was in full leaf above them, and the sky was full of stars.

(It made no sense that it was snowing when the sky was clear, but there you go. Dreams follow their own rules.)

I watched as Urd and Verdandi did as they had once before. There could have been a silent signal, for they both moved in the same instant without saying a word. They put aside their work and Urd reached for the bucket, the one she sent down the well. I knew that Verdandi would pull a ladle out from under the snowdrift and that they would water the great tree.

It was soothing to watch their quiet and efficient routine, so I settled back to doze. This was a mark that all was right with the world.

But this time, they surprised me. When Urd pulled the full bucket out of the well, she set it on the ground. A bit of water sloshed over the edge of the bucket; then the three sisters gathered around it to peer into its depths.

There was no ladle. I frowned and sat up to watch.

Skuld shoved her shears into that holster on her belt. She reached under the snowdrift and pulled out a handful of items that reminded me of sugar cookies or gingerbread cut into shapes. But these shapes were black.

They were the remains of the shattered NightBlade.

Urd chose one from the collection in Skuld's hands and held it up. She blew on it, as if to remove the black dust, and I smelled ash.

But it stayed black, whatever it was.

It was shaped like a griffin.

Granny did get her ladle, and she filled it with water from the bucket. Instead of pouring it on the tree, she carefully poured it over the shape that Urd held in her hand. It seemed to be very important that Urd's own bony fingertips weren't touched by the water.

To my astonishment, the shape swelled. It rounded. It grew. And by the time Granny poured the third ladle of water over it, it had become a griffin that towered over the three sisters. It could have been a black sculpture, a griffin carved of dark marble.

All three sisters blew on the griffin, and the blackness that covered it fell away like soot.

It was beautiful. It had the head and wings of an eagle and the body of a lion. Its coat was all in shades of gold and black, an elegant and beautiful creature. I could see the fur on its sides and the gleaming ebony of its nails. Its eyes were as dark as bittersweet chocolate. Its beak could have been made of hammered gold and it shone like the fierce weapon it was.

But its wings were astonishing. They shaded through every color of the rainbow: yellow at the tips, then orange and red and violet and blue, and green where they joined its body. Each feather glistened and each one was tipped in gold.

Then Skuld clapped her hands. My eyes nearly fell out of my head when the sculpture came to life. It could have thawed or awakened from a long sleep. The griffin flapped its wings; it stretched and let out a fearsome cry. That cry could curdle the blood of anyone. And those wings were even more stupendously beautiful when they were spread wide. Just when I thought nothing more weird could happen, it shimmered blue.

A familiar pale blue, a blue light that illuminated its perimeter and danced through its veins.

And the griffin shifted shape into a woman with long dark hair and elegant strength. She embraced the three sisters, then turned to face me. I saw the tears glisten in those beautiful dark eyes as she bowed low and touched her forehead to the ground before me.

"Thank you, Wyvern," she said, the words resonating in my thoughts like old-speak. She blew me a kiss, changed back to her griffin shape with a roar of delight, then launched herself into the air. She circled once over the great tree, dipped low in triumph, then gave that fearsome cry before she flew into the starry night.

"Always liked them," Skuld mused with satisfaction. "Even if I did have to wrestle one once in a while over a choice morsel."

"I'm glad they're back," Urd said.

Granny gestured with her ladle, returning her sisters' attention to the business at hand. Urd chose another shape, a shape I now realized was a shadow, the shadow of one of each kind. The extinction of each kind of shifter had added to the NightBlade, strengthening it, creating new layers like mica that were made of shifter shadows. We'd broken the bonds that enchanted them, and the Wyrd sisters were setting all those kinds of shifters loose in the world again.

I watched the sisters work, my mind filling with questions and possibilities. How many kinds of shifters were there in total? How would we all get along? It looked like I'd be learning a lot from my dad about alliances and treaties.

I thought of the chart I'd made just days before and envisioned it becoming a massive spreadsheet. Did these other shifters live openly among humans or hide themselves? The *Pyr* were charged with defending the earth and its treasures, but what were the quests of all these other shifters? What could we shifters do together to make the world a better place? What would humans think of so many myths coming to life among them?

No doubt about it—the world had become a much more interesting place.

I'm ready for the adventure.

Are you?

Deborah Cooke has always been fascinated by dragons, although she has never understood why they have to be the bad guys. She has an honors degree in history with a focus on medieval studies and is an avid reader of medieval vernacular literature, fairy tales, and fantasy novels. Since 1992, Deborah has written more than forty romance novels under the names Deborah Cooke, Claire Cross, and Claire Delacroix.

Deborah makes her home in Canada with her husband. When she isn't writing, she can be found knitting, sewing, or hunting for vintage patterns.

CONNECT ONLINE

www.deborahcooke.com
www.thedragondiaries.com
www.delacroix.net/blog
facebook.com/authordeborahcookefanpage

Don't miss the book that
launched the Dragon Diaries series!

Flying Blind

Available now from
New American Library

$\mathcal{T}$here was a guy in my bedroom.

It was six in the morning and I didn't know him.

I'm not much of a morning person, but that woke me up fast. I sat up and stared, my back pressed against the wall, sure my eyes had to be deceiving me. No matter how much I blinked, though, he was still there.

He seemed to think my reaction was funny.

He had dark hair and dark eyes, and he wasn't wearing a shirt, just jeans—and he had one heck of a six-pack. His arms were folded across his chest and a smile tugged at the corner of his mouth.

But he seemed insubstantial. I could see through him, right to the crowded bulletin board behind him.

Was he real?

I was going to try asking him, but he abruptly faded—faded and disappeared right before my eyes.

As if he'd been just an illusion. I jumped from the bed, then reached into that corner. My fingers passed through a chill, one cold enough to give me goose bumps. Then my hand landed on a pushpin holding a wad of drawings, and everything was perfectly normal.

Except for the hairs standing up on the back of my neck.

I took a deep breath and looked around. My room was the pit it usually was. There were some snuffed candles on my desk and bookshelves, a whiff of incense lingering in the air, and the usual mess of discarded sweaters and books all over the floor.

No sign of that guy. If I hadn't seen him, if I'd woken up two minutes later, I wouldn't have thought anything was wrong at all.

I shuddered one last time and headed for the shower. Halfway there I wondered, had Meagan's plan worked?

The visioning session had been my best friend's idea. Her mom calls herself a holistic therapist, which makes my mom roll her eyes. I was skeptical, too, but didn't have any better ideas. And Meagan, being the best friend ever, had really pulled out all the stops. She'd brought candles and mantras and incense for my room, and even though I'd felt silly, I'd followed her earnest instructions.

When the candles had burned down and she'd left—and my mom had shouted that I should open a window—I'd been pretty sure it hadn't worked. Nothing seemed to have happened.

But now I didn't know what to think. Who had that guy been? Where had he come from? And where had he gone?

Or had I just imagined him? I thought that if I was going to imagine a guy in my bedroom, it wouldn't be one who thought I was funny when I wasn't trying to be, never mind one who kind of creeped me out.

I'd have imagined Nick there.

In fact, I frequently did.

I heard my mom in the kitchen and my dad getting the newspaper and knew I had to get moving. I did my daily check in the bathroom, but nada. No boobs. No blood.

Four more zits.

At its core, then, the visioning session had failed.

I'm probably not the only fifteen-and-a-half-year-old girl who'd like to get the Puberty Show on the road. Even Meagan got her period last year, which was why she was trying to help. But my best friend didn't know the half of it.

That was because of the Covenant. I couldn't confide in Meagan because I'd had to swear to abide by the Covenant of our kind. I come from a long line of dragon shape shifters—*Pyr*, we call ourselves—and we pledge to not reveal our abilities to humans on a whim.

That would include Meagan.

The Covenant goes like this:

> I, Zoë Sorensson, do solemnly pledge not to willfully reveal the truth of my shape-shifting abilities to humans. I understand that individuals may know me in dragon form or in human form, but I swear that I shall not permit humans to know me in both forms, or to allow them to witness my shifting between forms without appropriate assessment of risk. I understand also that there will be humans who come to know me in both forms over the course of my life—I pledge not to reveal myself without due consideration, to beguile those who inadvertently witness my abilities, and to supply the names

of those humans whom I have entrusted with my truth
to the leader of the *Pyr*, Erik Sorensson.

Do humans know we exist? Sure. Humans always have—
thus the dragon stories they tell. But knowing dragons exist,
believing that there are actually dragon shape shifters, and
being convinced that your neighbor is one of them are
entirely different things.

That's probably a good thing.

The Covenant came about pretty recently. During the
Dragon's Tail Wars, some *Pyr* decided they wanted to be
more active and visible. My dad, though, remembers when
we were hunted almost to extinction. The Covenant is a
compromise between putting it all out there and living in
secret. So humans might see Sloane on the news, appearing
at the scene of natural disasters to help—he's the tourmaline
dragon—or Brandt, the orange dragon, making another daring rescue, but they don't know their names or where they
live in their human lives.

We teenage *Pyr* had to pledge to the Covenant after Nick
tried to impress the twin girls living next door, and his dad
caught him.

I still thought it was funny that they hadn't been impressed.

I, in contrast, was awed by Nick in dragon form.

The fact is that most humans don't believe they could per-
sonally know a dragon shape shifter. Those twins thought
Nick had pulled some kind of illusion to make himself look
cooler than he was.

So, in a way, we might as well be a myth.

Which is funny, if you think about it.

The trick is that the dragon business is all theoretical
when it comes to me. I'm the daughter of a dragon shape
shifter, so I should also be a dragon shape shifter. Sounds

simple, doesn't it? Except it's not happening. Nothing special has happened to me. I can't do it and I don't know why— much less what I can do to hurry things along.

Dragons are by nature patient. That's what my dad says. He should know, seeing as he is about twelve hundred years old. That's supposed to reassure me, but it doesn't.

Because dragons are also passionate and inclined to anger. I know that from spending my life around all those dragon shape shifters who are my extended family. And the fact that my dragon abilities were AWOL—despite my patience—was seriously pissing me off.

The *Pyr* are all guys—men and their sons—except for me. The story is that there's only one female dragon at a time, and that she's the Wyvern and has special powers.

Yours truly—I'm supposed to be the Wyvern.

The issue with there being only one female dragon shape shifter at a time is that the last one died before I was born. And it's not like anyone has her diary. Zero references for me. Zero advice.

Zero anything.

Just an expectation from my family and friends that I'll become the font of all dragonesque knowledge and lead the next generation to wherever the heck we're going.

Sooner would be better.

No pressure, right?

My dad says I was a prodigy, that I was already showing special powers before I could walk. Then I started to talk and all the Wyvern goodness went away. *Poof.* Instead of being special and a prodigy, I was just a normal kid.

I'm still waiting for the good stuff to come back.

No sign of it yet.

Some incremental progress would be encouraging. It's one thing to be a disappointment to everyone you care about, and quite another to just sit back and accept that inadequacy. In fact, I was starting to think that those dragons who believed I wasn't really the Wyvern might have it right.

Thus Meagan's session.

An act of desperation.

Because the one thing I did know was that the other dragon teenagers like Nick had come into their powers with puberty. Their voices cracked and bingo, they were shifting shape like old pros. So being a late bloomer has bigger repercussions for me. Meagan thought we were doing the ritual for my period to start. She didn't need to know I was after a little bit more than that.

Instead I got a guy mocking me in my own bedroom at the crack of dawn.

Like I said, it wasn't the best way to start the day.